Critical Acclaim for Penelope Lively's *Passing On*

"Writing with both wit and compassion, Ms. Lively conjures up Edward and Helen's mid-life dilemmas with uncommon sympathy. . . . Her command of narrative is fluent and self-assured, the mark of a novelist completely at ease with her craft."

—Michiko Kakutani, *New York Times*

"*Passing On* feels like real life drawn to scale, where private dreams dwarf the daily routine. . . . An expert at articulating character through place . . . Lively has a gift for invention and control . . . the slow unfolding of secrets gives the book tension without melodrama."

—Roz Spafford, *San Francisco Chronicle*

"Engrossing. . . . Lively writes in a deceptively simple style passed down from 19th-century novelist Jane Austen via Barbara Pym to a new generation of British women authors. . . . The writing is sophisticated, with witty observations of people and their foibles. And the characters' narrow lives shed light on much larger issues of personal—and global—concern."

—Judith Rosen, *Boston Sunday Herald*

"Engaging, comic, occasionally surprising and thoroughly—well, lively."

—Clarinda Harriss Raymond, *Washington Times*

"Sly subtleties, keen observations and raw emotional power. . . . Remarkably fuses the comic and the tragic in a graceful, fluid narrative."

—Sarah Gold, *Newsday*

"This is a marvelous work, filled with Lively's almost magical insights into how our distorted self-images can betray us into crushing our own dreams."

—Paul Craig, *Sacramento Bee*

PASSING ON

Books by Penelope Lively

PENELOPE LIVELY

PASSING ON

Harper Perennial
A Division of HarperCollinsPublishers

A hardcover edition of this book was first published in the United States in 1990 by Grove Weidenfeld. It is here reprinted by arrangement with Grove Weidenfeld.

First HarperPerennial edition published 1991.

Library of Congress Cataloging-in-Publication Data
Lively, Penelope, 1933–
   Passing on / Penelope Lively. — 1st HarperPerennial ed.
     p. cm.
  ISBN 0-06-097370-6
  I. Title.
[PR6062.I89P38   1991]
823'.914—dc20   90-55666

92 93 94 95 FG 10 9 8 7 6 5 4

To Josephine and Steven

PASSING ON

ONE

The coffin stuck fast at the angle of the garden path and the gateway out into the road. The undertaker's men shunted to and fro, their hats knocked askew by low branches, their topcoats showered with raindrops from the hedge. The mourners halted around the front door and waited in silence. Birds sang effusively. At last the men managed to pivot the coffin on the gatepost and proceeded to the waiting hearse. The coffin was loaded. The mourners straggled out into the road and hesitated, unwilling to commit themselves to the attendant limousines.

Louise said, 'It's daft using cars to go such a short distance. At least we could have squashed into one, surely?'

There were two Daimlers. Helen and Edward got into the first, the four Dysons into the second. First time I've ever ridden in one of these, thought Helen. The last too, let's hope. They moved off at walking pace, past the Britches, radiant still with birdsong, past the builders' yard where Ron Paget, heaving planks of timber from the pick-up, suspended the operation and stood in respect, his eyes lowered. Helen nudged Edward: 'The old rogue – look at him.' Edward nodded. He said, 'At least he's not coming to the church – I wouldn't have put it past him.' Now they were passing the shop, where the Birds Eye van driver continued to lift out cartons without looking up. From within, faces watched furtively. Two women with prams paused, tucking themselves into the wall as the cortège went by. A small child pointed, questioning. They are having to explain, Helen thought. About deaths, funerals. Probably they will dodge the issue with distractions – an iced lollie, a sweetie. All the same, mother has disrupted the lives of others, just a little, for the last time.

Now they were at the church, unloading. The coffin, the

1

flowers, the mourners. Through the lych-gate, along the path, a halt at the door to make adjustments before entering. Two of the undertaker's men were young, Helen noticed; what a very curious choice of occupation. Earlier, she had looked out of the window at Greystones and seen one of them filling in a football coupon while they waited in the hearse. Now, their faces were composed into expressions of noncommittal sobriety.

'You three should go in first,' said Tim Dyson. 'I'll follow with the children.'

Only two of the family wore black. Tim's suit was a dark pinstripe but Edward's was green, shiny around the seat and elbows, brought out for school speech days and probably twenty years old. Helen had put on her camel coat; the late May morning was quite cold and she felt the coat to be more subdued than her maroon suit, the only other garment suitable for a formal occasion. Louise was in a hotchpotch of unashamed colour and pattern. The two adolescents, alone, were appropriately funereal, clad from head to toe in black leather.

There were twenty or thirty people in the church. The front pew had been left empty. The family shuffled into it. Helen, between her brother and sister, observed the coffin, which had been placed in the aisle just below the steps to the chancel.

It seemed, now, much too small. Helen thought of her mother's stocky form, eyed the coffin, and could not imagine her squeezed into it. She gazed at the varnished wood and the brass handles and waited to hear cries of protest and complaint. She half expected to have to rise to her feet and set things right. Glancing at Edward, she knew that he was thinking exactly the same.

'Let us pray . . .'

Helen sank obediently to her knees. She said, O God, now that she is Thine rather than mine, do something about her. If she was created in Thy Image, then the system is an imperfect one.

'We consume away in Thy displeasure: and are afraid at Thy wrathful indignation . . .'

No, not mother. She wasn't much more of a Christian than I am. A token one, being a natural conservative. But I doubt if she

2

ever gave a thought to Thy displeasure, any more than to anyone else's.

The service proceeded. The congregation sang a hymn, creakily. Louise and the children were silent; Edward and Helen moved their lips; Tim Dyson gave tongue firmly in a light tenor. Helen allowed herself a glance sideways and backwards to see who was there. Expected faces. Village faces, more distant relatives, Doctor Taylor, someone middle-aged who must be Mr Carnaby from Carnaby and Proctor, solicitors, to whom Helen had spoken on the phone but had not met. Dorothy Glover, at eighty, had not had friends. Indeed she had not had many at sixty or at forty or even, perhaps, at twenty. Helen could think only of someone she did voluntary nursing with during the war, who sent Christmas cards, and a woman who shared her interest in a mystical form of healing involving a black box with a lot of wires and buttons, with whom she corresponded.

Mother was not a nice woman. I have always known that, and I can say it, because I am her daughter and so in the nature of things came nearer to loving her than anyone else ever did. As did Edward. Louise's attitude is rather different, for various reasons.

Louise, right now, appeared to be suffering. Her face had become contorted; she was reaching for a Kleenex with which she scrubbed both eyes, angrily. As the hymn ground to its end she hissed to Helen, 'Bloody hay fever! It's those blasted flowers. Why did we have to have them?'

'Because they were sent.'

The flowers were rather awful: gladioli and enormous white daisies that looked artificial, and tightly budded roses fanned out behind windows of cellophane. And a couple of wreaths of shiny, hard-looking leaves. These offerings had ridden in the hearse and were stacked now outside the church door. Helen hoped they would not be brought back to the house: she was vague about what the etiquette was here. She longed to be rid of the flowers, of the appalling hours that loomed in which she must dispense hospitality and talk to people, of the whole disagreeable day. She simply wanted to get on with life, which would now be different. She wanted, quite dispassionately, to see what this difference would be. She was also extremely tired. Her mother had died indignantly and demandingly. Neither she nor Edward had had much sleep for quite a while.

And out now into the churchyard, trailing behind the coffin. The hole; the pile of fresh-dug earth. Oh God, thought Helen, this is too awful. Why isn't she being cremated? She is not being cremated because she specified that it should be like this. All in black and white, it appears. Burial in the churchyard of St Peter's, Long Sydenham, in a plot in the far corner near the big sycamore that she laid claim to several years ago, apparently – after, it emerges, a row with the rector that none of us knew a thing about. Now I know why he's been giving us funny looks for so long. So mother envisaged us all here, gathered round staring down in this ghastly way, looking at anything rather than each other, wishing they'd get on and get it over. You could have spared us that, mother.

Earth to earth, ashes to ashes, dust to dust. The words, in fact, are beautiful – the rhythms, the resonance. The meaning is another matter, for us unbelievers. Mercifully. Eternal life is an appalling idea, especially in mother's case.

And that, at last, was that. They could start to turn away, look at each other, they could leave her there under the sycamore and go. And now, damn and blast it, Helen feels tears prick her eyes, surge up, begin to trickle – and she looks at Edward and sees that he is the same. They both scowl and furtively dab. We can't leave her here, thinks Helen, we can't just put her in there and leave her. Mother.

But they can. And do. She is dead. Helen thinks, almost for the first time, mother has died. She is not here any more. Incredulous, she searches the group around the grave: Edward, Louise, Tim, Suzanne and Phil. No mother, any more.

'I thought they'd never go,' said Louise. 'Cousin Phoebe – may I be preserved from cousin Phoebe, now and for ever. Who was the good-looking bloke with the silver hair?' She stood at the drawing-room windows, open into the garden, sniffing and mopping her eyes. 'Oh those bloody flowers . . .'

'Surely,' said Helen, 'there must be *some* flowers in Camden?'

'Not a lot. Anyway florist ones are worse, for some reason. Was he the solicitor?'

'Yes. He's writing to us all. About the Will.'

'Oh, all that bumph . . .' said Louise vaguely. 'I suppose you wouldn't think of selling the Britches now? Make this place a bit more comfortable? It's perishing cold, as usual – frankly I don't know how you endure it.'

'Of course we're not going to sell the Britches,' said Edward.

They stood at the window, the three of them, and looked into the garden, on which rain now fell once more, after a tactful intermission for the funeral. It was defiantly unkempt; the lawn was a hayfield, the yew hedge drooped almost to the ground, the only surviving plants were vigorous shrubs and a few creepers swarming up above the general level of growth. None of them saw this, since it had been ever thus.

Louise saw fuming pollen, and longed for the tarmac of North London. Helen saw their mother, thick-set, irritable, wearing brown corduroy, stumping across the grass with a query or an order on her lips. Edward saw a flycatcher, a pair of great tits and a collared dove. He looked for the flycatcher's mate, and wondered where the nest was.

They did not look like siblings. Helen and Edward, at fifty-two and forty-nine respectively, were not physically alike though they shared a certain style: Edward's shiny suit, Helen's rather unbecoming dress, obviously chosen without interest or pro-longed thought. Edward was fair, thin, blue-eyed, and slightly stooping; Helen was shorter, brown-haired and fresh-faced, a woman who would be unremarkable in a group – only a second glance would reveal distinctive features: the bright eyes, the neat set of the nose. Louise, ten years younger, seemed of another generation and culture – her clothes raffish but also metropolitan, her hair unruly but tinted with salon highlights.

'Of course not,' said Louise, turning from the window. 'I never really imagined you would.' She patted Edward's arm. 'You'd feel uncomfortable being comfortable, wouldn't you? I'll help you wash up and then we'd better push off. Where are the others?'

'Taking glasses into the kitchen,' said Edward. 'Don't bother about the washing-up.'

Louise flung herself into a chair. 'All right. Maybe the kids'll do it. Wonders never cease.'

Helen picked up a plate of uneaten bits and pieces and took them through to the kitchen, where Tim Dyson stood looking with distaste at the crammed sink. It was a large, low ceramic sink, of the kind more often seen nowadays in a garden, planted with alpines. Quite possibly Tim did not recognise it as a sink, being accustomed to stainless steel. He always avoided the kitchen at Greystones; in fact Helen could not remember having seen him in there before. Normally, he kept to the drawing room and the dining room while domestic chores were being undertaken; he had not spent a night in the house for many years. Louise, during her mother's illness, had visited on her own.

The children – it was hard to think of them now as children, given their appearance, but fifteen and sixteen is more child than adult – were eating sausage rolls. Suzanne swallowed quickly and said, 'I'll wash, Helen – I don't mind.'

'Don't bother. We'll do it when you've gone. I think Louise wants to be off.'

Suzanne's metamorphosis was less startling than Phil's. Her hair stuck up spikily from her scalp in a way that seemed to defy gravity, her eyes were black-rimmed and there was a general impression of leather and metalwork. Phil, though, was almost unrecognisable. Helen's first reaction had been that someone had followed Louise and Tim into the house, then that Louise had let Phil bring some undesirable friend, that it was too bad of Louise, that he certainly couldn't be allowed to come to church, and at last, with pure astonishment, that this *was* Phil. He too was black-leathered and slung about with chains; his boots had spurs; there were chrome studs all over his back. It was his head, though, that startled most: the shaven scalp, the jet-black crest with streaks of emerald. Helen, punch-drunk with strain and exhaustion, had been on the edge of hysterical laughter. Neither Louise nor Tim had apparently thought the matter worth comment. Presumably they were so used to it. Helen had not seen either of the children for almost a year, she realised. A year is a long time, in more eventful lives. Louise and Tim led eventful lives. All Louise's phone calls were catalogues of activity and disaster; they were both always over-worked, over-stressed, on the brink of startling achievement or notoriety, and plagued by minor illness. Louise had hay-fever, cystitis and migraine; Tim had high blood pressure and sinus trouble. They were always in need of holidays for which they could not be spared. Louise worked for a firm of design consultants; Tim was in advertising. Long ago, Louise had been Helen's baby sister – adorable, charming, vulnerable, to be looked after and protected. This Louise seemed very far away and inaccessible now: from time to time, though, she surfaced, weeping over the telephone of betrayals, impositions and the cruelty of fate. More often, the Louise of today scolded Helen for conservatism, retrenchment and, above all, for not standing up to their mother. 'I live with her,' Helen used to say. 'You don't. That is the difference.'

Louise got out, as she put it, when she was seventeen. She had a series of rows with Dorothy and flounced off to art school, where she conned the authorities over the question of parental consent and support. There was more trouble. Eventually Dorothy gave in, reluctantly and vociferously, and Louise, from then on, was at one remove from Greystones, returning for Christmas and the occasional weekend, an unruly emotive draught of alien worlds. 'You and Edward can't just stay here for ever,' she said, each time. 'I mean, for God's sake, Helen, you're *thirty* . . .' 'I'll have to see what turns up,' Helen would say.

And in the event nothing did. Or not enough.

When the Dysons had gone Helen and Edward got down to the washing-up. Edward stooped over the sink – always inconveniently low – while Helen dried. Helen would have preferred to be left to deal with the mess on her own, in which case she could have brought out her illicit bottle of Fairy Liquid, but Edward would have been hurt to be shooed away at this moment. He wanted to talk. A scum of grease floated on top of the washing-up water; the dishes were slimy. Edward, an ardent conservationist, ignored the fact that detergents had been biodegradable for fifteen years. Lurid still in his mind's eye were the foam-packed rivers of the sixties, the rafts of dead fish, the blighted vegetation. Detergent never disgraced Greystones, or at least none that Edward knew about.

He said, 'How did Phil's hair get like that?'

'It's dyed, I suppose.'

Edward pondered. 'He seems a perfectly nice boy still. What an awful day. The bit in the churchyard was worst of all.'

'Yes. Do scrape that plate before you wash it. Shut up, Tam!'

Tam, Edward's rough-haired white terrier, squatted in the middle of the floor moaning with lust. He was a dog of unassuageable greed. Edward looked down at him, and then at the table, on which was a dish piled with sausage rolls and vol-au-vents. He said, 'Would we eat these, do you think?' Without waiting for an answer he slid two sausage rolls and a chicken vol-au-vent into Tam's bowl. Helen said nothing. They looked at each other, both realising that this had never before been done openly and unashamedly. Tam, as though in recognition that from now on things were going to be different, belched with roomy satisfaction. Dorothy had fought, for forty years, a vigorous and vindictive campaign against Edward's animals, from the kitten smuggled in when he was a schoolboy to the official but resented dogs of later years.

'Now I feel guilty,' said Edward. 'Is it always going to be like that?'

'That's what we're going to find out, I suppose.'

Edward, dabbling inefficiently in the murky sink, said 'I've never seen these plates before, where did they come from?'

'They were a wedding present of mother's, I think. We never used to use them, but I had to get out everything for today, or there wouldn't have been enough.'

As it was, nothing went with anything else, a medley of glasses, cups, plates surviving from once complete sets. Chipped cups, rogue saucers without a partner, pieces of cloudy pre-war Pyrex. 'There is absolutely nothing at Greystones that is nice to look at,' said Louise once, in a fit of rage, and Helen, dispassionate and not caring one way or the other, could see that she was absolutely right.

'Actually,' said Edward, 'they're rather pretty.' He held the plate clear of the sink to inspect it and it at once slid from his fingers to crash into several pieces upon the tiled floor.

They scrabbled for dustpan and brush, bumping into each other. Edward, assembling the bits on the draining-board, said anxiously, 'Isn't there some process for mending things like this? Riveting or something?'

'Why bother?' said Helen.

'But . . .' He looked at her. 'No. I see what you mean. All the same . . .' He stacked the pieces on the shelf beside the Coronation biscuit tin where, Helen suddenly saw with awful clarity, they would stay for the next five years.

They finished clearing up and went back into the drawing room. It was early evening now and the wet garden glinted in the low sunshine. Beyond it was the shaggy mass of the Britches and above the blackbirds and robins came the shrill whine of a chain-saw in Ron Paget's yard. The mantelpiece clock struck six and the chain-saw ceased abruptly.

Helen watched him walk towards the Britches. She knew exactly where he would go. He would sit on the fallen tree-trunk somewhere in the midst of that muddle of vegetation, doing nothing. He would come back in half an hour or so, apparently in some way renovated.

The village, at the outer rim of the Cotswolds, was also on the edge of notability. It was not one of those places that people tell each other they mustn't miss. The church was good but not exceptional. There was a respectable acreage of limestone, mullioned windows and drip-moulding but few single buildings of any distinction. There was nothing much to take a photograph of. Nor was there any antique shop or anywhere selling country jams, dried flowers and basketry from Hong Kong. The village store was a small supermarket and sold food only, rather expensively and of second-rate quality. Most people shopped ten miles away on Saturdays, by car.

Most of them also worked ten or fifteen miles away. They worked in offices and hospitals and shops. There were a few schoolteachers and a scattering of retired people, the rector and his wife in a new Barratt's Executive Home and an industrialist and his family in the Old Rectory. Sociologically classified, they would have come out as preponderantly A's and AB's with a sprinkling of C's; council housing had been kept to a minimum in Long Sydenham and what there was was mainly built before the war. The Glovers, Edward and Helen, and – hitherto – Dorothy, were presumably AB or thereabouts, by occupation (Edward taught, Helen worked as a part-time librarian). In terms of income and life-style, though, they were a bit of a puzzle, to the rest of the village, at any rate.

Within the village wealth was unequally distributed. Of course; it always is. There were the Hadleys at the Old Rectory who were so very much richer than everyone else that they were beyond competition, outside the fray. Their sleek cars, Mrs Hadley's even sleeker hunters, the rumoured house in the West Indies and yacht at Fowey were like the attributes of gods, only to be expected. Beneath them, nearly everyone else jostled within an income band narrow enough to allow for plenty of resentment, aspiration and emulation. The matters at issue were housing, cars, electrical and electronic appliances, holidays and children's schooling – probably in that order. Right at the bottom were those poor enough to be immune from competition, concerned only with survival. There were not many of these, Long Sydenham being geographically fortunate: a handful of old age pensioners, a couple of large families (considered feckless), a single parent (ditto) and a few unemployed, most of whom were very young. While none of these were in danger of starvation, they were nevertheless obliged to contemplate daily the lavishness around them, from the Hadleys' Mercedes gliding past their door to the five pound box of chocolates in the village shop, almost equally inaccessible. The advertisements on their television screens made certain that they should be in no danger of forgetting the range of consumer goods available and the urgency and intensity of normal need for these things.

The Glovers were a problem, where wealth status was concerned. The house, one of the largest and – at least potentially – most valuable in the village, put them in one category. So did their accents and their education; old Dorothy's self-confidence was generations deep. But patently there was no loose cash swilling around at Greystones. You only had to look at their cars, at the furnishings within (nothing new within sight, no central heating, no dishwasher, only the most decrepit old twin-tub washing-machine); none of them was known to go abroad at all. As for their clothes . . .

The failure of the Glovers to fit properly into a category troubled the village, which liked to know where it was with people. The inhabitants of the Barratt Executive Homes did not know whether to defer or to be kindly patronising and ended up doing both, disconcerting themselves. The Hadleys were so set apart by wealth that, like old-fashioned aristocrats, they saw everyone else as a featureless proletariat and were uniformly bland to everyone; they would never have noticed the Glovers. The older inhabitants of the council houses had had a barbed relationship with Dorothy Glover for many a long year. Their children and grandchildren, less conditioned and more broad-minded, thought her a bad-tempered old bag but rather liked Edward and Helen, who were in no way stuck-up and not given to complaining about noisy motor bikes.

There were only two industrial enterprises in Long Sydenham. At one end of the village the Old Forge made wrought iron garden gates, firescreens, lampstands and candlesticks. It wouldn't have known what to do with a horse if it saw one. At the other, divided from Greystones by the *cordon sanitaire* of the Britches, was Ron Paget's builders' yard, a place of noise, mud, lorries, churning cement-mixers and stacks of bricks.

The Britches was a piece of mixed scrub and woodland about two acres in extent. It was known as the Britches to everyone in the village for reasons now lost; that was its name, simply. It belonged to the Glovers; their garden, indeed, melted into it at an indeterminate point where the back of a shrubbery gave way to docks, elder bushes, and a few diseased apple trees long past producing anything but a sparse rash of blossom in spring. Beyond that was an expanse of grass that was waist high by August, and huge billowing clumps of nettles, and beyond that again a thickly tangled place of beech, birch, elder and an undergrowth of brambles and low bushes above a blanket of leafmould. There was a vague belief at Greystones that the Britches had once been a quarry; certainly the ground was very uneven. Long ago Edward had constructed a rockery in the garden with large stones hauled from there. It was divided from Ron Paget's yard by a high but battered fence through which came marauders by way of dogs, cats and children. From time to time unpleasant things turned up: animal corpses, hanks of lavatory paper and used condoms.

The village had long marvelled over the Britches. Throughout the rapacious seventies, when every other morsel of waste ground within miles, every barn, shed, pigsty, dilapidated cottage, every orchard and a good many back lawns had been turned to financial advantage by their owners, Dorothy Glover had disregarded the blandishments of speculative builders. Foremost among them, naturally, was Ron Paget. He had tried everything, varying his approach from brisk outright proposals to more subtle manoeuvres, moving from periods of relentless pressure to times of tactful neighbourly solicitude. Dorothy ignored him.

From time to time people raised the matter, driven by curiosity and perplexity. If you sold the Britches, they said (circuitously, delicately, wrapping it up in euphemisms . . .) you could buy a new car, put in central heating, have a holiday in the Bahamas, go and live in Hove. Helen and Edward could have cars, holidays, new clothes, consumer goods. You would all inspire respect and envy. You would look nicer. You would be asked out more. Helen and Edward would have sexual clout. Money is power.

The years went by and the Britches remained unsold and untouched. It became apparent to the village that you were dealing with people who were beyond reason and impervious to common sense. Those who had attributed to Dorothy Glover financial acumen and patience greater than their own – the old bat was waiting till land prices rocketed even higher – came to realise that they were mistaken. Land prices peaked, and peaked again; planning permissions poured forth from the offices of the county council, and still she did not sell. She wasn't ever going to sell: she meant what she said.

Dorothy herself never went into the Britches, Helen only rarely. The only person who visited it regularly was Edward, to monitor the ecology. There was a surprising amount of it if you knew what you were looking for. A pair of tawny owls nested, as did green and spotted woodpeckers. Warblers abounded. There were treecreepers and occasionally a nuthatch, goldfinches and every kind of tit. There was a good assortment of butterflies and moths. Flora did rather less well; the surviving patch of bluebells was imperilled by ranker growths, the few wood anemones had vanished along with the purple spotted orchids that were now almost legendary. But there were some ramsoms and plenty of celandine and self-heal and ground ivy and more ordinary stuff. Edward fought a half-hearted battle with grey squirrels and magpies, considered to be a threat to the choicer forms of bird life. Helen, from time to time, pointed out the irrationality of this: 'You're interfering, in fact. Tampering with the system. And why is one bird more desirable than another?' Edward, while admitting the ambiguity, said that one couldn't help feeling that way. As it was, all he was able to bring himself to do was to make shooing noises and, on occasion, destroy a magpie nest. When, years ago, Ron Paget had spotted what he was at and offered to come over with a shotgun, Edward had been appalled. Helen pointed out the irrationality of this, also.

It was starting to rain again. Helen continued to stand at the window and after a few minutes Edward appeared, breaking out of the gap in the shrubbery that was the normal route to the Britches. He had not changed out of the suit, his only one, which would now have bits of twig and leafmould on it when next it was required. He looked exactly what he was: an absent-minded well-intentioned school teacher approaching fifty.

TWO

During the ensuing days Helen felt as though her mother were continuously present in the house as a large black hole. There was a hole in Dorothy's bedroom, in the bed where she was not, on which, now, the blankets were neatly folded and the cover spread. There were various other holes, where she stood at the kitchen table preparing one of those unappetising stews, or shouting instructions from the landing or inspecting a caller at the front door. There were perambulant holes in which she creaked down the stairs or came in through the front door. Almost, Helen stood aside to let her pass or manoeuvred around her large black airy bulk as she occupied the scullery or the narrow passage by the back stairs. It was weeks before Helen could walk straight through her, or open her bedroom door without bracing herself for the confrontation.

Louise telephoned, almost daily. 'Are you all right?'

'Of course I'm all right.'

'And Edward?'

'Edward's all right too,' said Helen, rather crossly. 'Why shouldn't we be?'

'After all this time. You're so used to her. I mean, I can't quite take it in myself yet. It's a shock.'

'No it isn't,' said Helen. 'We all knew she was going to die.'

'Yes, but we didn't properly believe it. One doesn't. She didn't, certainly, which I suppose was just as well. O gosh . . .' – Louise's voice trailed away – 'I still can't . . .'

Dorothy, who had seldom had a day's illness in her eighty years, had disputed the diagnosis. She had contradicted it flatly. 'The stupid man says I've got something foul,' she announced. 'I told him not to be so silly.' As the disease progressed she blamed

14

the consultant for ineffective or faulty treatment, baying at him across his desk in the hospital or railing over the telephone. When eventually it reduced her to bed, and at last to a glaring silence, the specialist came into his own, able to commend her fighting spirit. 'Your mother never gave in,' he told Helen and Edward, portentously. 'One can tell the truth to someone like that and know that it will inspire strength rather than despair.' Helen hadn't had the heart to say that her mother had never for one moment believed him. Her dead face had worn, it seemed, an expression of outrage and incredulity.

'You should have a holiday,' said Louise. 'Go off somewhere. Look, we've this friend who's got a cottage in the Lake District . . .'

'No thanks. I'm too busy. I'm getting back to the library as soon as I've got the house sorted out.'

During the long weeks of her mother's illness Helen had had to take leave from the library. She looked forward, now, to a return to those brisk impersonal days. First, though, there were chores. The paraphernalia of nursing had to be disposed of, bills attended to, those things done which had not been done. She saw that the drooping gutter at the front of the house was now quite unsupported, and that there was yet another slate off the roof. Ron Paget had been asked to come and had not. Foolish to have imagined that one request would suffice. With the back of the Morris Minor piled up with the things for the Red Cross – the commode, the back supports – she stopped off at the yard, spotting Paget loading one of his lorries.

'Mr Paget!'

He came across. They were old sparring partners. He was almost pleased to see her, she saw – gingered up at the thought of a little contest. Over the years there had been plenty: questions of noise and dirt from the yard, the dominant continuous issue of the Britches, Ron's need to keep in with Greystones offset against Greystones' frequent need for minor repairs and services. We have grown middle-aged together, thought Helen. Except that Ron has also grown richer and richer, and shed his dull old wife and got a glossier younger one, and progressed from a beat-up van to a flashy new car every year. The times have been good to Ron. More so than to me. She thought of him as Ron, but always addressed him with formality, for good strategic reasons.

'Mr Paget, you said you'd see to that gutter for us. And the slates.'

'So I did, Miss Glover, so I did. Will do. Tell you what – I'll send a couple of the men over tomorrow morning. How's that?'

'Thanks. I'll expect them, then.'

'A sad time for you,' said Ron piously. 'We've been thinking about you, Pauline and me. You're keeping well, and your brother, I hope.'

'We're fine, thank you,' said Helen briskly. She started up the Morris again.

Ron Paget laid a hand on the bonnet. 'It's done you well, hasn't it, your old jalopy. How old would it be now?'

'I wouldn't know,' said Helen. 'I'm not very interested in cars.'

The Morris Minor, in fact, was fifteen years old but had seldom been more than fifty miles from Long Sydenham. The mileage was barely forty thousand and it was in pristine condition, exquisitely maintained by a fond mechanic at Willough-by's Garage in Spaxton.

Ron, eyeing the Morris, said, 'I'll tell you what, Miss Glover, I've had an idea. I'll do you a favour. My sister's wanting something to potter around in. She doesn't need anything fancy. I'll buy your old rattle-trap off you and do it up for her.' Amazing what a good Morris would fetch now, collector's items, they were. This particular one was hot stuff, in the right market. Old Miss G. wouldn't know that, of course, not in a month of Sundays she wouldn't. 'Get yourself something more up to date,' he went on. 'Nice little Escort, that sort of thing. You deserve it.'

'Do I?' said Helen. 'Well, you may be right.' She got out and contemplated the Morris. 'What do you think it's worth, Mr Paget?'

'Well . . .' Ron considered. ''Course, they don't make them any more. Gone right out of fashion. You can't get the spares. And that's long in the tooth, that one.'

'Mmn,' said Helen.

16

'Hartwell's wouldn't look at it. Not as a trade-in for a newish Escort.'

'I daresay not,' said Helen.

'I'd like to do you a good turn, though, Miss Glover. I can tinker about with it myself and see if I can put it to rights. Tell you what, I'll give you five hundred for it.' He slapped the Morris's rump, scraped at a small scratch mark and frowned. 'I'm a fool, but I'm feeling generous. Five hundred.'

'It goes very well still, as it happens,' said Helen. 'I doubt if you'd need to do much tinkering. I'll think it over. Or I could put an advertisement in the Morris Minor Owners' Club magazine. Did you see that article in the *Observer*?' She got into the car and started up the nicely tuned engine. 'Thanks for the offer, anyway. And that's a promise, is it, about the gutter?'

Ron watched her go. Crafty bugger. Not so daft as she looks. Like the old woman. But where does it get them?

Helen, experiencing the first little glow of pleasure for quite a while, turned out of Ron's yard into the road. In fact, Edward was more in need of a new car than she was. The Morris had many miles in it yet, but Edward's old Beetle (also, one understood, of rarity value nowadays but in this case, alas, too far gone) had packed up again that morning and he had had to go to school on the bus, a tedious process involving a change with a long wait.

Edward taught at Croxford House, a private girls' school catering for the daughters of the more prosperous local farmers, the less prosperous gentry and upwardly mobile business people from Spaxton. It had few educational pretensions. Hardly anyone went on to university. A few of the more aspiring girls took vocational courses and became physiotherapists or nurses. Most settled for clerical work, jobs as receptionists or, if the worst came to the worst, shop assistants. Marriage was very much on the cards, too. There might no longer be any stigma on spinsterhood in Hampstead or Fulham, but down here things were a little different. The girls still married at twenty; marriage remained their objective and the means whereby they acquired status. Mrs Hadley of the Old Rectory gave a great many parties, the purpose of which was to infiltrate her two daughters into the local aristocracy. No nonsense about universities or interesting jobs for them. Here was a tacit agreement on what life for a girl was all about. And Croxford House, while paying lip-service to more up-to-date ways of thinking, would not have entirely disagreed.

Edward taught English, History and Biology to the juniors, and Current Events to the seniors. He was the only male teacher except someone who came on Wednesdays to coach tennis in the summer, and he was regarded with kindly patronage by everyone save the headmistress, who thought him distinguished (in a social rather than an intellectual sense) and had hired him for that reason, fifteen years ago.

The girls liked him. They recognised that his disciplinary powers were so weak that there would simply be no point in challenging them. Also he was amiable, he listened to what they told him with apparent interest, and he never gave them bad conduct marks or reported them to the Head. He demanded little of them, so they demanded little of him. His lessons were gentle, dreamy affairs that seemed to go on and on for ever, with sunlight lying in bars across the desks and flies buzzing at the window. He had long since been removed from teaching duties involving anyone old enough to be within hailing distance of such public examinations as Croxford House bothered with, and simply pottered around with the eleven and twelve year olds in the more decorative areas of English history. He also read to them from books that he himself remembered having enjoyed when he was their age. Modern children's fiction had passed him by. He read *Alice*, *The Wind in the Willows* and *The Water Babies* to the juniors while they handed notes to each other, knitted under their desks or lay with their heads on their arms, apparently asleep. Edward still loved *Alice* and had never noticed that the children did not. He read, effectively, to himself and was happy. It reminded him of being read to by his mother – except that this was an elusive memory since Dorothy had seldom done so. She was profoundly bored by books. It was Helen who had read to Edward, and subsequently to Louise. What Edward was reviving was a cloudy, luxurious sensation of acquiescence to

18

someone authoritative, more skilled and with access to a wondrous other world. Helen would have been about nine at the time.

Helen, disposing of the invalid equipment in Spaxton, was reminded not of reading to Edward but of her mother's antipathy to the printed word. One of the accelerating problems of her final years had been the entertainment of a vigorous old woman, sound of mind and body, who had no interests.

Dorothy Glover's attention was concentrated on a personal reference system. She read the Births, Marriages and Deaths columns only of *The Times*, with a practised eye that could pick out any known name in three seconds flat. Novels met with approval only if the setting was familiar. 'I'm extremely fond of *Persuasion*,' she would say, 'I went to school near Bath. It's by far her best book.' Her knowledge of personal connections was compendious – she knew of cousins unto the tenth degree, she remembered everyone she had ever met, their names, their occupations and their attributes. She knew all this with the dry detachment of an official at Somerset House; she had no interest whatsoever in people as such. She was expert and scholarly in disposing of extraneous material; there was the world which related to her, to which she had been or to whom she had spoken, and there was the rest, which was irrelevant. Needless to say, she could not see the point of history and ignored politics. She never voted. She was a Tory by inclination, but would have denied political affiliations with indignation, claiming that she had no time for politicians and owed her opinions to common sense and using her head. 'Stupid' was her favourite term of abuse; interestingly, though, 'clever' was not a word used in praise. She was more likely to call someone 'too clever by half'.

She read books only for good reason, and noisily when she did so, pointing out the personal resonances whereby the work satisfied her – the familiar place or the name with associations of some kind. She had once written to a well-known novelist to ask if a character in her novel was related to a family of the same name Dorothy had known. The author's polite but acid response had been read to Helen and Edward over breakfast, as they squirmed: 'What on earth does the woman mean – ". . . your

19

unusually literal view of fiction"? Is she trying to be funny or something?'

As Helen, Edward and Louise grew up they had come to recognise their mother's outlook for what it was. They realised with discomfort that she was not so much egotistical as fettered – trapped within a perpetual adolescence. She moved for ever within a landscape whose only point of reference was herself.

The Red Cross lady received the commode and the backrest with nicely gauged murmurs of sympathy. Helen parked the Morris and set out to do some shopping. Spaxton, a medium-sized market town, supplied all those needs that the village could not meet. Helen and Edward, unfastidious eaters and exception-ally unacquisitive, had fewer needs than most people. Even so, there were occasional requirements. Today, a screwdriver with which to do something about the broken lamp, Earl Grey tea (one of Edward's few indulgences) and a sweater for herself. She walked down the High Street and plunged into the new shopping precinct, a futuristic place in which the shops had no fronts but opened straight into the shining heated covered walk, like some awkward parody of eastern booths. Her mother walked beside her, in her more strident persona of ten years ago, criticising loudly and attracting glances. 'I know,' said Helen. 'I don't care for it either, aesthetically, but I see no reason why people shouldn't have a better choice of things to buy, if that's what they want.'

She stopped to contemplate a display of sweaters. Blue. Interestingly patterned.

'You can't wear that sort of thing,' said her mother. 'It's too young for you. You're fifty-two. And too short and too fat. Louise could get away with something like that, I daresay. Not you.'

'I may be a little more adventurous,' said Helen. 'For a change.'

'Brown,' snorted her mother. 'Brown's right for you. That's what you always wear.'

Helen left her outside and went into the shop. She held garments up against herself and tried to see both face and garment with detachment. The face was – well, unassuming was the word

20

that sprang to mind – neither particularly attractive, nor unattractive either, the complexion better than average, something interesting about the eyes, the chin a touch stubby. She saw age and decay, but did not too much care. She would not have especially wanted to be younger, but would welcome change. Brown, she now observed, sent her face into compliant anonymity; she held up a sweater rich with stained glass window colours – blues and reds and a spice of green – and thought she saw an answering glow above. She bought the sweater. Her mother, waiting outside, made noises of disapproval. 'Well,' said Helen, 'maybe. And again maybe not. We shall see. I shall see. Anyway, I need uplift.' She turned away and her mother, with a curious, unprecedented look of vulnerability on her face, began to fade, like the Cheshire cat in *Alice*. Help me, she seemed to be saying, save me, keep me. And Helen, with tears pricking her eyes, treacherous and deaf, marched out of the shopping precinct, clutching the sweater, the screwdriver and the packet of Earl Grey tea.

'We've each got a letter from the lawyers,' said Helen.

Edward stood at the kitchen door, eating Puffed Wheat out of a bowl and throwing bread to the birds, who lurked in droves. Greystones, it sometimes seemed to Helen, sustained entirely the local wildlife, if it could be called that; they bought a loaf a day just for the birds, in winter. The garden was festooned with coconuts and mesh feeders as though with exotic Chinese decorations.

Edward turned back into the room. 'I shan't have time to read mine – I'll have to get the bus again. Have you seen a pile of exercise books anywhere?'

Helen opened her letter. Edward prowled the room, went out into the hall and returned, still murmuring plaintively about exercise books.

'It's about mother's Will.'

'Yes,' said Edward. 'Did you see me with them last night, can you remember? Maybe I never brought them back at all.'

'Mother hasn't left Greystones to us. Just the Britches.'

Edward halted. He stared at her.

'The house is left to Phil.'

'*Phil*?' Edward gaped. 'But why?'

'It's to do with tax. Inheritance Tax. At least up to a point it is. This lawyer seems a bit puzzled. He's a new one. The old one did the Will, apparently, five or six years ago. It's left to Phil because that way some tax is saved, but there is a proviso that we go on living here till our own deaths.'

'Oh,' said Edward. 'Then I suppose it doesn't really make much difference.'

'I suppose not.'

They looked at each other. 'I wonder why mother never told us,' said Edward, at last.

'So do I.'

Edward, now, opened his letter and read it. The letters were identical.

'I don't think Louise is going to be awfully pleased about this,' said Edward.

At that moment the phone rang. Helen went into the hall to answer it.

'I don't *believe* it!' shrieked Louise. 'What on *earth* is all this about? What the hell was mother thinking of? It's crazy. Why didn't she ask us about it? Oh God – I can't talk now, I'm half an hour late already and I've got an important meeting. Look, we'll come down on Saturday, we've got to talk about this.'

Helen returned to the kitchen. 'She isn't.'

Edward was hunting for his exercise books again. He opened the bread bin and peered inside. 'Oh dear . . . Could I have left them on the bus? Louise is furious, is she? Do we have to answer these letters?'

'They're fairly conclusive,' said Helen. After a moment she added, 'I'll ring him up – Mr Carnaby. It does seem to need a bit of explanation.'

'Oh, good,' said Edward, relieved. He lifted the bread board and found his exercise books underneath. 'There they are . . .! I knew I'd brought them back.' He sounded quite happy now. 'Can I borrow your car this evening – there's a Naturalists' Trust meeting in Spaxton.'

Helen, as she moved around the house that morning, thought about responses to possession. She owned very little: a car (coveted, admittedly, by Ron Paget, which gave it an enhanced status), a wardrobe full of clothes (which no one would covet), some books and knick-knacks. She owned also some stocks and shares left to her by her father, which brought in, nowadays, about a thousand pounds a year. Edward and Louise had received the same legacies when John Glover died in 1958. Everything else had gone to Dorothy, naturally enough. Helen recognised that she, and Edward, and Dorothy herself, for that matter, were not as others are when it came to possession. She seldom wanted anything. Edward was the same. Her mother had hated spending money, not out of parsimony but laziness. Whatever it was in the make-up of most people that responds to the sight of goods for sale had been left out, in their case. Equally, they derived no pleasure from ownership. Helen could just remember a certain frisson induced by an evening dress when she was eighteen, but this had seldom been repeated.

Louise was rather different. Louise had a lot of clothes and a big untidy house in Camden Town crammed with furniture acquired at sales and from junk-shops. She bought pictures and then got tired of them and shoved them in cupboards and bought others. She owned, probably, a considerable bulk of material goods, obtained impulsively and without calculation, and frequently disposed of in the same way. Louise was generous, vague and impatient.

And now Phil owned Greystones.

Pondering this, Helen went out into the garden. Something ought to be done about the garden, she supposed. There were obstacles to anything being done, though, quite apart from apathy. Insecticides could not be employed, nor fungicides or weedkillers or any of those labour-saving devices used by everyone else. Just as mice and moles could not be trapped, or flies and wasps sprayed. Neglect and conservational sensitivity together had turned the garden into a fine acreage of cow parsley, buttercup, dandelion, bindweed and nettle. In fact, Helen rather liked it as it was, though it was annoying not to be able to walk across the lawn without getting wet to the calves. It really should be mown.

Tam was hunched over something, gnawing. As she approached he laid his ears back and began to growl, still frantically gnawing. He had got the withered carcass of a blackbird, Helen saw. 'Drop!' she ordered. Tam snarled and shuffled sideways. Helen seized a corner of the blackbird and tugged. Tam tried to bite her hand, letting go of the blackbird in the process. Helen marched to the rubbish heap with it, Tam mobbing her heels and yapping hysterically. She flung it as high and as far back as she could. Tam watched balefully and then walked off with his whole rear end twitching, as though something were stinging him.

Helen supposed that she would live at Greystones for the rest of her life. She supposed that Edward would also. Edward's attempts to live elsewhere had never come to much. There had been the time when he worked in London with maladjusted children and shared a flat with a man he had been at college with. The children were uncontrollable and scared the wits out of Edward; also, he couldn't stand the traffic noise. After eighteen months he packed it in and returned to Greystones, where he was perfectly happy doing a bit of private coaching and spending the rest of his time on volunteer stuff for the Nature Conservancy people until a casual criticism by some relative sent him into a crisis of conscience. Edward announced that he was thirty-four, had no purpose in life, and ought to be serious about his career. He applied for a job at a minor public school and got it. When, after eight months, he resigned and returned to Greystones, Dorothy was put out. 'What on earth does he want to give up so easily for?' she demanded. 'It's not as though they'd be impossible boys, like that lot in London.' Helen, who knew why, said nothing. Edward got the job at Croxford House and lost that hunted look.

And Helen? Helen, too, had left Greystones. More than once. She had left to go to college, and had returned of course in the vacations. She had taken that first job in the county town fifty miles away, lived in a bedsitter and drifted back to Greystones at weekends. There seemed no reason not to do so, and anyway

Edward was usually there. 'Helen's looking for something to do locally,' stated her mother, to those who displayed any interest. 'It's ridiculous her trailing off like this every Monday morning.' And so inevitably the local opportunities had arisen – the part-time work at a school, then at a technical college, and eventually at Spaxton library. Helen herself saw, now, with crystal clarity, the slide from indecision to an inevitable self-perpetuating arrangement; she saw how what might have been an undistin-guished but useful career, dignified by such a title, had turned into a series of jobs. At the time, fatal steps are seldom recognised as such. There had been, for so long, the presumption that at any moment something would crop up to provoke change. There had been Dorothy, making assumptions. There had been Edward. And in any case she quite liked Greystones, and was, it would seem, pathologically short of territorial instincts of her own.

So, technically, Greystones now belonged to Phil. Techni-cally, it had belonged before to her mother. Did that matter? Well, of course it matters, thought Helen, but does it matter in any significant way? And, walking back across the lawn with sodden feet, her arms full of lilac with which to cheer up the house, she decided that it did not.

What was significant, of course, what did matter, was their mother's continuing effect; absent, she still prescribed.

'Ludicrous!' stormed Louise.

'Not necessarily. There seems to have been a tax incentive.' Tim, in the big armchair, was the still calm centre. Louise eddied around him. Phil and Suzanne perched on chair arms. Helen and Edward stood at either side of the mantelpiece.

'Mother didn't care tuppence about that sort of thing. Anyway, why didn't she *tell* us?'

'Ah,' said Tim. 'Now there you have a point.'

'I don' wan' it anyway,' said Phil comfortably.

'You haven't got it,' stormed Louise. 'It's Helen and Edward's home, just like it always has been. It makes no difference.'

'Exactly,' said Helen. 'So there's no need for any of us to get in a fuss about it. It's a technicality.'

'S'right,' Phil agreed.

Louise, glaring out of the window, swung round. 'It's the principle of the thing. In the first place she should have *discussed* it with us and in the second it's insulting to Helen and Edward technicality or not and frankly how far tax was a consideration I doubt. Mother never had a clue about finance and she wasn't interested so . . .'

'One assumes that this lawyer . . .' Tim began.

'Oh, sod the lawyer. Mother would have done what she'd decided to do. She always did. I daresay he put the *idea* into her head – that's quite possible – but from there on it would have been her. She should have *told* us, it's insulting to Helen and Edward and it's discriminating between Phil and Suzanne. Suzanne is left her jewellery. Her jewellery! Her *jewellery*! Her jewellery is that brown bead necklace and her wedding and engagement rings and the regimental brooch with half the stones missing and the copper bracelet for preventing rheumatism. That's what her jewellery is.'

'Oh, shut up, Mum,' said Suzanne. 'I mean, I don't *mind*. It's silly, all of this.'

'That's not the point. The point is that it's everything for Phil and nothing for Suzanne. The point is also that Phil is a boy and Suzanne is a girl. That's what the point is. Mother is making what might be called a political point.'

'Was,' murmured Tim, his hands folded behind his head, his gaze trained upon the ceiling. 'Was making, darling. Sad to say.'

Louise ignored him. 'It's a blatant piece of anti-feminism. Quite deliberate. Calculated to annoy. She wasn't particularly fond of Phil. She criticised him every time she saw him.'

'She got at me just as much,' said Suzanne.

'Oh, do let's stop talking like this!' cried Edward.

'S'right,' agreed Phil. 'S'all stupid, anyway. Anyone min' if I go for a walk?'

Louise looked for a moment as though she might strike him, then subsided on to the sofa with a groan.

'Think I'll go too,' said Suzanne, following Phil out of the room.

There was a silence. Edward took off his glasses and began to clean them meticulously, a thing he only did when emotionally disturbed; most of the time they were opaque with dust. Helen heard a creak from somewhere upstairs and reminded herself that no, that was not mother. Mother was not heaving herself out of the bed in search of something; there was no need to go up, no need to feel restive. Tim cleared his throat and glanced at his watch.

Louise sneezed violently. 'Oh, *Christ* . . . I don't care what they say, it's psychosomatic too. I always get it worse here.' She blew her nose and wiped her eyes. 'Apart from anything else, you realise it makes it difficult if not impossible for you ever to leave Greystones?'

'We don't want to,' said Edward. 'At least I don't.' He looked at Helen.

'How can you know?' Louise bounced to the other end of the sofa. She stuffed a cushion behind her head and lay back.

Tim was restive. 'Darling, I've got a thousand things to see to before . . .'

'All right, all right. Anyway the kids have pushed off somewhere. How can you know *what* you might want? Or Helen. I mean, it's perfectly possible that . . .'

'I doubt it,' said Helen. 'My market value has declined with the years. Come to think of it, I suppose it's even lower now.' She laughed. Tim looked embarrassed.

'That's not what I mean. You know perfectly well that's not what I mean. What I mean is that you don't know *what* might turn up. Specially now that you're not going to be dancing attendance on mother. Both of you.'

'We never did so very much dancing,' said Edward. 'Not till lately. Mother was always self-sufficient, that you must admit.'

Tim rose. 'Think I'll go and round up the children.' He left.

'Anyone can get *married*,' said Louise. 'I'm not interested in you getting *married*. I'm interested in you being able to . . . to . . .'

'Go where the wind blows?' suggested Edward. He put his glasses on again, looking unusually clear-eyed. He seemed rather cheerful now.

27

Louise scowled at him. 'You simply are not taking this seriously.'

'It isn't worth taking seriously.'

Louise swung towards Helen. 'Surely you can see?'

'I stand somewhere in the middle. I think Edward may well be ignoring possible future problems. But I don't think it's something we should get steamed up about. It is, in the last resort, a technical point. It's not going to make any practical difference to any of us.'

'I know, I know. It's the *effect*.'

'There's nothing that can be done about an effect,' said Helen.

Her own words came back to her that night, standing in front of her bedroom mirror. The new sweater was a mistake, it made her face look not more appealing but disturbingly furtive. It stared out over the unaccustomed colour and pattern with, it seemed to Helen, sly defiance. It was not at home. She took off the sweater, folded it and put it on a shelf of the wardrobe. It would do nicely as a *pièce de résistance* at the village fete jumble stall.

She got into bed. It was late. Edward had come up some time ago, while she was still pottering in the kitchen. Now, she heard his door open, quietly. The stairs let out a furtive creak. She knew exactly what he was doing. Assuming that she was asleep, he was going down to see if she had set a mousetrap in the larder. If she had, he would spring it with a pencil, guiltily, and not mention the matter. Helen, one step ahead in the mouse battle, now put traps under the sink; Edward – unlike the mice – had so far failed to discover them.

THREE

Helen had a clear memory of Edward as a toddler sitting in long grass contemplating with rapturous absorption a butterfly on some clover. She could see it now: the waving grasses, the crunchy head of the clover, the butterfly opening and closing its wings, Edward's baby face. Was that when it had all begun? Or later? For alongside that – the next slide in the box, as it were – was another scene featuring an upright, articulate Edward, aged three or four: a man shooting pigeons over a stubble field, the mound of pearly corpses at his side, Edward flinging himself at his mother screaming 'Tell him he mustn't shoot they! Tell him he mustn't kill they because they nice!' Dorothy pushing him impatiently aside: 'Don't be silly, Edward. Birds have to be shot.'

Nowadays the possibilities for distress were limitless, and had been for many a year. Edward's outrage had run from the abuse of donkeys and circus animals and battery hens to vivisection and otter-hunting. There were whales to worry about and ospreys and gorillas and the greater horseshoe bat, orchids and lichens, butterflies and toads. There was no end to it. And it got progressively worse, as far as Helen could see. Fuelled by the glowing testimony of television, in full colour, the scale of man's insensitivity was seen to be as never before. The destruction of South American rain forests, the draining of the Somerset levels, the pollution of Finnish lakes – it was all brought to your hearth now, to furnish sleepless nights for such as Edward. In the village, small boys no longer collected birds' eggs; propaganda in the primary school had seen to that, but five thousand miles away people were exterminating entire ecological systems. Edward's interest in protective organisations had extended from the Royal Society for the Protection of Birds and local naturalists' groups to Greenpeace and the World Wildlife Fund. Greystones had a television for one reason only – that Edward might indulge his passion for wildlife films, though these as often as not brought to his attention some new aspect of the endangered environment and gave him yet another thing to worry about. His rare holidays were spent with like-minded souls, camping on bird-infested islands and living off wild spinach and tins of baked beans. He always came back wonderfully exhilarated, which puzzled Helen. Surely the contemplation of vanishing riches should be dampening rather than uplifting? 'It's knowing that it's still there somewhere,' said Edward.

Helen, getting down before him in the morning, hurried out into the garden with the mousetrap, from which projected a stiffened corpse. Tam followed her, gazing hopefully upwards. When they returned Edward was in the kitchen, making tea. Helen said, 'I forgot to tell you – Mr Carnaby rang. The lawyer. He's going to look in this afternoon.'

'I shan't be here,' said Edward at once. 'Why?' he added.

'That's not clear. He just said he'd like a word.'

'Well, he'll have a much more satisfactory one with you than with me. You can tell me all about it afterwards.' He gave her a propitiating smile and left for work. Habitually, Edward side-stepped all confrontations with the world of affairs; he would have avoided having a bank account if he could, and had great difficulties with the income tax people. He never answered letters that came in typed envelopes, and often did not open them.

'I hope you don't mind me inviting myself here,' said Giles Carnaby. 'I felt that my office would be inappropriate. People can feel at a disadvantage.'

'Supplicants. And all those filing cabinets. Of course,' Helen added hastily, 'you have to have the filing cabinets, I realise that.'

'Quite. And in any case I think it is I who am the supplicant. I'll come straight to the point. I'm feeling somewhat concerned – and embarrassed – about your mother's Will. We were not aware, in our office, that you and your brother had never been informed of the terms of the Will – that this house was to be left

30

to your nephew, with the proviso about your continued occupancy. The fact of the matter is that when my predecessor advised your mother, and the Will was drawn up, he appears from the correspondence to have suggested to her that she should consult all of you – all three of you. It now seems that . . . um, well, that she didn't.'

'That's right,' said Helen.

'Which is a bit unfortunate. So my predecessor seems to have been under the impression that she had, and proceeded accordingly, and of course it wasn't up to him to inform you, and indeed he would have been acting unprofessionally had he done so on his own initiative.'

'Oh goodness,' said Helen. 'No one's blaming him.' She shifted slightly; the sun was in her eyes, obscuring her view of the visitor. Thick silvery hair and a face beneath that looked younger than the hair. Actually, she thought, my age – give or take a year or two. Nice voice.

'All the same. We feel . . . concerned. I feel concerned. Not of course that it makes the slightest difference to . . . to your living arrangements. But obviously there is . . . there is . . .'

'An effect,' suggested Helen.

'Precisely. Which could have been avoided.'

'I don't think my mother wanted to avoid it,' said Helen. He looks like a film star, she thought, the one in that film about a man being chased across enormous fields by a plane. What's he called, for heaven's sake? Man with a nice face and thick hair. Bit younger.

'Oh,' said Giles Carnaby. 'I see.'

There was a silence. Got it, thought Helen. Cary Grant. Why on earth should I think of that? I haven't seen a film in years.

Giles Carnaby coughed. He ran a hand through the thick hair. The hand wore a heavy gold ring. Married? wondered Helen. Wedding ring? Some men wear them. Oh, married, presumably. Everyone's married.

'The other rather unfortunate thing is that – and I feel I really have to mention this – the tax advantage is not, to be frank, all that great. My predecessor was – well, his initial enthusiasm for the scheme turned out to be somewhat misplaced though, to be fair to him, he did put this to your mother. But by that time she appears to have got up a certain enthusiasm of her own. At least this is my impression, from the correspondence.' Giles Carnaby looked at the floor, uncomfortable; he stirred the carpet with his foot, ran a hand through the hair again. Don't take on so, thought Helen, please, it's not *your* fault. It's perfectly all right, honestly. Would you like a glass of sherry? No – heavens, it's only half past four. Tea. Would you like a cup of tea?

'Yes, mother would have,' she said. 'I can imagine.'

'I hope it's not causing family problems, anyway.'

'My sister's rather put out. She'll calm down.'

'The boy himself . . .'

'He's got green stripes in his hair,' said Helen. 'I don't imagine they mean anything serious. He was always a perfectly nice child.'

Giles Carnaby laughed.

Helen sprang to her feet. 'Would you like a cup of tea?'

'I'd love a cup of tea.'

He followed her into the kitchen, a move she immediately regretted. From time to time she saw Greystones as others must see it; this was one of those occasions. The cracks in the flagged floor. The green mould creeping up the wall by the back door that one just ignored because if you redecorated it simply crept up again within a month or two. The rusting cake tins. The crockery. That sink.

'What a marvellous kitchen,' said Giles Carnaby.

Helen threw him a quick look of suspicion. No, perfectly sincere.

He wandered around. 'I say! *Country Life* calendar for 1962!'

'It's got some photos of bats that my brother is rather fond of.'

'Doesn't he get confused over dates?'

'He's never very bothered about that sort of thing,' said Helen. She put the kettle on. Biscuits? She opened the Coronation tin and closed it again quickly. You cannot offer slightly mouldy Tea-Time Fancies (Dorothy's favourites) to a visitor. Cake? No cake available.

'Earl Grey!' said Giles Carnaby. 'I haven't had Earl Grey since my wife died. I never know where to get it.'

'Oh,' said Helen. 'Have this one.' She thrust the packet at him, an extraordinary, unaccustomed sunny smile on her face. 'I can get another.'

'I wouldn't dream of it.'

'Please . . .'

'All right,' said Giles Carnaby. 'But only on condition you come and drink a cup of it with me sometime.'

The kettle boiled. Violently, as always, spewing water all over the stove. Helen leapt for it, this absurd smile still pasted to her face. How tragic. When did she die? Come and drink a cup of it with me sometime.

'You would probably have to make it also,' said Giles Carnaby. 'I'm hopelessly inefficient. Not professionally, of course – I mustn't let you think you've got a dud lawyer. Professionally I am a whizz.'

Don't just stand there, you stupid woman. Put hot water in teapot, cups on tray, and milk in jug. The man will think you're half-witted. Don't look at him like that, either. God knows what he will think.

'Let me carry the tray for you.'

'Thank you,' said Helen.

They returned to the sitting room.

'Oh – I've forgotten the sugar.'

'I don't take it,' said Giles Carnaby. 'My wife always went on at me about getting fat. I am a bit too fat.' He peered down at the front of his trousers. 'Don't you think? No – I'm not asking you, you'll be too polite to do other than prevaricate. Anyway, no sugar. Your delightful time-slip kitchen has completely distracted me from the matter in hand. Is there anything you – or your brother – would like any further advice about?'

Helen racked her brains. Advice? Surely they needed advice? Of course they needed advice; she reviewed, in a flash, the whole unsatisfactory condition of Greystones, of her state of mind, of life itself. How can we stop the drain flooding whenever it rains? Why do I have to feel guilty because my mother has died? How can I achieve a comforting complacency?

'I can't think of anything.'

'Oh dear. What a pity. I don't in the least want to go back to the office. Let's have another cup of tea and perhaps something will spring to mind.' He held his cup out. 'I like this house. It feels so . . . established. I imagine you've lived here a long time.'

I must remember 'established', thought Helen. Next time Louise is on at us about brightening the place up a bit. Established. 'Nearly thirty years. We came here just after my father died. We'd been living in London and mother always hankered after a village.'

'And it came up to expectations?'

'Of course,' said Helen. 'Villages are red in tooth and claw and my mother was naturally contentious.'

'Really? How interesting. What is it that is being contended about?'

Helen reflected. 'Who owns what, on the whole, and what they are doing with it. Conservation versus making money. All that. Oh – and with side-issues about noise and personal vendettas and things people's children have been up to. There's no end to it.'

'And do you take part? And your brother?'

'Only in a desultory way. Edward not at all, I suppose. We are considered a bit eccentric. And then there's the Britches.'

'Ah. The bit of woodland. What about it?'

Helen explained. Giles Carnaby listened with attention. When she had finished he said, 'Yes. I can see how this would be seen as perverse. Your mother was not acting according to the spirit of the times. She could have made a hundred thousand or so. Was it that she was ecologically minded, like your brother?'

'Not in the least. She just liked saying no to people. She especially liked saying no to Ron Paget.'

'Who?'

'The builder along the road.'

'Ah yes. Does he drive a very affluent-looking red car? I think I saw him coming out as I arrived. You realise it would be perfectly possible to sell the – what's it called? – this land now if you wished?'

'That's out of the question,' said Helen. 'Edward would be terribly upset.'

'Then so long as your finances are healthy there is absolutely no reason why you should. Perhaps that's why your mother didn't include the . . . the . . .'

'Britches.'

'Curious name – what does it mean? Why she didn't include the Britches with the house. Maybe she didn't feel confident that your nephew would share the family resistance to material prosperity. Maybe she thought he'd sell it to your builder friend – in the fullness of time.'

'Yes,' said Helen. 'I should imagine that was precisely why. She knew we never would.' She thought of her mother with a flash of respect, successfully pursuing her struggle against Ron Paget from beyond the grave.

'The whole situation is a touch bizarre, but nothing for you to worry about. The lad can't ever evict you, even should he turn out a villain and who's to suppose he will? The green hair tells us nothing, I assume – it's purely totemic and tribal. Anyway, at sixteen, he remains an unknown quantity. I speak from authority – my own son didn't solidify, as it were, until he was well over twenty. And you have no need to sell the land so your brother can go on enjoying his ecology.'

'Good.'

'You're protective about your brother, aren't you? Oh dear – I'm sorry, none of my business. Now I'm exceeding my brief.' He smiled. 'I'm seduced by the ambience – I keep forgetting I'm here in a professional capacity.'

Ambience, thought Helen. Ambience and established. Just you wait, Louise. She smiled back – no, beamed: felt her face fixed in this idiot grin of well-being and response.

'More tea?'

'What did the lawyer say?'

'He said they never realised mother hadn't told us about leaving the house to Phil and it didn't save much tax anyway. And he liked the kitchen.'

'What was he like?'

'Do you remember that old film with a man being chased across an enormous field by an aeroplane?'

35

'No.'

'Oh, never mind,' said Helen. 'Nice, anyway. Very nice, actually.'

Protective.

That, yes. One had no choice, really. Given mother. Given Edward.

She had taken them, aged maybe four and seven, to someone else's birthday party. Children skittering all over polished parquet floors: children more practised and assured than they were. Musical chairs. Hunt the slipper. Balloons. Attendant nannies. They did not have a nanny. Mothers gathered in a drawing room.

She had tugged at her mother's sleeve, whispering, 'Edward's wet himself – what shall we do?'

'I'm talking to Mrs Carew,' said her mother. 'Be quiet, Helen. If you've got something to say wait till I've finished.'

'But mother . . .'

Her mother turned on her a scalding gaze. 'Don't interrupt, Helen. And go away, please. Play with the others.'

Helen led Edward to the bathroom. His pants dropped, damply. Once there she took his things off. His socks, too, were sodden. She tried to dry them on the bathmat. Edward simply stood, compliantly lifting a foot when required. Once, he said 'Will there be crackers for tea?' She wiped him down with lavatory paper and put his pants back on; they were still wet but there was nothing else for it. She stuffed his underpants and socks behind the Carews' radiator. Then she washed her hands and his and led him downstairs again. He was talking once more about crackers. All she could think of was whether anyone would notice that he had no socks on.

He was sent to boarding school at nine. It was inevitable. 'Don't be silly, Helen,' said her mother. 'Of course he won't hate it.

He can play football and all that sort of thing. What do you mean – he doesn't like football? All boys like football. And there's no point in going on at Daddy about it. Daddy agrees with me.'

Or so she said. And so he appeared to do – backing into the study, newspaper in hand, with deprecating gesture. Distant, hazy, dead Daddy. Long since drowned out by other voices, other opinions; bleached now to a faded outline, a few mannerisms, a vague remembered preference for anchovy paste as opposed to jam. Could a lifetime be reduced to that?

But in the event Edward, who might have been expected to suffer deeply and conventionally at school, in fact went through it in some kind of trance. He retreated so far into himself, became so withdrawn and unresponsive, that in another age he would probably have been classified as subnormal. As it was, he was simply left alone to operate some private sensual filter system, which admitted air and nourishment but excluded the grinding scatological barbarity of his peers and the ugly monotony of the nine years' imprisonment to which he was condemned. He must also have admitted instruction, since he passed examinations – though only just. He was no good at games, but survived again by a system of practised self-effacement – dreaming long afternoons away in the long grass of the cricket pitch at deep square leg, trotting helpfully around on the wing at football. From time to time he was bullied, but his anonymity was so expert that after a while even the bullies lost interest. There is no fun in negative response; screams of pain are essential.

'How did he get into the kitchen anyway?' said Edward. 'Lawyers don't go into kitchens. Didn't you receive him in the sitting room?'

'One thing led to another, somehow.'

'I see.' He was busy fiddling with the knobs on the television set. It was an ancient model and required much coaxing; Edward's favourite programme was due in five minutes. 'Do you think mother did it all on purpose? The Will, and Phil and everything.'

'I suppose so,' said Helen.

The television screen shuddered into life and produced a delicate Seurat landscape composed of coloured dots, with just discernible trees and moving figures. 'Blast!' said Edward. He hammered the side of the set and the dots turned from green to red. He turned to look at her for a moment: 'There's really no point in us getting worked up about it now. About her, I mean.'

'Absolutely none.'

'I suppose she couldn't bear the thought of not dictating things any more. It's bad enough for anyone to know they're going to die eventually but I suppose it's even worse for people like mother. Like medieval kings. Poor mother. We never realised what she was going through, really.'

'Hmn. Maybe not.'

Upstairs, a window slammed. Involuntarily, they both leapt to their feet. And sat down again sheepishly. 'God!' said Edward. 'Are we ever going to get used to it?'

'Eventually, I imagine.'

Edward hit the other side of the television set and a head and shoulders shot into clarity, talking about pesticides. He sighed and slumped into the armchair.

The programme, that evening, dealt among other things with the Barnacle geese of the Arctic. The Barnacle geese migrate north in the breeding seasons to a wide river valley bordered by low mountains. In order to preserve their young from the marauding foxes of the plain the geese nest two or three hundred feet up a mountain cliff. As soon as the young are fledged it becomes necessary to get them down off these crags to the feeding grounds below. To this end, the parents lead the chirping fluffy bundles across the rocks until they reach the precipitous edge. Then the adult birds, squawking anxiously, launch themselves into the air and circle around, calling the babies.

The camera dwelt unflinchingly on the ensuing horror as, one by one, the pathetically cheeping goslings hurled themselves over the edge. It lingered on the plunging balls of fluff as, embryonic wings outstretched, small feet flailing, they plunged to the rocks below. There, a fox trotted up and down sniffing. The parents rushed around calling frantically. It came as a surprise to learn that about fifty percent of the chicks survive this charming natural arrangement.

Edward and Helen watched in appalled silence. The programme ended with some stunning *tour de force* photography – a blood red Arctic sun hanging low in an orange sky above an exquisite wilderness in which wolves and caribou, foxes and geese were left undisturbed to do what they liked to one another.

Edward, after that, found it difficult to sleep. In his head, the goslings churned around with other, more personal, matters. The peculiarly savage twist to the distress he felt about the goslings was that there was nowhere to direct one's outrage. It was easier, in a way, to lie awake boiling about the barbarities of Canadian seal-slaughterers or the ecological insensitivity of English farmers. There was no one and nothing to blame for the goslings. There was nothing to join, no one to whom to send a contribution, no letter to be written to a newspaper.

In the darkness at the end of the bed Tam snored in loud staccato bursts; from time to time he changed position in his sleep and tried to shove Edward's foot out of the way. He was a dog entirely devoted to the pursuit of self-interest; Edward and Helen, discussing this, always came up against the intractable point that presumably there could be no other kind of dog, or indeed of animal. Animals always act out of self-interest, unless in the interests of their young, and that too can presumably be defined as self-interest in a genetic sense.

Tam, Edward suspected, would not even act in the interests of his young, should he have any. Since he was rising ten and had never given more than token attention to the village bitches this was unlikely. Edward loved Tam, in the complex and distorted way in which people can be said to love animals, though he had loved other dogs more. Tam was one of a series; he had predecessors and would no doubt have successors, and Edward sometimes thought of the others in the way in which people review other children or other spouses. He also knew quite well that these were the terms in which he thought of them, and why.

He had never shared his bed with a person. He had come near

to it, once or twice, but a long time ago. Even those occasions, now, were dimmed; they were rosier, too, in recollection than in cold reality. He flinched from the thought of the people involved. What was left was the memory of something else: his own feelings.

He had a vivid, and much earlier, memory of the first occasion on which he had realised that feelings were something to which a word was attached, and that they were recognised by others. He was quite small – his head did not reach above the windowsill below which he stood – and through the open window came Helen's voice, high-pitched in indignation, crying out to their mother, 'You've hurt his feelings! Why did you say that!' And three things fused within his head: Dorothy's derision of his ineptitude at something, what he felt in consequence, and the fact that Helen understood how he felt even though it hadn't happened to her. Now that he knew what they were called, he realised also that he had them all the time, with kaleidoscopic intensity, and hence that others must do so too.

Their mother also, presumably, though in her case expressions of feeling more usually took the form of anger. Dorothy found outbursts of rage exhilarating; she would descend the next morning blithe and invigorated, while everyone else crawled around punch-drunk from emotion. Louise was the only one who was a match for her. She learned in infancy to throw spirited tantrums in response to her mother's anger, holding her breath and going blue in the face in a way that alarmed even Dorothy, who held that most childish ailments were put on. The tantrums were, of course, up to a point, but they were impressive all the same. When too old for tantrums, Louise resorted to argument and shouting matches. And, eventually, she left.

Helen and Edward, on the other hand, withdrew. Once they grew beyond being afraid of Dorothy's temper, they dealt with it by evasion; they simply got out of the way whenever she brewed up. Living with her, they learned to treat her as the weather – elemental and inescapable.

Feelings also may be inescapable, Edward learned, but there are ways of cheating them. Of diverting them. Of hiding from them. Your own howls can be drowned out by the howls of the rest of the world, if you set about it properly. If you are naturally self-deprecating, and exceptionally under-endowed with egotism, the process comes almost naturally. Eventually you are exercised only about the atrocities around. Or so it can seem.

Helen also thought about the Barnacle geese that night, though with less intensity. The image of the plunging chicks lurked in her head, nagging, but it was other matters that kept her awake. Feelings, of course – those maddening unquenchable onsets of disease. She reviewed Giles Carnaby's visit and was aware of having existed, during that hour or so, on two different planes; at one level she had listened to Giles Carnaby and talked to Giles Carnaby, at some other level she had undergone strange physical and emotional experiences. She had gone hot and cold; she had felt slightly dizzy; she had been unable to take her eyes off him. All this while discussing her mother's testamentary arrangements.

She had not felt thus for roughly fifteen years and had not expected to do so ever again.

Edward – in so far as he thought about the matter – had always assumed that his sister was a virgin. He was wrong. Other people's sexual lives are of course deeply mysterious; even so, Edward's assumption was understandable. To his knowledge, she had had few abiding relationships with men and not many transient ones either. It was lack of opportunity as well as his knowledge of her character that made virginity seem likely.

In fact, Helen had first gone to bed with a man when she was twenty-three. She found the whole performance embarrassing but distinctly pleasurable. She quite liked him but was not in love with him, and recognised the experience as a purely sexual one. The man made vague suggestions about keeping in touch, and then vanished. Helen settled down wretchedly to await the outcome; she doubted if the correct precautions had been taken and knew that copulation leads, more often than not, to pregnancy. She told no one and sat it out stoically. When, on the seventeenth day, her period arrived the relief and elation she felt were like a religious experience. Indeed, she went down on her knees beside her mother in church that Sunday and thanked the Lord, furtively and guiltily. She did not say to Him that she wouldn't do it again because she did not expect the opportunity to arise. Nor did it, for quite a while.

Dorothy's attitude to sex was one of withering contempt. She did not disapprove, she despised. The subject brought out in her a particular look – an expression of obstinate rejection, a clamping of the mouth, a hardening of the eye. Each time Helen saw it she thought of her father, and shivered for him.

Louise, at sixteen, discovered boys. The row with Dorothy and Louise's flight to London and to art school was about sex rather more than about educational opportunity. Dorothy had opened the front door at the wrong moment late one evening and discovered Louise on the top step, in a fervent embrace with the publican's son. The ensuing commotion kept everyone up till the small hours of the morning. 'You're disgusting!' bawled Dorothy. 'You're a revolting little trollop, do you hear me?' And Louise, incoherent and weeping but primed with righteous outrage, shouted back that Dorothy didn't *own* her, that other people's mothers didn't . . . that every other teenager in the country . . . that this wasn't the nineteenth century, for heaven's sake!

Louise and Dorothy kept up a spasmodic battle about Louise's sex-life until Louise married Tim, at which point Dorothy lost interest. Helen and Edward were an altogether simpler matter. So far as Dorothy was concerned they had nothing to do with that sort of thing; they weren't 'silly' like Louise. When Helen struck up friendships with men Dorothy moved into the offensive with a strategy of disparagement: 'That poor young man – one wonders what he can possibly fetch up doing, with that voice and those looks.' She was given to assessing people in terms of appearance. Girls were classified as pretty girls, nice girls and clever girls. Pretty was best; clever was worst. One could not help noting that Dorothy herself, in youth, could not have fallen into any of these categories, but then Dorothy always saw herself as apart. Not in any sense of superiority: simply as apart. There was her, and there was the rest of the world.

At first Helen was upset by Dorothy's disparagement: 'Just as well you're prepared to put up with that chap's acne – no one

42

else would, I imagine.' 'Why hasn't anyone ever told him about his teeth?' Then she ceased to bring her friends home, unless it was unavoidable. Eventually what Dorothy said no longer mattered. During the long-ago weeks and months when it had seemed possible that she might be on the brink of a permanent alliance she explained to the man in question about her mother, and he appeared to understand. As it turned out, she need not have bothered.

The hall clock struck four. Edward and Helen, apart and awake, heard it. Edward remembered that he had to coach the remedial French class in a few hours' time, always a taxing business; he turned over and made a resolute attempt to sleep. Helen felt an odd little tingle of interest at the approach of the new day: another unusual sensation. In the Britches a cat yowled.

FOUR

'Why are there ladders everywhere?' said Edward.

'Ron Paget's men are mending the broken guttering.'

'The house looks like some medieval siege. Do tell them to be careful of the martins' nests.'

'They've been told. Though I don't see why the martins shouldn't do some rebuilding. Here is Ron.'

Edward made a dive for the door, but too late. Ron Paget was already there.

'Better to come round to the back, I thought, this time of day. Don't let me interrupt your tea. I heard Mr Glover's car go past so I thought I'd just pop over and see the men are getting on all right. What about that window-frame — shall I have them see to that while they're about it?'

'I suppose they may as well,' said Helen.

'No problem.' Ron's glance slid around the kitchen. 'The damp's really got a hold in here, hasn't it? You ever thought of having a proper damp course put in?'

'Well . . .' Helen began.

'Tell you what — why don't I have a look round later this week? Work out what we could do and how much it would set you back. Just to give you an idea. It'ud be a biggish job, mind, but I'd make a special price — we've been neighbours a heck of a long time now and I had a soft spot for your mother.'

Helen and Edward looked at each other.

'You leave it to me,' said Ron. 'I'll suss out the damage and we can talk about it later.' He turned sideways to look out into the garden. 'Lovely place, this. Of course it's bound to get out of hand, you've neither of you got the time to give to it. You know, if it was me I'd have a patio. Cut down on some of the grass —

give you an area for sitting out – York stone paving, swing seat with an awning, very nice.'

The Glovers made no comment.

'Yes. Well, of course you've gone rather more for the natural look, the way it is. Is that a yew hedge?'

'I believe it is,' said Edward. 'In theory, anyway.'

'It needs the clippers taken to it, certainly. And beyond it there's what you'd call the kitchen garden, right? Your mother did a bit in the veg line, I seem to remember.'

'Not for quite a while,' said Helen, wondering how to curtail all this. 'Anyway, thanks very much, Mr Paget, we mustn't keep you, the men seem to be . . .'

Ron took a few steps backwards and stared up at the house. 'There's a bit of re-pointing needs doing up there, too. We'll see to that. And I tell you what, Miss Glover, I've had a thought. About your garden. Our Gary'll come in for a couple of hours, Saturday mornings.'

'Gary?' There were several Paget offspring. Gary must be the adolescent, from marriage number one.

'He's a big lad now. Fourteen. Muscles on him like nobody's business. You can put him on to the rough work – dig over the vegetable garden, that sort of thing. Give him one fifty an hour, that'll be quite enough. Maybe two quid by Christmas, if you think he's worth it.'

'But we don't grow vegetables,' said Edward.

'I'm surprised, Mr Glover.' Ron sounded quite censorious. 'I thought everyone was doing their own veg these days. Nouvelle cuisine and all that. Mangetouts and yellow zucchini – that's what I'm into this year. Fantastic. I'll tell you the varieties to go for.'

The Glovers, intrigued by this unsuspected bent, gazed at him. Helen suddenly thought – well why not? It's absurd the way we waste the garden. Never mind yellow whatsits but new potatoes would be nice. And he could clean up that old mower and do something about the grass. 'All right. Maybe it's not a bad idea.'

'Oh,' Edward began. 'We'd never . . .'

'Tell him to come on Saturday,' said Helen.

Ron grinned. 'Spot on, Miss Glover. You won't regret it. And I'll drop by myself and have a think about your damp. Cheerio for now.'

'What was all that about?' said Edward, when he had gone. 'Falling over himself to be so helpful.'

'The Britches, of course.'

'He never gives up, does he? But do we really want this boy messing about?'

'Might as well.'

Edward shrugged. 'If you say so.'

Life was reasserting itself. Days had trundled by and it was now two weeks since the funeral. Helen, going into Dorothy's room, saw that it had become dusty. Her presence was still loud and strong, but patchily so; there were occasional moments when she was not there at all, when it was possible to walk up the stairs or into the kitchen without expecting to see her. The black holes were becoming grey; Helen could see the substance of the house behind them, as though brick, stone and wood were extinguishing her mother.

She began to manifest herself in other ways.

'At least get new curtains,' said Louise. She had come down for the night, for purposes as yet unclear. 'These are all of thirty years old. They've got moth *and* mildew. I've always hated them. They're the precise colour of pee.'

'Mother made them.'

'I *know* mother made them. That's why the hems are uneven. That's why they're such a nasty colour.'

Remnants, thought Helen, from a sale at Elliston & Cavell's in Oxford, which is no more, subsumed into Debenham's. I helped, if that is the right word, mother to buy the material. Stood about, in actual fact, while she yanked bales of stuff around and hectored shop assistants. I murmured things about the colour at the time. She pointed out that the fabric was cheap and service-able. And indeed here it is, still serving.

'And another thing,' said Louise. 'The downstairs loo. Cloak-room, as mother called it. Something must be done about it –

46

there are strata, quite literally strata, of defunct raincoats in there. There's stuff of *father's*. Do me a favour and clear it out.'

'It's part of the ambience,' said Helen.

'The *what*?'

'This house feels so established.'

'What's all this about? Who's been giving you that sort of crap? Here . . .' Louise rummaged in a carrier bag. 'I brought a bottle of plonk. What are we eating? And where's Edward? Don't tell me he's sloped off somewhere – I want to talk to both of you. Tim's at a weekend conference, so I damn well didn't see why I shouldn't have a break myself. God knows what I'll find when I get back, but still.'

'Edward's in the Britches putting up some nest-boxes that came this morning, and we're eating a sort of stew.'

'Mail order nest-boxes!' said Louise. 'I don't believe it!' She wandered around the kitchen opening cupboards. 'I hate these glasses – where are those green ones? Ah, there . . . You need a proper corkscrew – this kind is hopeless. Here – let's take a drink through to the sitting room. It's perishing in here.'

Settling into the corner of the sofa she continued, 'It feels so *peculiar* here now. I keep expecting – oh God, I don't know quite what I keep expecting. And I keep wishing I hadn't fought with her so much. You know I kept trying, all this last year, to . . . well, to have a sort of great *rapprochement* . . . and each time she'd spoil it by coming out with . . . well, the things she always did come out with. You know.'

'I know.'

'So now I feel . . . Ugh! Guilty. Nasty.'

Edward came in. 'Hello. What are you feeling guilty about?'

'Mother, of course,' said Louise morosely. 'Here's a glass and the bottle's on the book-case. Listen, was she the way I think she was or did I imagine her?'

Edward poured himself a glass of wine and looked doubtfully at it – not because he questioned its quality but because drink was unusual at Greystones and had connotations of ritual celebration – Christmas and birthdays. The note struck right now did not seem to be one of celebration. He took a gulp and sat down at the other end of the sofa.

'She once threw a plate at me,' Louise went on. 'Did you know that? One of those blue and orange ones. It missed.'

'I thought they were supposed to be Crown Derby, those,' said Edward. 'It shows what a temper she must have been in.'

Louise glared at him. 'I was seventeen and a half at the time. All I could think was – other people's mothers don't do things like this.'

'There's probably more of it around than one imagines.'

Helen had finished what was in her glass. 'Mother was the way you think she was. And the way I think she was and the way Edward thinks she was. She was demanding and assertive and dogmatic and possessive and she always thought she knew best about everything. She bullied us. She bullied everyone who gave her the chance. She was prejudiced and inflexible and opinionated. She never listened to what anyone else said. She had a vile temper. There are also other things that she wasn't. She wasn't avaricious or malicious or cruel in any deliberate sense, though the result of some of the things she did was cruelty of a kind.'

The others stared at her. 'I'm not sure you should say all this,' said Edward rather wildly.

'What's the difference between saying it and thinking it? And it's true. And it can't hurt her now because she's dead. Also, it doesn't mean I feel any differently about her.'

There was a silence. Louise, eventually, spoke. 'What did you feel about her?'

'I loved her, I suppose,' said Helen. 'One does, willy-nilly.'

'Sometimes I hated her,' said Louise.

'Oh, that too.'

Further silence. Louise reached for the wine bottle and shared out what was left. 'Edward, that dog of yours is disgusting.'

Tam was sitting under the standard lamp, salivating lavishly as he gazed at a fly that wandered across the shade. Edward poked him with a foot. Tam gave a propitiating wag of the tail, licked his lips and concentrated once more on the fly.

Edward said, 'Well, it's over, anyway. Poor old mother. She's not here, quite simply. We're on our own now.'

Helen laughed. 'Clearly that is just what we are not.'

Edward gave her a stern look. 'Wine always sets you off. Don't give her any more, Louise.'

'For Christ's sake!' cried Louise. 'She doesn't get *enough* booze, that's the trouble. This house has always been like some Temperance cell. Mother again – just because she didn't care for it herself. Oh – enough, enough! Look, I came here to talk about myself, not mother.'

'Good,' said Edward comfortably. The *sturm und drang* of Louise's private and professional life gave him all the vicarious satisfaction of television soap opera. 'What happened over the row in your office about the new restaurant contract?'

Louise looked at him sharply. 'My life isn't some sort of spectator sport, you know. Anyway, it's nothing to do with the office. It's Phil. Classic teenage stuff, I suppose, but it's got a bit beyond a joke. He wants to leave school, go and hang out with a bunch of down and out friends, all that nonsense.'

Edward was losing interest. 'Talk to him,' he advised kindly.

'That's pathetic!' snapped Louise. 'Frankly we feel more like hitting him at the moment. I have a permanent stress headache. If I was anyone else I'd be on tranquillizers.'

The telephone rang. 'I'll go,' said Helen. Out in the hall, she picked up the receiver. 'Hello?'

'Miss Glover? Helen . . . May I? Giles Carnaby here. I have one or two further little things I ought to discuss with you. I wondered if you might like to meet me in Spaxton for a spot of lunch?'

She returned to the sitting room. Louise was still talking about Phil. Edward was picking burrs out of Tam's coat. They both looked at her. Louise said, 'That wine has turned you bright pink – it must be even more vicious than I thought. Let's open another bottle. And your stew's burning – I can smell it.'

When Louise was a little girl Helen had been immensely proud of her. 'Louise is going to be the pretty one,' Dorothy said, when Louise was about two; and said it rather too often, thereafter. In fact Louise was not pretty, but she had a quality of vibrancy that

49

did very well instead. Nowadays, in the company of good-looking women she appeared louche – her skin was bad and her hair messy. But beside most women – Helen included – she was a curious illustration of why one woman is attractive and another not. You were simply more inclined to look at Louise than at others. And as a small child she had been compelling, with her bounce, her bright eyes, her mop of hair. Helen, escorting her along a street or into shops, had delighted in it: 'Yes, she's my sister. Yes, she is quite a handful – come along, Louise.'

She sometimes saw a shadow of Louise in her own face, with interest and quite without rancour. Patently, the life of an attractive woman is different from that of a plain one – and not exclusively in a sexual sense: a personable appearance conditions the world's response to most people. Louise's looks invited attention; Helen's did not. But, that being said, Helen knew that the gulf between her experience and her sister's could be attributed to personality and inclination quite as much as to the cast of nose or mouth. Louise was extrovert and unwary; Helen was reserved and cautious. Louise, from the age of two, had fought their mother; Helen had propitiated and avoided confrontation. Louise had grabbed at opportunities (and, on occasion, paid for it); Helen had hesitated, considered the pros and cons, and then found that it was too late.

She had never envied Louise; rather, she had feared for her. She had stood in the wings, over the years, and watched with apprehension as Louise was crossed in love, had rows and reconciliations, got the sack, went broke, suffered a fallopian pregnancy and an attack of shingles and smashed up a car. She came to realise, too, that while temperament may condition experience it also determines how we overcome it. She herself would have been felled by any of these things, she suspected; Louise shrieked her protests, and prospered. The mystery, as Helen saw it, was that two people could emerge from the same circumstances and set about dealing with the world so differently: follow the thread back and you reached, in each case, the same hearth, the same cot, the same indoctrinations, Dorothy's uncompromising lap.

*

'Will this do?' said Giles Carnaby. 'I thought of the Crown, but I can't stand all the bucolic laughter from Rotarian lunches. And that wine bar place is too young and the White Hart is too elderly. I hoped this might fill the gap – it's new, apparently.'

The restaurant struck Helen as unlikely to survive long in Spaxton: the menu was ornate in every sense and the prices high. There was hardly anyone else there. It was also elegantly under-lit; she had difficulty in picking out Giles until she spotted the gleam of his silver hair in a far corner. He jumped to his feet as she approached and fussed around with her coat; his hand lay for an instant on her shoulder.

'It's fine,' she said.

'Are you sure? I've been having misgivings about the decor. We could always do a bolt somewhere else.'

'Not now they've got my coat. And you've unfolded your napkin.'

'So I have. Sheer nervousness.' That winning smile. 'Well, we're stuck with it. Shall we get the rather boring business bit over first or do you want me to stow it away until the coffee?'

There was some matter of the whereabouts of share certificates, it turned out, and an explanation about probate and how long it took. It occurred to Helen that all of it would have gone nicely into a letter; quite a short letter. She sipped her sherry and thought about this.

'There!' he concluded. 'Honour is satisfied. Now tell me what you've been doing? How is the young man with green hair? By the way – the Earl Grey has been an absolute treat. I think about you every time I brew myself a cup – not that I wouldn't do that anyway but the combination vastly cheers up breakfast, always a slightly dismal time these days. What do you have for breakfast? I've been imagining you in that amazing kitchen, and your brother except of course that he is a blank since we haven't met.'

The trouble about this multi-faceted style of conversation was that it left you not knowing quite which bit to deal with first. Helen, a little breathless, tried to talk and attend to various unspoken responses and queries. She felt both heady and in some way disadvantaged. The food was rather good; wine at lunch-time was of course always a mistake but one could repent that at leisure, later on.

Various things emerged, also to extend their impact later. Carnaby & Proctor had only become thus four years ago, when the Carnabys had moved down here from London since Gillian Carnaby, already ill, had wished to spend her last years elsewhere. Then old Mr Proctor had retired, as anticipated, leaving Giles in partnership with young Simon. Giles rather missed London at times, but was adjusting. There were compensations. (What were they? Who were they?) The house was pleasant enough but Giles was not good at housekeeping. The son, a marine engineer, was abroad. Giles enjoyed long muddy walks, preferably in company (whose?), opera, sweet and sticky puddings (the choice of dessert occasioned much heart-searching) and travel books of the 1930s. He sang in an amateur choir on Monday evenings, voted Liberal, was allergic to strawberries and had bicycled across France when he was twenty. He didn't know one end of a car from the other, could never see the point of Picasso but accepted that he was probably an ignoramus, seldom drank spirits and liked to do a little mild gardening. He had a gold filling rather far back in his mouth that glinted when he laughed heartily. He paid bills with Access.

'Good grief – it can't be three-thirty! Is service included, do you imagine? I can never tell with these things. I feel as though I've been going on about myself in the most shameless way. What a nice patient woman you are.'

He laid his hand on hers. There it rested for several seconds, until the waiter arrived and there were things to be done with wallet and credit card.

'And you never did report on the green-headed nephew.'

'He seems to be giving trouble,' said Helen. 'My sister was complaining.'

'Adolescence is quite fearful. Be thankful you're not a parent. Though you would be a marvellous one, I'm sure. I do wonder . . .' He checked himself. 'Anyway, your sister has my sympathy. The boy too. Tell them it all works out in the end.'

They rose. Coats were fetched. At the door he said 'Where are you going?'

'I left the car in the Market Street car park.'

'I can go back to the office that way.'

Out into the street, the humdrum Spaxton street, butchers and building societies and banks, known for thirty years but somehow today transformed – gay and quirky and inviting. Pails of summer flowers outside a greengrocer. Small children skittering home from school with enormous satchels banging against their backs. Sunlight on old brick. A boy whistling.

He took her arm to guide her across a street in which there was no traffic. '*What* a treat! I usually spend my lunch-time in the pub on the corner. Or having a brisk walk. Or sandwiches in the office.'

'I enjoyed it too,' said Helen. 'Thank you so much. Perhaps . . .' she hesitated.

'It's for me to thank *you*. Sparing the time . . . Letting me natter on. Oh dear – here's the wretched car park.' He pulled a face, then beamed the smile upon her, laid a hand on her arm.

'Perhaps . . .' she began.

'Anyway – goodbye and thank you, my dear.'

And that was that. A quick squeeze of the arm and off. My dear. Perhaps, she said to his back view – diminishing, vanishing, dodging away among passers-by – perhaps you'd like to come and have a drink sometime and meet my brother. Oh well.

I am unpractised in these things, she thought, driving home. I have forgotten the codes, if indeed I ever knew them. I don't know the to and fro of it.

Aflame, she glared at the road ahead. Her mother, sitting squatly in the passenger seat, told her she was fifty-two years old, no beauty and never had been and would do better to pull herself together and think about something else. Go away, said Helen. I'm sorry but go away. This is something you know nothing about, nor ever did.

She removed all her clothes and stood in front of the long mirror in her bedroom. She saw a body with heavy thighs, legs with the purplish blotches of incipient varicose veins, breasts that sagged and a belly that was far from flat. Viewed dispassionately, she could not see how this body could arouse desire. It was demonstrably female, but very distant from the female bodies displayed in advertisements or on the covers of magazines. It looked to her more like an illustration in a medical journal.

Edward, returning at the end of his school day, found Helen on the upstairs landing amid what appeared at first glance to be the final sediment of a jumble sale. Shoes and clothing were spread around in desultory heaps. Helen, her arms full, moved uncertainly among them. Reaching the top of the stairs, Edward recognised his mother's garments.

Helen looked at him uncomfortably across an armful of pinkish-grey elastic net, boning and suspenders. 'It had to be done eventually. I suddenly thought – now. And get it over with.'

'Yes, of course. Where can it all go?'

'Well . . . Oxfam, I suppose, except that I believe they're rather fussy nowadays. And . . .' Her glance strayed guiltily to a couple of black plastic rubbish sacks, stuffed full. She had already come to the conclusion that very little re-cycling could be done; Dorothy had been a parsimonious dresser at the best of times.

Edward averted his eyes from what Helen was holding: distant *malaise* lurked there.

'I never realised she had any hats.'

'Nor did I. They must have been for weddings, ages ago. I'm afraid a lot of this has got the moth. Such as the fur coat. She hardly ever wore it and it dates from before the war.'

'What is it, do you imagine?' enquired Edward with distaste. He remembered the fur coat, which used to emerge in his childhood for rare visits to the pantomime or the ballet. It gave his mother the appearance of a small purposeful brown bear and he had hated it.

Helen picked it up. There were balding patches and a rip in one sleeve. Bear was still the animal that it most closely evoked. She held it out to Edward, who shook his head and pulled a face. Helen laughed. 'Whatever it was, it died an awfully long time ago. Too long ago to get exercised about now.' She dropped the coat onto one of the piles.

'That's not what I was thinking about,' said Edward. His glance shifted from the coat to the pink tangle in Helen's arms. He took his glasses off and began to scrub them violently with a grubby handkerchief.

The sensual feel of fur was one of his earliest memories. Live fur. The warm flank of the cat from next door, to be precise, in which he had buried his face and been rewarded with the consoling reverberation of its purr. An amiable, unrejecting maternal cat.

He had been under the impression, as a very small child, that his mother was armour-plated, like the rhino in London Zoo at which he had gazed in astonishment. You could not touch the rhino, but it looked like his mother felt. Beneath her tweed skirts and her thick jerseys there was a carapace, a plated stiffness that rejected infant limbs and hands. Later in life he learned about female corsetry and realised what it was one had been up against, but the impression lingered yet of some unyielding natural structure.

Dorothy did not encourage physical contact. 'Don't paw me like that, Edward,' she would say. 'No, you can't hold my hand/ sit on my lap/have a cuddle. Don't be silly. You're not a baby now, you're two/three/four.' The cat never said things like that; it simply provided a gently throbbing flank until called away on more pressing matters. Hence, perhaps, the disturbing emotions aroused by the sight of dead fur and, even more, that dingy flaccid heap of canvas and elastic, which prompted, now, another murky response, another distant moment. He had lain in bed once, in infancy perhaps, and watched with furtive distress as his mother dressed; presumably she had thought he was asleep. Why was he sharing her room? Some crisis induced by visiting relatives, maybe. At any rate, the sight was with him still: that shadowy figure revealing undreamed-of clefts and protuberances. He had cowered under the bedclothes, mesmerized, and watched her flopping breasts as she stooped to haul pink drawers up over heavy thighs, had seen hair where surely no hair should be, had printed on his vision for ever the pucker of nipples and the black valley between buttocks.

He started to retreat back down the stairs. 'You might at least take some of the stuff down for me,' said Helen, in a tone of reproach.

Edward grabbed the black plastic sacks. 'I'll help if you want, but I'm sure I'd . . .'

Helen vanished into Dorothy's room, saying tartly that it didn't matter; it was the nearest they had come to ill feeling for a long time and Edward was left with a further layer of disquiet. He dumped the sacks outside the back door by the dustbins, called Tam and set off for the Britches.

He checked the nest-boxes. There was evidence that something might already have been roosting in one of them, which was satisfactory. They were sold by an organisation that provided work for the mentally handicapped, which made them doubly benign; the only displeasing thing about them was the aggressively rustic appearance – a cross between a cuckoo clock and a miniature *cottage orné*. Edward had tried unsuccessfully to knock off the superfluous gables and twiggy excrescences. They would mellow, he hoped, in the raw winter climate of the Britches.

It was June now and still warm though past six. The evening sunlight that came down through the leaves suffused the whole place with a golden glow. Edward sat down on his usual log and noted, while thinking of quite other things, that he could hear a robin, assorted tits, rooks, a chaffinch and a magpie. He observed a delicate collar of fawn and pink fungus around the base of a dead tree, vivid green cushions of moss, the crimson flicker of a cinnabar moth against leaf mould, a very small spider with white spots on its back. He heard, but did not register, the screech of the chain-saw in Ron Paget's yard, the rattle and thump of an articulated lorry taking the bend in the road, the roar of an American F1-11 fighter some two miles above his head. A few feet away Tam was gnawing at something dubious he had found in the undergrowth.

Edward tried to think of nothing at all; like Tam, like the birds, the cinnabar moth, the fungus, the Britches itself. He felt

56

unsettled, uneasy, disquieted in his very depths, as indeed he had felt since his mother's death. He had felt like this from time to time all his life and had conquered the feelings eventually, on each occasion, by stern application to other matters and by refusing consideration of what he felt. If you denied a name to something perhaps it would no longer exist. Thus, as a child, had he driven away the shadows on the bedroom wall – the witch-shaped, wolf-shaped shadows. And thus, today, he sat on his log – a delicate pink-grey log furred here and there with green moss – and tried to concentrate on what he could see while thrusting aside what he knew. He watched the moth and the spider, followed the movement of the tits and the robin, saw the valiant growth of a six-inch beech seedling. The Britches rustled and flickered comfortably around him. Tam chewed the ancient corpse of some small creature.

And Edward, not unfeeling, not impervious, began presently to howl within. Nothing lasts, he wept, everything goes. My mother is dead, who had always been there, for better and for worse. Mostly for worse. And I am forty-nine and getting old and soon it will be too late for all the things I know nothing of but which torment me in the middle of the night and here now in this place which is supposed to be a comfort and a solace. I am lonely and hungry and I have never breathed a word of this to anyone. Nobody knows or cares. I don't want anyone to know or care.

Tam dug a hole and stowed away his prize. Then he came and nosed at Edward's foot, ready to move on. Edward pushed him away, quite violently, and Tam, unused to even such half-hearted maltreatment, looked up in surprise.

FIVE

When, after eight days, Helen had heard nothing more from Giles Carnaby she was bleakly self-contemptuous. Her heightened condition persisted, there was nothing she could do about that: the swerves of mood, the burning senses. In an animal, she told herself savagely, it would be called being on heat. Her mother, who had been fading hitherto, returned to fill the black hole by the kitchen sink or to confront Helen on the stairs, saying smugly that she could have told her all along what to expect.

Louise came again, towing Suzanne, who spent the entire time shuttered off within the earphones of her Walkman; if spoken to she smiled with bland and tolerant self-absorption, like the very old. There was much complaint of Phil. And, obliquely, of Tim. Helen, alarmed and suspecting infidelity (there had been an episode in the past concerning which Louise had boiled away on the telephone for months on end), asked what was wrong with him.

'Nothing's *wrong*,' said Louise irritably. 'Tim is precisely as he always is. That's the problem, I suppose.'

'Don't you love him?' asked Edward.

Louise rolled her eyes in exasperation. 'God! You simply don't know the first thing about marriage, do you? Well, bless you – how could you? Listen – *tout passe, tout casse, tout lasse*. Right?'

'What?'

'French expression suggesting instability.'

Edward appeared to think hard for a few moments and then got up and left the room abruptly.

'And what's the matter with *him*, come to that?' said Louise. 'He's the nearest I've ever seen him to snappish, for someone constitutionally incapable of bad temper. The trouble with

Edward is that he's practically a saint. I honestly think he's never thought anything nasty about anyone in his life, which is what makes him occasionally so impossible. Just as well *he* never got married – no one could have stood that. Not of course that it was ever on the cards.'

'He has been a bit edgy,' said Helen. 'Mother, maybe.'

Louise sighed. 'He's left it about forty years too late to get uptight about mother.'

'*Is* there some trouble with Tim?'

'Tim and I,' said Louise heavily, 'are going through what is called a bad patch. We get on each other's nerves, to put it bluntly. Hence me here and him there. He is not, so far as I know, having it off with anyone and I certainly am not, more's the pity in a sense, though to be honest I've never felt less inclined in my life.' She stared glumly at the window. 'Frankly, I seldom get a glow about anyone these days, including Tim, which I daresay is partly what's wrong. How sex does bugger things up . . . Sorry. I shouldn't talk like this. I know you . . .' The sentence was left unfinished.

'You know I what?' said Helen tartly.

Louise gave her a searching look. 'Now you're starting to sound like Edward. I don't know what's got into you both. I just meant I know you're . . . it's not a subject you get very enthralled by. Sex, I mean. There! Your expression's gone all peculiar at once. Anyway . . . Tim and I are just simply out of sync at the moment – I can't think how else to put it. We're not connecting. Don't worry – we're not going to split up, at least I trust not.'

Suzanne came into the room, the earphones clamped to her head, exuding a distant tinny jangle. She sat down by the window, smiling vaguely.

'It's not that we don't love each other,' explained Louise. 'Within the context of how long we've been together. It's that . . .'

'Ssh . . .' murmured Helen.

'She's dead to the world. Lucky little beggar. Extraordinary, isn't it? Were we like that? No, of course we weren't. Not even me. Anyway, as I was saying, Tim . . .'

Edward appeared, looking agitated. 'There's a boy digging up the old kitchen garden.'

'Yes,' said Helen. 'It's Ron Paget's son. You know about it. This is Saturday.'

'Do I? Oh – yes. Is this a good idea? Surely we're not really going to grow vegetables?'

'Ron Paget?' said Louise. 'Nobody told me about this. Anything set up by Ron Paget has got to be suspect.'

Helen explained.

'One fifty an hour would be considered exploitation in London but I daresay it's par for the course round here. I wouldn't put it past Ron to be taking a cut for himself. Mind you give it to the boy personally. What's he like?'

'I didn't notice,' said Edward. He went to the window and stood there wiping his glasses: they could all hear, now, the distant thwack and flump of spade-work. Edward turned round, walked irresolutely around the room and then headed for the door, where he halted. 'I'm off now. There's an RSPB field-trip – I won't be back till late. 'Bye Louise . . . and, er . . .' – he glanced at Suzanne, who smiled blankly and placatingly. 'Oh Helen, by the way, I forgot – that lawyer rang, he wanted you to ring back.'

'When did he ring?' asked Helen after a moment.

'Um . . . Yesterday, the day before . . .'

Edward left. Suzanne, who had neither moved nor altered her expression, continued to jangle by the window in her private world. Louise began to recount further discontents, unheard now by either her daughter or her sister.

Helen postponed telephoning, as one might hoard some delicacy, to savour it the longer in anticipation. When at last she did so Giles Carnaby was warmly effusive. 'Oh, what a relief! I was beginning to think I must be in the doghouse for some reason.' He spoke as though they knew each other well and over a long period. 'You didn't get the message? I shall have to speak severely to your brother. Anyway – now that I've got you at last . . . I have a proposition. The choir . . . my little Monday diversion . . . We have our big night next week – performance evening. Towards which we've been striving for weeks. Will you come?

We all bring friends and family – please come and be mine. We perform and then everyone gets together over wine and cheese. Usually quite good fun. Please say you will.'

Later, released from the spell of that voice, she was plagued by niggling incredulity. Me? *Me*? Why? What does he mean by it? Does he mean anything at all by it? Why me out of all the other women in Spaxton?

They're all married, said her mother. Not that that would bother most people nowadays. He must wonder why you're not, come to that. And look at you jumping to conclusions, going the right way to make a proper fool of yourself. Why should the man mean a thing by it? You're a client, aren't you?

If he took all his clients out to expensive lunches, invited them to concerts . . .

Maybe he does, said her mother. Once in a while. How are you to know?

She was working in the library her regular three days a week now. It seemed amazing to be able to leave the house each time without feeling furtive, and irritable at being obliged to feel furtive. Her mother had never grasped that a job is a commitment. 'I want you to put off the library today,' she would say. 'I need help with bottling the plums.' In bad weather she would watch Helen's preparations for departure with contempt: 'It's completely ridiculous to go out in this. I can't imagine why you don't leave it till tomorrow.' During her final illness, when Helen took unpaid leave, she had announced to visitors, with satisfaction, in moments of clarity: 'At least I've been able to make Helen see sense about trailing off to that wretched library day after day.'

Edward, on the other hand, had always been accorded a mysterious potency: 'They do so depend on him at Croxford.' This was curious; in all other areas she treated – always had treated – Edward as negligible. If he embarked on a task she stepped in and took it from him; she interrupted him when he spoke. 'Let him do it!' Helen had raged, time out of mind ago, aged fifteen, eighteen, twenty-one. 'Leave him alone. Let him finish what he's saying.' 'He'll only break it,' would come the reply. Or do it wrong: too fast, too slow, not in the prescribed way. And he doesn't know what he's talking about: he's too young, too inexperienced, too Edward.

When, in his thirties, he took driving lessons and passed his test Dorothy refused to go out in the car with him: 'I intend to live to a ripe old age, thank you very much.'

In fact, Edward was a good driver, if somewhat decorous. Dorothy waited patiently and had her moment of triumph when someone went into the back of his car at a traffic light – clearly his fault for not getting a move on quicker.

Helen worked because she needed the income, quite apart from anything else. Her mother had never understood that, either. 'You've got Daddy's money,' she would say. 'I can't think why you want to go grubbing around for more.' Helen's dividends, like her own, had dwindled to smaller and smaller sums; even for someone as uncommitted to possession or luxury as Helen was it had become necessary to top them up.

But the library was a refuge, most importantly of all. It was an impersonal sanctum that was not Greystones. There, Helen became someone else; she became brisk efficient well-liked Helen. Helen who had been there years and years, knew all the ropes, could be relied on to deal tactfully with difficult customers, with the intransigence of the county library system, with errant books and tiresome children. Helen who evinced endless patient interest in others, who remained politely anonymous herself. Her colleagues came and went; they had got younger and younger, it seemed, as time went by; those who were career-minded departed for lusher pastures, more Susies and Karens took their places, giggling in the cloakroom, muddling up the reservation cards. Only the senior librarian remained constant, Joyce Babcock, a contemporary of Helen's, stuck as far as she would get on the ladder of professional advancement, suspicious of the girls but tolerant of Helen, who offered no threat. Part-timers did not become senior librarian, however highly regarded. She was a woman without vision or curiosity; her distaste for books was equalled only by her dislike of people. She sat out her days behind the central desk, complaining of her superiors, of technological innovation, and of the weather. Helen, marvelling at Joyce's capacity for self-protection, often wondered at her choice of career. It had something to do with order, she decided; Joyce mistrusted books for their content, but liked the way they could be marshalled. The readers were simply an unlooked-for hazard.

Now, she sensed a shift in Joyce's attitude towards her. 'I suppose,' Joyce said, with studied carelessness, 'you may think of going full-time now you haven't got your mother.'

Helen understood. Joyce feared potential rivalry; her status might be threatened if Helen, a favourite of the county librarian, were more available. 'Possibly,' she replied. With an uncharacter-istic spurt of mischief she added that she was considering the matter. Joyce flipped feverishly through a reference book; her neck had gone red with emotion. Helen, relenting, said, 'I daresay not, in the end. I rather like the idea of some time to myself.'

'I should think so!' cried Joyce. 'I mean, if anyone deserves it you do. Oh, I don't think you should take on any more, definitely. You want to spoil yourself a bit, that's what.' Restored to normal confidence, she gave Helen a sharp look. 'You've had your hair cut differently. It suits you. Was it that place on Market Street? They're pricey, mind, but good if you want something a bit out of the ordinary.'

'I'm glad you approve,' said Helen, applying herself to the acquisitions file. The library was empty except for an elderly man pottering in Biography and a couple of schoolchildren in the reference section; there was opportunity for what Joyce called a natter, and no escaping it.

'You'll miss your mother,' stated Joyce. 'I know. Paul wasn't himself for months after his went.' Paul was her husband. 'It's a shock, however much you know it's coming. It'll take you time to adjust, you'll find.'

'Mmn,' said Helen. Comment was neither possible nor invited.

'Of course, you've got your brother. Let me see now, I always forget – is he older or younger?'

'Younger.'

'It's funny he's never married either – funny coincidence, I mean.'

'Isn't it,' said Helen. This was familiar ground. Joyce, frustrated, moved on to consideration of yesterday's weather, complaints about the new trainee and an attempt to enlist Helen's support in resisting the county librarian's enthusiasm for a local history section at Spaxton. Joyce had a special hatred for history. She was interrupted, however, by a schoolchild in search of a reference and had to break off to give grudging and limited assistance. Helen returned to the new acquisitions. She had been noting various titles during Joyce's discourse; there was a new book about bats that Edward would want, and one or two things she would like to get hold of herself – the sole perquisite of this trade was a surreptitious early pick of incoming titles before they went on the shelves.

Helen read a great deal. The feel of a book in her hands was an ancient solace – not, originally, because of what lay between the covers but as a screen, a defence, a shield. The book she was reading had once been the physical barrier between her and her mother. 'Head in a book as usual,' Dorothy would say with contempt. 'You should be doing something, not just sitting there.' Helen had drawn Edward into this sheltered place, and read aloud to him. And presently what was within the books became significant also – quite small books would do, she discovered, because of what they said, one did not always have to get behind Bartholomew's atlas or the bound volumes of *Punch* that lurked in the bottom of the sitting-room bookcase. She read her way through what was in the house – not a daunting process, given her mother's resistance to the printed word – and then resorted to libraries. Her choice of occupation, she realised, had perhaps been fore-ordained, written into the scheme of things like some genetic prescription, laid down by her mother's inclinations. Dorothy did not care for books, so Helen became a librarian.

She read anything; she read in all directions. She read to learn and she read to experience. She identified areas of special interest – Greece and Rome, popular science, cathedral architecture, arctic exploration – and burrowed happily away; she reconsidered herself and others through the lens of that well-constructed lie that is a good novel. She became book dependent, for better or for worse.

'Anyone would think we were some kind of free education service,' grumbled Joyce, having disposed of the child and returned to her central eyrie.

'That's just what we are,' said Helen.

Joyce shot her a look in which surprise and indignation were nicely fused.

Edward, at the same time and eight miles away, was dispensing some moderately expensive education to the Lower Fourth at Croxford House. The Lower Fourth numbered eighteen ten- and eleven-year-olds, sagging over their desks in assorted attitudes that were meant to indicate intense attention, dreadful weariness, shrewd insight or rapt admiration. Most of them weren't listening. Some of them were whispering to each other. Edward was talking about the Galapagos finch. This was a new series of lessons, rather grandly called Biology, in which he wandered happily around various special fascinations of his own and tried to tell the children something about natural selection and the origin of species. He had brought along several exhibits, including a portrait of Darwin he had found in a junk shop and an assortment of feathers and fossils that the children were passing from hand to hand. None of them took any notice of Darwin, but the feathers and fossils aroused mild interest. Edward was now drawing a diagram of a feather on the board – with some difficulty and much rubbing out – to illustrate its complexity and lead up to a discussion of the evolution of birds.

Sandra Willmot put up her hand. Edward was not fond of Sandra; she was a prissy little girl, always fastidiously turned out and given to exclamations of disgust and revulsion. Her parents were prominent local business people; her mother was chairperson of the Parents' Association.

'Yes, Sandra?'

'Please, Mr Glover, my mother says things like feathers prove there must be a God.'

'Really?' said Edward, stalling.

'Yes. Because they're so complicated. Somebody must have made them.' Sandra stared smugly at the blackboard. 'I mean, they couldn't just happen, could they? So someone must have made them.'

'Who?' enquired Edward with resignation.

'God, of course,' said Sandra, buffing her fingernails on her sweater. She looked round piously for support and approval.

Edward knew that he was on treacherous ground. Those of the children who were not squabbling over fossils or sticking feathers in their hair gazed expectantly at him. He said carefully that while everyone was entitled to feel and believe what they liked about God it really wasn't possible, given what we now know, to say that His existence is proven by feathers or fossils or by anything else in the world. He continued in this vein for a couple of minutes, tripping himself up several times. The trouble was that imprinted in Edward's own mind was a charming array of creatures like a Noah's Ark procession, from ant to man, that sprang from the illustration in a fatally misconceived nature book he had had himself as a child. An image of the Great Chain of Being was at the very heart of him; he often had considerable difficulty in marshalling the arguments for apostasy. It must be a bit like being a lapsed Catholic, he thought; you knew you were right but felt you were wrong. He waxed vehement about dinosaurs and extinction, about continental drift and the good old Galapagos finch. He concluded by saying that if you believe in God you have to find other ways to convince people that He exists, and that was not something to be discussed in this lesson.

Sandra Willmot listened – or appeared to listen – with an icy stare. Several hands shot up.

'Yes?' said Edward unwarily.

'Please, Mr Glover, don't you believe in God, then?'

'No,' said Edward, after a moment. A rustle of interest ran around the classroom. One or two people announced that they didn't either; others declared loudly that they did. Croxford House was given to morning prayers and all the outward trappings of Church of England belief; it even had a chapel. Now that he came to think of it, Edward was surprised this point had never cropped up before; Biology was obviously a dodgier area than English and History.

'Anyway,' he said firmly, 'what I believe or don't believe is neither here nor there. We were talking about feathers. I want you all to get out your exercise books and copy what is on the board . . .'

The children subsided, more or less. Most of them applied themselves to their exercise books, their faces contorted with intellectual effort. Some continued to daydream. Sandra Willmot was whispering urgently to her neighbour, with occasional furtive glances in Edward's direction. 'Would you please get on with your work, Sandra,' said Edward with unusual severity. She was a peculiarly unlikeable child, he thought; the sort of child – or person – who refuted any notion that *homo sapiens* is the pinnacle of creation. The Galapagos finch was a darn sight more valuable than Sandra Willmot.

When Helen arrived at the hall in which the choir concert was to be held she could not at first see Giles Carnaby. There were a great many people milling around, the cream of Spaxton society, indeed, many of whom she knew or recognised. She was about to find herself a seat when she caught sight of him, in conversation with a rather pretty dark young woman, both of them laughing a lot. Looking at them, she experienced a curious sense of exclusion; she wondered who the woman was; she wondered how well Giles knew her. And then he looked in her direction, smiled and waved over the woman's shoulder, continued to talk to her for a few moments, then laid a hand on her arm for an instant and moved towards Helen.

Later, she saw the woman among the sopranos, and noted her. She noted everyone in the choir, indeed, as part of a determined effort not to gaze all the time at Giles Carnaby, who was in the back row, in the middle of the tenors, straight ahead of her, where she could consider him in detail – silvery hair, grey herring-bone tweed jacket, greenish shirt, paisley patterned silk tie (so much for not gazing . . .)

And then there was the wine and cheese, in an adjoining room where tables were laid out and choir and audience enabled to mingle. Giles seemed to know everyone. Indeed he seemed to have to keep rushing off to have a word with this person and that; Helen found herself on her own a good deal of the time, glimpsing him across the room in spirited conversation. She saw a lot of his back, of his distinctive head moving from one group to another. She talked to various acquaintances. One woman asked curiously 'Do you know Giles Carnaby well?' Helen, faintly ruffled, replied that she didn't – not all that well. 'He's very charming, of course,' said the woman.

The room thinned out. Giles returned to her side. He seemed cheerful and stimulated. 'Oh dear – I kept getting caught by people. Have you had enough to drink? Are you all right? And there hasn't been a chance to talk . . . You will come back for a cup of coffee, won't you? Or the tea – the famous Earl Grey.' He took her arm, shepherded her out of the building, into the street. 'You've got your car? Bother – so have I. We shall have to go in a convoy – it's only five minutes away. Sunderland Road.'

The house was unexceptional, one of those in Spaxton's prosperous Edwardian suburb. Within, there was an atmosphere of chintzy comfort. Helen, thinking of the wife, sat almost apologetically on a plump sofa. On the mantelpiece was a photo of a pleasant-looking woman, fair hair, not beautiful, not glamorous, quite ordinary really.

Giles went to the kitchen to make coffee, refusing offers of help – 'I should get in a fuss and make a fool of myself if watched.' Helen inspected the room. Other people's houses always intrigued her by the contrast they offered to Greystones; she would see suddenly – with detached interest and quite without envy or criticism – the extent to which other people's preoccupations differed from her own. Here, someone had gone to considerable lengths to get the cushions toning in nicely with the curtains. There was a fireplace with realistically glowing coals and the cosy flicker of flames around them that was, she soon realised, a gas fire; no bother with cleaning it out, then. The pictures were unprovocative landscapes or flower paintings that neatly fitted the spaces allotted to them. The books were all behind glass. A low table carried some tidily arranged journals and newspapers; letters on the desk top were pinned down by a silver paper knife. She felt again the presence of the wife, looking kindly and securely at her from the photograph; don't resent me, said Helen, I am really neither here nor there, I very much doubt if I signify, you needn't mind.

Giles returned. There was a bottle of brandy on the tray as well as the coffee. 'You will, won't you? We need warming up – that hall is arctic, I perish every Monday evening.' He poured out, sat back at the other end of the sofa, looked at her. 'Thank you so much for coming, Helen. Did you enjoy it? I kept taking quick glances but you always looked inscrutable. It went quite well, I thought – a bit shaky at points in the Britten. Good fun, anyway – but oh dear, people do nobble one, don't they? It was wonderful having you as a defence. Provincial life is very demanding, don't you find? All these nice people wanting you to join things. But of course you've known Spaxton for so long.'

'Yes,' said Helen. 'I'm generally regarded as a lost cause by now.'

He laughed. 'I wish I were! Anyway, you have your village to cope with – that must be quite enough. Except that you're regarded as eccentric – is that right? You and your brother – I do want to meet your brother, by the way. I think I must cultivate eccentricity – would I make an eccentric?' He beamed at her. Charmingly. Helen gazed at him. The room lurked at the edges of her vision – chintz, pictures of woodland or roses, that paperknife. No, she thought. Something else brooded, indefinable, padding doggily around; she tried to ignore it.

They drank the coffee, the brandy. Giles talked of Spaxton acquaintances, of a visit to the opera, of an entertaining incident in his office: bland impersonal discourse, given somehow an edge of intimacy. It seemed to Helen that the room became very warm and enclosed: she basked, as she later thought of it. And then suddenly it was midnight, a clock delicately chiming outside in the hall, and she was getting up, with him protesting – really quite fervently protesting. 'No, I must,' she said. 'Edward will wonder where on earth . . .'

'Then if you must, you must. Please drive carefully. I'm inclined to ring in half an hour to see you've got there safely, but I suppose I'd have your brother hopping out of bed.' He helped her into her coat; again, his arm lay on her shoulders after he had done so. He escorted her out into the street, held the car door open for her, leaning in the window as she started the engine, exhorting caution. His hand closed on hers as it rested on the wheel: 'Thank you again, my dear, God bless.' And he turned and was gone, briskly, into the house.

Greystones, when she reached it, seemed even colder than usual. The lights were all out and Edward in bed. Helen, climbing the stairs, burned with a curious mixture of exaltation and foreboding.

'You were very late last night. I didn't even hear you come in.'

'It was only about half past twelve. I went to that concert in Spaxton.'

'Oh yes – with the lawyer. What on earth for?' Edward added after a moment. 'I mean, one *pays* lawyers, surely. There's no need to go and hear them sing as well.'

Helen appeared to be distracted by the back of the cereal packet.

'Well, it was very charitable of you,' said Edward. 'By the way, we're out of bread. Is it my turn to shop or yours?'

'Mine. Edward, if people phone when I'm not here do please remember to tell me.'

Edward looked across the table at her in mild surprise. 'Of course. I thought I did. You always say you're glad they didn't catch you.'

Helen was now bent sternly over a shopping list. She had written 'bread' three times, Edward saw.

'I never realised you felt like this, Edward,' said Mrs Fitton petulantly. 'It really is the most awful nuisance. Parents just

70

don't like it, you know – quite a lot of parents.' From outside the window came the shrill piping sound of the juniors playing netball. The school secretary put her head round the door; '*No!*' snapped the headmistress, 'I'm in a meeting.' She was a small round woman, puffed out with frilly blouses and an energetic hairstyle. When crises arose she went into a condition of sustained fizz; you almost expected bubbles to come popping out of her head. She was in this state now.

'I mean, Mrs Willmot won't be the only one – or rather, Mrs Willmot will see to it that she isn't the only one. I wish you'd told me before, Edward, I mean, it's entirely your own affair of course but if I'd known forewarned would have been forearmed and we could have avoided this sort of thing.'

'You never asked me,' said Edward reasonably.

'Well, I suppose not . . . One just assumed . . . I mean, we are a C. of E. school. Oh dear – what a *bother*. And most other parents one could have calmed down – smoothed things over somehow – but Mrs Willmot, well, we know Mrs Willmot, don't we? On the phone to all her cronies at this moment, I don't doubt, and this is the year we hoped to get the swimming pool appeal off the ground.'

'Sorry,' said Edward.

'What I can't understand is why God had to be dragged into it in the first place. Can't you simply leave that sort of thing out? I mean, tell them about natural selection and all that and don't mention God. After all, it was Biology, not Religious Education. Charlotte Havering does R.E. She expects to cope with that side and she's C. of E.'

'I was leaving God out,' said Edward. 'The children brought Him in. Sandra Willmot, to be precise.'

'Tiresome child. Well, the damage is done now. All we can do is hope that Mrs W. will cool off and in the meantime, Edward, I'm sorry but honestly I think Mary or Janice had better take over Junior Biology.'

There was a silence. Mrs Fitton began tetchily shuffling a pile of letters. Edward looked out of the window, where rooks beat across a turbulent sky. At last he said 'I suppose really I should resign.'

Mrs Fitton bucked in her chair. 'What nonsense, Edward. What absolute nonsense. Of course you don't even have to *think* of resigning. All right, we're a C. of E. school but that doesn't mean every single one of the staff has to be a signed up communicant. In fact come to that I myself . . . What I mean is, it's a personal matter except in so far as it affects the syllabus. If you stick to English and History like you used to and . . . well, just avoid the issue . . . then we shan't have any more problems.'

'I don't mean resign because I don't believe in God,' said Edward. 'I mean resign because you won't let me teach biology because I don't believe in God.'

Mrs Fitton gazed at him. Her hands twitched on the letters; she blinked once or twice. 'Well, that I simply wouldn't have thought of. I don't know what's got into you, Edward, you don't seem to be quite yourself. You can't possibly resign. I won't hear of it.'

'Then can I teach biology?'

'*No!*' cried Mrs Fitton. 'Edward, be reasonable!'

They stared at each other; Mrs Fitton crackling with emotion, Edward apparently tranquil. Behind Mrs Fitton's head the rooks were now tossing and tumbling like blown leaves. It occurred to Edward that he knew little or nothing about rook behaviour.

'You're not serious?' demanded Mrs Fitton wildly. 'You're not really going to resign?'

'No,' said Edward with a sigh. 'I don't suppose so.'

It was Helen who pointed out that Mrs Fitton would have been concerned about the newspapers, as well as with her regard for Edward and for Edward's welfare.

Edward looked incredulous. 'Would there really have been a fuss?'

'Of course,' said Helen. 'Properly handled.'

'It would almost have been worth it. Perhaps I'll change my mind. I'd have been a martyr, wouldn't I? Victimised for my beliefs. But that wretched Sandra would have had a field day too – her picture in the local rag in her best dress. No, it's not worth it, on reflection.'

Helen made no comment.

'You think I should have done, don't you?'

'Most people would have, I suppose.'

'But not me,' said Edward with sudden bitterness. 'Oh, I know, I know. The thought of finding another job . . . And it all seemed so silly. And I know perfectly well Croxford is a crummy school, but it suits me and I suit it, which doesn't say a lot for either of us.' He was pulling on his anorak now, no longer even apparently tranquil. 'I'm going out for a bit.'

He drove to a favourite spot and walked, in the late afternoon, up the long flank of a hillside, in the lea of an old hedgebank. On one side of him was the complex inhabited thicket of the hedge in which flocks of bullfinches competed for fodder and invisibly singing warblers were stationed at thirty-yard intervals; on the other was a great sloping reach of field, the earth a reddish copper colour and patterned like a Japanese garden with the swirls and furrows left by machinery. The sun, a scarlet disc, was perched just above the horizon. The land folded in on itself as far as you could see – green and brown hillsides sinking down in repetition, marked by the dark masses of trees and hedges. Here and there a grey farmhouse or cottage was tucked into a hollow. In the far distance was the blue outline of yet further hills. The impression was of some sparsely populated, unchanging landscape; it was hard to realise that Birmingham was less than thirty miles away.

At the top of the hill the bridle-path entered a small copse. Immediately, the sense of distance gave way to intimacy and detail. Edward stood still; he had once seen a whole flock of long-tailed tits here, swinging like pink jewels among the flickering leaves of a silver birch. He told himself that this was what he was now searching for again.

In fact he was waiting for the place, its calm and its unconcern, to make him feel better. To make him feel less alone, less disturbed, less hungry. He was howling once more, within. And the place did nothing, nothing at all. It simply went about its business. And its business, of course, at this fecund point of the year, was that of survival – survival and reproduction. As

73

Edward looked around he saw everything determinedly perpetuating itself – buds forming, leaves unfurling, seeds setting, the whole place off again on the same mindless uncaring cycle, while Edward stood there in the midst of it, quite alone.

SIX

'I been having a little think,' said Ron Paget. 'About your patch of waste ground.'

Edward and Helen gazed at him without expression, a practised process. They were all three standing in the lane outside Greystones. Ron had pounced from his car, screeching to a halt ten yards ahead of them. He had opened with a solicitous enquiry as to whether young Gary was giving satisfaction.

'I mean,' he continued, 'it's a bit of an albatross, isn't it? The upkeep and that. What I was thinking was . . .'

'We don't keep it up,' said Edward. 'It keeps itself up.'

Ron shook his head censoriously. 'That's just the point, Mr Glover, if I may say so. There's a lot of work needs doing in there. You've got dead and diseased trees need felling, you've got bramble and stuff needs clearing out. It's not healthy, the way it is. But with a bit of money spent you could have a nice little spinney there – be pretty in the spring. You could do a bit of landscape planting, azaleas and rhododendrons and that, camellias maybe – you know, like your National Trust sort of place.'

'Those things don't grow on limestone soil,' said Helen.

Ron opened his mouth and then closed it again. Behind him the engine of his new red Rover was still running – a barely audible hum. Ron stepped aside, opened the door and turned the ignition. 'Point is, to do something about the place you need finance, right? I know what it's like these days – we're all stretched as far as we can go' – he sighed – 'but I've had a little think and I see a way round it for you. Now you've got quite an area there – two acres, is it, two and a half? What you do is you make one half of it finance the other. You do a little development on the far side – three, four nice houses, something along those

75

lines. I can see to all the nitty-gritty for you – I know you're not a family for bothering your heads with that sort of thing, you've got better things to do. I can handle it for you and see you clear enough to lay yourselves out something really nice with what's left, really classy bit of landscaping. And a fair bit left over to put away for a rainy day, I daresay.'

'No,' said Edward.

Ron looked sadly at him. 'You're saying that off the top of your head, Mr Glover. Think it over. There's the question of what's good for the community, too. You'd be doing the community a favour. Desperate shortage of housing these days.'

'Was it council houses you had in mind?' asked Helen.

'Well, no,' said Ron. 'I mean, what's needed in the village is more by way of quality housing, isn't it? Another nice little executive estate, like the Barratt.'

'I don't see that as fulfilling a social need,' said Helen.

Ron gave her a bad-tempered look. There was a sense of time and patience running out. He opened the car door and got in. The engine purred again. The driver's window slid down; 'Well, think about it, anyway. It would be in your own best interests, believe me.'

The Rover accelerated round the bend. Edward, who had seemed despondent hitherto that morning, laughed. 'You have to hand it to him, he's never short of a new idea.'

They were on their way to the churchyard. The firm from whom the gravestone had been commissioned had telephoned about dimensions and other details. Having reached the initial, simple decision about lettering (plain, unadorned and to the point) and material (unpolished limestone slab) they were now floored over questions of layout and surroundings. Did they want chippings? Did they want a flower container?

They walked slowly up the church path, past the old graves, those so seared by time and weather that they stood as grey shapes furred with lichen, names and dates no longer legible, uniform in obscurity. Where the seventeenth and eighteenth centuries gave way to the nineteenth, things became crisper: you read of a profusion of Elizas and Thomases, of beloved wives and lamented parents: white marble crept in with the grey limestone.

It was round the back of the church, though, where the more recent graves reached away to an expectant area of bare grass ending at the village allotments, that variety and self-expression were rampant.

'I realise what chippings are now,' said Edward. 'No. Definitely not.'

Most of the newer gravestones presided over a neat granite-edged rectangle packed with green crystal chips. The effect, from a distance, was disconcertingly like a series of little swimming pools. Closer to, memorial detail became apparent: elaborate confections in the form of open books inscribed with the particulars of the departed, weeping cherubs and angels, praying heads and exuberant crosses. It disposed entirely of any notion of the rural midland English as a phlegmatic and undemonstrative lot. Many of the graves had flowers on them – wilting asters and marigolds in jam-jars, or vases of plastic roses and daffodils in luminous colours. One unkempt mound bore a glass with a Harp Lager insignia, filled with greenish water.

Edward and Helen approached the sycamore tree and stood before the raw earth of Dorothy's grave. In the month since the funeral, infant weeds had sprung up, and some blades of grass.

'No chippings,' said Edward. 'No thing for vase. I'm not even sure about this kerbstone business.'

'You can have granite chips, but they're almost as bad. Just grass, then?'

'Just grass, yes. It would be nice to try to naturalise some fritillaries. Or those small grassland orchids – Lady's Tresses.'

'Oh, Edward,' said Helen with a sigh.

'Just a thought.'

They stood there uncomfortably. Both had a fleeting vision of what lay beneath the mound of earth: the varnished wood, the brass handles, their mother. Edward, fighting the thought, imagined decay; Helen remembered the posy of flowers from the garden that she had tried to fix to the coffin lid with sellotape. Sellotape will not stick to varnish, she had discovered; she ended up with hammer and tintacks, shrinking at the unseemly noise and violence. The flowers would be withered now, down there.

Both recalled the funeral, calculated time: a month, already, when we have been without her. Both examined their feelings.

I am adjusting, thought Helen, I am stepping aside. But funny things are happening. In some way she is more here than she ever was. It is as though she had not died but been transformed.

Edward thought: It is as though I were adrift, untethered. I don't think of her much, no more than I ever did, but something terrible is going on. At moments all is well, and then at others I think that I am flying apart.

Helen took a tape-measure out of her pocket and suspended it above the grave.

'That height? Or a bit more? They want to know.'

'It doesn't matter,' said Edward.

'Two foot six, then. And just "Dorothy Edith Glover: April 10th 1907–May 24th 1987". They seem to feel it's a bit stark.'

'It is. Compared with everyone else.' Edward looked around. Deeply lamented. In loving memory. Pray for the soul of . . . R.I.P.

Helen rolled up the tape-measure and pushed it into her pocket. 'Well, I shall just have to be firm, then. They obviously think it most inadequate.'

They turned and walked back towards the lych-gate. 'Presumably,' said Edward, 'they take it to mean we weren't all that fond of her.'

'Or else that we're hard up. More lettering costs more. Polished granite is more expensive than limestone. The angels and open books and things cost a packet – I looked at the brochure.'

It was Saturday morning, which meant that the village was fairly populous; on weekdays it was emptied of all but the old, the very young and those tending them. The central green had cars scattered all around it. Ron Paget's Rover stood outside the Swan, the more plushy of the two pubs. A sinister looking cluster of motor-bikes huddled in front of the other one, the Goat and Compasses; as the Glovers passed two more arrived with a deafening roar and two androgynous figures, clad in skin-tight leather as though for a bout of deep-sea diving, went into the pub, stripping off immense gauntlets. From within came the crash of reggae music. A BP oil tanker was blocking the narrow lane down to the Old Forge, towering over the thatched cottage to which it was attached by its pipe-line as though with an umbilical cord. Beyond, the post van hooted indignantly. An old man sat on the bench by the War Memorial. From the gravelled sweep of the entrance to the Old Rectory came Mrs Hadley on a gleaming chestnut horse; she clattered past the Glovers, the old man, other passers-by with the age-old superiority of the mounted over those on foot. A car slowed down to pass her and she raised her crop graciously.

'We need something for lunch,' said Helen. 'And dog food. And cereal.' And detergent, she added to herself. 'You may as well stay outside, there's an awful crowd in there.'

She stood in a queue at the single check-out; the village store had supermarket aspirations without the amenities. Two young women in front of her were murmuring confidentially. One said 'I gather Brown Owl *has* resigned . . .' It took Helen a moment or two to realise the affairs of the village Brownie pack were under discussion. She looked over their heads and caught the eye of an acquaintance, who smiled faintly and dipped away in embarrassment, observing the quarantine imposed upon those recently bereaved. There we go again, she thought, mother is still here, still making herself felt. She paid for her purchases, tucking the detergent under the other things.

Outside, she found Edward in conversation with Peter Sidey, the leader of the preservationist element in the village. The preservationists, over the years, had lost ground – quite literally. They tended to be schoolteachers, academics and the recently retired; against them were ranged builders, farmers and most of those who, by luck or good management, owned a half acre or derelict cottage ripe for profitable transformation. Such people were adept at the manipulation of planning committees, the lobbying of local government officers. The preservationists, pinning their faith to moral superiority and persuasive argument, were beaten back every time.

The cause at issue right now was the planning application for half a dozen houses in the orchard attached to a cottage in the centre of the village, the property of a local farmer. The farmer, himself a member of the planning committee, had recently removed his stockman from the cottage and built him a modern bungalow on the farm, an arrangement now recognised as less altruistic than it might appear. Peter Sidey was explaining all this to Edward. Edward, Helen could see from his stance, was bored: he had his head tilted on one side and was watching a bird in a tree behind Peter Sidey's left ear. People believed that Edward, as an ardent nature conservationist, must be similarly passionate about all environmental matters. This was not so. He found it difficult to get worked up about buildings and tended to think of landscapes as habitats rather than objects of aesthetic concern.

'Clegg will make about a hundred thousand,' said Peter Sidey, 'if his application goes through. And the village will lose its last open space. I've seen the plans for the houses and they're peculiarly insensitive – more suitable for Milton Keynes.' He was a retired architect, past seventy now, who had exhausted himself over mainly fruitless endeavours to obstruct the likes of this opportunist farmer. He would have had a much more tranquil retirement, Helen thought, in some already brutalised corner of the country.

The Glovers made appropriate noises of concern. Peter Sidey outlined the opposition plans and urged them to write letters and attend a protest meeting. 'If that piece of land is developed there will be no large open space left in the village except the Green itself. And of course the Britches, thanks to your mother's public-spirited stand over the years. By the way, had you ever realised the name is Saxon by origin? From *braec* – a word meaning land newly taken into cultivation.'

'Well, it's the opposite now,' said Edward. 'Extremely uncultivated.'

'Quite. Interesting, though – the indestructibility of a name.'

Helen and Edward broke away as soon as was decently possible. They were both tickled at the image of Dorothy as a defender of the public good. 'Perhaps we should have told him she spent twenty years not selling the Britches simply to annoy the people who wanted to buy it,' said Edward.

'Certainly not. The result remains the same, whatever her reasons.'

As they approached the front door of Greystones Helen heard the telephone ringing within. She felt a rush of excitement and anticipation, and realised that in the preoccupations of the last half hour she had not thought of Giles Carnaby once – definitely a record. Fumbling with the latch key, she rushed for the telephone, thrusting the shopping basket at Edward.

It was Joyce Babcock. Reminding her at length, in case she hadn't made a note of it, of the Christmas holiday schedule for the library. When at last she put the receiver down and went into the kitchen she found that Edward had unpacked the shopping. The bottle of detergent stood in reproachful isolation at one end of the table.

Thinking of Giles Carnaby, of course, was not so much a considered process as an involuntary twitch. She did not want to think of him but could not help it. Indeed he was there most of the time, presiding within her head, dimming a little when her attention was engaged, all-pervasive in times of relaxation. At night he filled the room. She heard again every word he had spoken; she reconstructed his face, his body, his clothes.

A man she had met three times. With whom she had spent six hours or so. Who had displayed a friendly interest in her.

She saw herself, and did not care for what she saw. She stood to one side and observed this pathetic self-deluding fifty-two-year-old in a state of romantic yearning and sexual excitement. Given to the observation of others, she now observed herself, but without charity. She agreed with her mother: riding for a fall, driving nails in her own coffin, only herself to blame.

And there was nothing, absolutely nothing, to be done.

Edward, offended by the detergent, wandered out into the garden and was instantly distracted by the sound of digging from beyond the yew hedge. Rather desultory digging. Of course – that boy was here. He went to the gap in the hedge and saw

Gary at the far end of the kitchen garden. He was not digging at all now but taking a breather, evidently. A prolonged breather, during which he took a bar of chocolate out of his pocket and unwrapped it in a leisurely way.

Edward stood there.

Gary half-turned, spotted him out of the corner of one eye and began to dig again with great fervour.

Edward continued to stand there for another minute or two. Then he plunged off into the Britches to check the nest-boxes.

'He *what*?' exploded Louise. 'A row with the headmistress about *evolution*? Only Edward could have a row about evolution.'

'On the contrary,' said Helen. 'It was the stock subject for argument in the late nineteenth century, in some circles.'

'Oh, *then* . . . Trust Edward. I wish he had resigned – it would have been hilarious. So what else is new?'

Helen reached out for Edward's anorak, lying on the oak chest, and put it round her shoulders. She wished, not for the first time, that the telephone was not in the hall, always the coldest place in the house. The telephone was in the hall because Dorothy had said that telephones had to be in halls; it occurred to Helen that there was no longer any reason for this to be so. In one moment of combined panic and acceptance she knew that the telephone would stay exactly where it was.

'I've ordered the memorial stone.'

'The *what*?'

'Gravestone. Sorry – it's what the brochures say.' She described the choice. 'Do you think that sounds all right?'

'I suppose so. God! What a thing to have to do. I'm sorry – everything gets shoved on to you.'

'Edward helped.'

'Well, good. But now I'm feeling guilty. I ought to be there. Actually life has been fairly murderous lately. The office. And Tim has been having a go of his sinus plus conjunctivitis and something else he describes as *angst* and is being generally unsupportive. And Phil is playing up. Actually I think I may come down this weekend, just to escape. So . . . anything else?'

Helen put the anorak on. 'Ron Paget tried to get us to build on the Britches again.'

Louise laughed. 'Tell him Edward's turning it into a conservation area for endangered species. Actually, Ron doesn't know it, but he's got a point – you really ought to think about money a bit. Tim wants you to see some people he knows who do investment advice – then you'd get more out of those shares. Apparently they're all in the wrong things.'

'We don't want . . .' Helen began.

'Don't be silly. Tim's going to fix it up. You can have a nice day out in London – do you good.'

'We don't . . .' But Louise was off on another track. Helen stared at the oak chest and wondered what was in it. She couldn't remember anyone having opened it in years. There was a torn squab cushion on the top and it was traditionally used as a place to dump coats, scarves and gloves. Helen thought she could distantly recall having seen it open with her mother upended over it, rummaging. It had been Dorothy's territory, as indeed had all of the house, except for areas of communal use. It occurred to Helen – listening to Louise, contemplating the chest – that in all the years she and Edward had lived at Greystones they had fully occupied only their own bedrooms; elsewhere, they perched.

As soon as Louise had rung off she removed the cushion and opened the chest. The contents reeked of damp. On top was a rug, colourless with age and stained with mildew. Helen picked it out and dropped it on the floor; beneath was a tangle of string. So that was where mother had kept all that string from parcels which must not be discarded lest it be needed. There was a stack of crumpled brown paper, some of it addressed to herself and to Edward or Louise and bearing injunctions about not opening before Christmas; she recognised the handwriting of aunts and godmothers.

Beneath the layer of string and paper was a foetid mass of material: old curtains and cushions, felted blankets, a porridge of gloves and belts, garments decayed almost beyond identification. Moth and mouse had thrived down here. Helen reached in and stirred with distaste; a brown knitted pixie hat surfaced that her

83

mother used to wear long ago, unravelled now to a skeletal condition. She spotted a sweater she once gave Edward for a birthday, and various throw-outs of her own. She remembered her mother, standing squarely at the front door, fending off supplicants from the village school Parent-Teacher Association, the Darby and Joan Club, the summer Fete; Greystones never had jumble. Had her mother harboured some primitive superstition about the totemistic quality of one's possessions? Rejected the thought of her things in other hands?

She poked again – dug right down to the bottom and up through the shambles came something that signalled with painful clarity. Honey-coloured muslin. *Mousseline de soie*, to be precise; a grandeur of definition that she had cherished, aged eighteen. Faded now to dirty cream, and thrust down in a crumpled ball to the base of the chest – but still instantly known. That dress.

She pulled it up and shook it out. There it was – complete with the taffeta underskirt that had once (once only) rustled so satisfyingly. She sat down and examined it minutely – spread it over her lap and investigated. It was undamaged; creased into a wrinkled network, yes – its honey glow extinguished – a poor drab thing but unstained, untorn, unshrunk.

She smoothed the dress across her knees and pondered this.

The cupboard in which it was not. The moment of surprise, of faint alarm. The rail of intimately known clothes – her two tweed skirts, her three cotton frocks, her winter coat, her wool pinafore dress. And an airy space at the end where should have hung, in all its glory, the honey-coloured muslin – her first and only evening dress, the amazing, unexpected, enhancing present from her godmother.

'Mother! My evening dress isn't in my cupboard!'

Dorothy's back view, squat and priest-like before the altar of the kitchen stove. Stirring a pan, her head wreathed in steam, hairpins jutting from the bun at the nape of her neck.

'*Mother*!'

'I heard you. No need to shout. That dress went to the cleaners.'

'But *mother* . . . It didn't need cleaning. I've only worn it once. And I need it for Saturday – for the Clarks' dance.'

'It had perspiration marks.'

'Oh mother, it didn't . . . Never mind, I'll go and get it. It will be ready, won't it? Where's the ticket, I . . .'

And Dorothy turns, red-faced from her brew, or so it seemed. 'They had some disaster with it, apparently. No point in going round there. It was spoiled. The stuff they use – these chemicals.' And turns again to the stove, furiously stirring.

'No! Oh no . . . Oh, *mother* . . . But then I've nothing for Saturday. Nothing at all.'

'Nonsense,' says Dorothy. 'I'll take in my old brown silk for you. There's a good hem on it, too, it can be let down. That'll be perfectly all right – Rose was out of her mind buying you that ridiculous creation anyway, far too low cut and tight in the bust.'

And what, one now wonders, happened to the brown silk, of which there is no sign – neither here in the chest nor upstairs among mother's things. It is all too well remembered: the slimy feel of it, hanging limp and unfitting around her as she stands awkward on the threshold of the Clarks' drawing-room, where the carpets are rolled back, the parquet gleams and in the corner the big hired radiogram is asserting that the lady is a tramp. She prays to be noticed; she prays to be ignored. Gone is the rapturous unfamiliar feeling of equality, of authority, induced by the *mousseline de soie* at her cousins' dance two weeks before. She does not look nice; she knows that she does not look nice. A few yards of material have changed her from one person into another. Is one's grip of things to be always so fickle?

'I've emptied the hall chest. I thought you might use it for your files.'

'I didn't know there was anything in it,' said Edward.

'It was bung full.'

'Stuff of mother's, I imagine.'

'Not entirely. There was a dress I had when I was eighteen.'

Edward looked at Helen warily, alerted by her tone.

'A dress mother said the cleaners ruined. Not the case, it now seems.'

Edward, shying away from disagreeable exposures, supposed that mother must have made a mistake.

'Mother didn't make that kind of mistake.'

'So long ago,' murmured Edward, sidestepping. 'I don't know how you can remember . . .'

'Since when,' said Helen, 'does one forget?'

He remembered now, though would not have done so otherwise. He left Helen and went to have a bath and in the cold steamy bathroom there came to him this vision of a distant unreal Helen looking – well, radiant was the unexpected word that came to mind – looking not her usual self at all in some frock that glowed and billowed and rustled as she came in at the front door late, pink-cheeked, a touch dishevelled and greeted by the stone wall of Dorothy's disapproval. Where had he been then? Lurking on the stairs; listening from his bed?

Edward lay in the bath as the water cooled around him – as usual it had never been adequately hot – and allowed physical discomfort to complement his state of mind. He thought of Helen, with distress and in helplessness. He did not know quite what was implied by all this business of dresses, but he sensed something ugly – and flinched. His mother trundled around on the edges of his thoughts and he tried to push her away. She came back, unquenchable and impervious.

When he was very small Helen had been all that he was not; wise, mature, equipped with skills and resources. He sheltered under her wing; above all, he sheltered from their mother. And then had come the awful perception that Helen too was vulnerable; he had seen her exposed, humiliated, disappointed. He had realised that the refinement of distress is that you are obliged to suffer not just for yourself, which is the easier part, but for others as well. He suffered for Helen, and suffered again now – in retrospect in the chill bathwater in the dank Greystones bathroom where condensation sent rusty trails from the pipes down every wall. He thought of Helen, and felt for Helen, as some wincing extension of himself. If anyone had asked him – God forbid – what were his feelings for his sister he would have replied that he was fond of her.

When Edward was about twenty he had once intercepted the look exchanged by a young married couple. He could no longer remember who they were, but their faces were with him still, and that look: those two pairs of eyes, from which shone a brilliant collusive intensity – an intensity that excluded the rest of the world.

On that occasion he was awed and intrigued; he hoped and expected that one day he too would share such a look with someone. Subsequently, he came across the look on various faces – a mother lifting a baby from a pram, a child running towards its father, a woman sitting beside a hospital bed, lovers by the dozen. Awe gave way to a certain bleakness; he felt the excluding quality of those eyes – they were never looking at him. The only eyes that ever gazed thus into his were those of a succession of dogs.

Nor did he ever so gaze himself. At the only time in his life when he would have liked to he was so crushed by doubt and diffidence that he kept his eyes scrupulously trained upon the ground, or the table in front of him, or the wall behind the shoulder of the person concerned. Whole conversations took place during which Edward stared out of windows, or at carpets or pavements or the branches of trees.

'Do you realise that you have this exasperating habit of never looking at one, Edward?'

Oh yes. Only surreptitiously, when unobserved – soaking up, then, the tilt of the jaw, the structure of the hairline, the wonderful singularity of nose, of mouth, of eyebrow.

'Edward, are you with me or are you not? I sometimes wonder.'

Only too much so, alas. Only too much so.

Those times were reduced now to a swirl of unchronological slides – images of a room, a street, a skyline – some with accompanying sound.

A tube train. Circle Line. Paddington, Bayswater, Notting

Hill . . . An advertisement about Amplex: two people staring in distaste at an unsuspecting third. 'Well, Edward – what *about* this Italian trip . . . Would it be fun?' And the whole scene becomes incandescent: the cheerful rocking train, the interesting faces of people, promise and potential.

The Chinese restaurant. Waiting; alone. Watching the door. Through which, at last, comes the expected face and with it another, known also, and the evening is dashed, the stomach twists, the chop suey smells sour.

Greenwich Park. The perfect ginger circles of autumn leaves beneath the trees. A tug hooting from the river. Sparrows at their feet. His own hand reaching out in despair to touch another, which is instantly withdrawn. 'Sorry, Edward . . .'

Trudging from one grey day into another, on and on, until at last it doesn't matter any more, or so it seems.

SEVEN

'This is a complete waste of time,' said Edward.

'Louise arranged it – at least Tim did. We could hardly say no.'

'Couldn't you just have written these people a letter?'

'Apparently they like to see you once to begin with.'

Edward, still rebellious, gazed out of the train window. He hadn't been to London in years, and didn't wish to.

'It's your money too,' said Helen reprovingly.

'There isn't much of it anyway.'

'That's the whole point. These investment people can make the capital produce more – put it into different things.'

Edward grunted, apparently intent on Didcot power station. In fact he was observing a flock of lapwings in a flooded field; his spirits lifted a notch. The lapwings were followed up by some tufted duck on a reservoir – a frustrating snatched glimpse but enough to dispel most of his gloom. By the time they reached Paddington he was more cheerful. They studied the Underground map to see how to reach their destination. Both were made nervous now by the prospect of the appointment and the tricky matter of timing. How long would it take to get there? Should they go at once or have a cup of coffee first? Too late would not do; too early would be awkward. They stood amid the station crowds, arguing. Edward was in favour of coffee; Helen wanted to go.

'It takes half an hour to get anywhere in London on the tube,' said Edward.

'Twenty years ago. And anyway we don't know exactly where it is. I forgot to ask Louise.' Helen was becoming flustered.

'Ring her up then.'

This presented a further problem. Neither of the Glovers had used a public telephone for a long while and were astonished to find themselves confronted by a totally unfamiliar contraption. They stood before it in perplexity, Edward banging his head against the plastic hood, and tried to work out what to do from the illustrative diagram shown, like foreign tourists. Behind them, other intending users glared in contempt. Eventually Helen got through; Louise was in a meeting, she was told, and could not be reached.

They took the tube. Emerging at the station in the City (with fifteen minutes in hand, Helen noted to her relief) they found themselves in an alien landscape. Blank-faced office blocks reared around them; everyone else carried a briefcase and a daily paper. They hesitated, getting in the way of this purposeful world. Eventually, Helen asked directions of a newsvendor.

Their destination turned out to be one of the largest and glassiest of the office blocks. The Glovers approached it with apprehension, unused to such places. The central lobby was several stories high. It included a number of thirty-foot trees and a tide of foliage that would not have disgraced Kew Gardens. One entire wall was constructed as a glass cliff down which fell a waterfall some six feet wide; the pool into which it tumbled smoked with spray and the whole effect was disconcerting, as of some plumbing disaster on a majestic scale. The Glovers stood around at a loss; this did not seem to be the sort of place in which business could be carried on. Eventually Helen spotted a reception desk, discreetly tucked away behind a large weeping fig; they advanced across wastes of polished marble and were directed to a lift. As it rose Edward said thoughtfully, 'One gets the impression that this sort of place must cost rather a lot of money.'

The lift stopped. The doors opened and they stepped into a thickly carpeted, perfectly silent and very large room, again rampant with greenery, in which a girl was sitting behind a desk smiling brightly. At the sight of them she sprang forward and offered to get them a cup of coffee. She ushered them into deep leather chairs, offered Edward a copy of the *Financial Times* (which he took, cravenly) and pranced off down a corridor. She wore an emerald green silk shirt, a very short black leather skirt and black tights.

Edward dropped the newspaper on to the carpet. He gave Helen a look of reproach and accusation. Helen stared doggedly at a Swiss cheese plant.

The coffee arrived, followed a few minutes later by two tall and thin men who introduced themselves and led the Glovers to another room, barely identifiable as an office except for one discreet filing cabinet. An immense window overlooked the river. More foliage. A large low glass table to one side of which the Glovers were directed. Their hosts drew up chairs on the other; the one who was apparently the senior of the two said, 'Julia, I think we could manage some more coffee . . .' The leather-skirted girl tripped off.

Courtesies were exchanged. The Glovers, cautiously, observed their hosts; both wore suits that spoke of much expense, the senior and thinner with a striped shirt, the other with a lilac shirt and pink silk tie. They sat there drinking coffee and looking at the Glovers with detached interest. Edward wore his green suit, Helen her camel coat. Both, in fact, were dressed as for their mother's funeral except that Helen had a new white blouse with a frill down the front and her pearl necklace. Edward's shoes were dirty and bits of the Britches still clung to his trousers.

The striped shirt man now began to talk about the portfolio. Pink tie tapped at a calculator. Striped shirt said that the position could undoubtedly be improved, with a judicious mixture of playing safe and maybe doing something a bit interesting with Japan or the Far East but of course unfortunately there wasn't all *that* much room for manoeuvre. He wondered if there were any other assets. Helen explained about the house. Striped shirt nodded. He asked if there was anything else. Edward looked warningly at Helen and Helen heard herself say that there was a small piece of land. Striped shirt and pink tie perked up a little. They asked for particulars; pink tie made some notes.

'But there's no question of selling it,' said Edward.

Striped shirt raised an eyebrow.

Edward lapsed once more into strangled silence. Helen explained why it was impossible to sell the Britches. This took a couple of minutes, during which striped shirt and pink tie sat back, long legs crossed and polite smiles of amusement or possibly incredulity on their lips. Pink tie tapped again at his calculator and wondered, with a quick glance at striped shirt, if Miss Glover and her brother had considered that realisation of the asset would bring in . . . well, at a conservative estimate around ten, fifteen thousand extra income? Helen replied that they had.

There was a short pause. Edward, who appeared to have detached himself from the proceedings, stared out of the window. Helen now had a curious prickling sensation up and down her spine. I am not to be intimidated by house plants and silk ties, she thought. Striped shirt tapped a gold pencil thoughtfully against his teeth and said that of course one had every respect for someone wishing to take such a stand and that in that case we must see what could be done with the portfolio as it was. Such as it was. He flashed Helen a nice white smile: 'We can certainly get the income up on what it is now. And I don't imagine you have particularly expensive tastes, either of you – vintage claret or fast cars.' Both men were now smiling genially; the sort of smile people give to earnest but not very bright children, or to social inferiors.

And why the hell shouldn't I have a *penchant* for claret? thought Helen. She felt as though, had she been a dog, all her hair would have been standing on end. She looked stonily across the table, telling herself that all she and Edward had to do was get out of here, as soon as possible compatible with the observance of social niceties and the maintenance of civilised behaviour. She forced herself to sit tight and retain a noncommittal but not overtly offensive expression while striped shirt talked about unit trusts and pink tie came in once or twice with deferential follow-ups or corrections. She counted to a hundred, in her head, twice, and tried to think about something wonderfully different. Edward was now looking at the river with great intensity; he leaned forward a little, as though to see something better.

And then at last everyone was shuffling chairs on the pile carpet and getting up and there was a lot of shaking of hands and

Edward and Helen were in the lift once more, smoothly and silently descending.

Edward said, 'What terrible people.'

'Mmn.'

'Do we have to pay them a lot of money?'

'I imagine so.'

But it was clear that his attention was now elsewhere. He set off across the marble lake at a canter, with Helen panting behind. Outside, he headed for the bridge and there, halfway across, he came at last to a halt, with traffic rushing past, the river gleaming below and the city reaching away in an infinite complex parade of shining white and pearly grey with light snapping from windows and cars. He leaned over the parapet and gazed.

Helen joined him. 'What are you looking at?'

Edward pointed. 'Terns.'

Helen looked down. The water was a greyish-green, streaked with gold by the sun, and above it wheeled and drifted numbers of birds. Others floated slowly downstream, sitting upright like bathtoys amid a flotsam of bottles and skeins of plastic and what seemed to be sandwiches, while several more patrolled a little shingly beach almost beneath the piers of the bridge.

'I thought they were just gulls at first,' said Edward. 'I could see them from the window in that place. Then I realised they were terns.'

'I thought terns liked coasts and estuaries, not the middle of cities?'

'They do. That's the point.'

The Glovers stood alone on the bridge and watched the terns. They dipped and swirled over the golden water, disappearing sometimes under the bridge, sweeping off in a flock to examine the wake of a passing launch. One small colony remained all the time on their beach, an isolated solitary place of grey pebbles below greenish breakwaters; high above them the blind-eyed office blocks glittered pink and yellow in the sun. Edward was enthralled; he leaned his head on his hands and gazed. Once, he turned to Helen and smiled apologetically; 'Sorry . . . We'll go in a minute.'

But Helen was in no hurry. She stood there beside him,

acknowledging the marvellous presence of the terns, and as she did so the thought came to her that striped shirt, and pink tie, and Julia of the leather skirt, presumably passed them by five days a week without knowing that they did so. One is supposed to feel a charitable surge at revelations of deprivation, but oh how satisfying not to do so.

Edward straightened. 'I'm hungry – aren't you?'

'Yes. We'll find somewhere for lunch.'

They were both, now, in a state of mild exaltation. This curious fusion of experiences had made them elated and slightly feverish. Helen clutched Edward's arm as they dodged through the traffic. They remembered details of the past hour, giggling. 'What *are* unit trusts?' said Edward. 'I couldn't understand a word he was saying.' 'I'm not sure – but did you notice his *socks*? I never saw such smooth socks on a man.' Forging onwards in this way, they found themselves away from the river and in a hinterland of commercial London that was as alien to them as New York or Hong Kong. Money reared up all around; it towered in the form of plate glass, stainless steel, polished marble, Portland stone, concrete, brick and slate. For Helen, London meant the leafy calm of Twickenham, where they had lived in early childhood, subsequent rare excursions to the Royal Academy or the Tate and occasional visits to Louise in Camden Town. For Edward, it was a bed-sitter in Bayswater, the rioting children of the secondary modern and the distresses of those disturbing years. For both of them the landscape in which they now stood was quite unrelated to any of this. They came to a stop. Edward said 'This doesn't look like the sort of area for restaurants.' He gazed at a glass block, soaring upwards, in whose mirror cliff-face swam the distorted white reflection of a Wren church spire.

'No. Where was that French place Louise used to take us to?'

'Somewhere near South Kensington tube station, wasn't it?'

Clutching at the safety of recollection, the Glovers set off for more familiar regions. And indeed, surfacing again at South Kensington, some atavistic instinct for the lie of the land took them directly to the street in which Louise had had an office, fifteen years or so ago, and where two or three times a year they had met for a meal.

'That's it!' said Edward. And then, more doubtfully, 'Isn't it?'

'I think so. The outside's different, somehow. Better go in and see.'

Once in, there was no going back. Handed from one briskly obsequious waiter to another they found themselves tucked into an upholstered corner, served up with menus and dealt drinks that neither of them was conscious of having ordered. It was very noisy; every other table was full and music babbled from the walls.

'It used to have check tablecloths,' said Edward. 'And artificial onions and fishing nets hanging from the ceiling.'

'Well, they're gone.'

'Never mind.' Edward picked up the menu. 'It's called Maggie's Wine Bar now, apparently. Looks rather expensive, I'm afraid.'

They ordered. Edward finished his glass of sherry; he seemed quite restored now.

'You were very good with those men. I'm afraid I rather backed down.'

'You did,' said Helen.

'They made me feel like . . . some species that had got into the wrong time slot. That ought to be extinct.'

'Do you feel more comfortable now?'

'Marginally,' said Edward, glancing round. 'I could put up some sort of valiant struggle for survival.'

'You'd have to adapt, not just survive. Even I know that.'

'True. That might be more difficult.'

They grinned at each other. 'So what do I say to Tim?' enquired Helen.

'Say we were too small fry for them. He ought to have known that anyway.'

'He meant well.'

'People are always meaning well,' said Edward. 'That's often the trouble.'

The food arrived, and a bottle of wine. Edward looked warily at it. 'Do you think we'll manage all that? I ordered a half carafe.'

'They've taken the cork out now.'

'Oh well . . .'

'The problem about us,' said Helen, 'is that we've never felt the same way about money as most other people seem to.'

'I've never thought of it as a problem.'

'It's the only way we seem to be like mother.'

'I hope so,' said Edward fervently.

'Louise isn't interested in money as such, but she quite likes *things*. Buying things. You and I can't manage even that to any extent.'

Edward was tucking in to his meal. 'This is rather good. Perhaps eating in restaurants is nicer than I think it is. I suppose the difficulty about us is that so far as money and possessions are concerned we're at a more primitive stage than the rest. We're not interested in surplus. It's like being aborigines or North American Indians after the colonists have arrived. When everyone else is busy accumulating they get bothered about anyone who is quite happy with a modest sufficiency.'

'And look what happened to the aborigines and the Indians,' said Helen.

'Mmn. Perhaps that's why I felt so uncomfortable with those men. But then there were the terns getting away with it on the other side of the window.'

'The terns get away with it because they aren't noticed.'

'I've always thought I did quite well at being inconspicuous myself,' said Edward. 'But I take your point. One hasn't a hope, really. With the likes of Ron Paget around, and those chaps in their glass skyscraper.'

Plates were removed. More wine was poured. Helen caught sight of a silver-grey head at the far side of the room and twitched; not Giles Carnaby, of course not, how could it be – here? And I hadn't thought of the blessed man in the last two hours – at least barely thought. Ten days now and he hasn't telephoned.

'What's wrong?' enquired Edward.

'Nothing. Do you imagine that we are the way we are about money because of mother or because we would have been like that anyway?'

'Interesting. I don't know. Conditioning must have something to do with it – it always does. We weren't trained to be acquisitive.'

'Presumably the children of the poor aren't either. And we've never been the poor, in a proper sense. Tim obviously thinks we're going to be, in our old age – that's why he got us involved with these investment people.'

Edward sighed. 'Old age will be quite bad enough without being patronised by people like that. I think I'll settle for poverty.'

'It's not just conditioning,' continued Helen. 'Presumably inheritance comes into it too. Inherited characteristics. Like we've both got slightly flat feet, the same as mother, and Louise has her wiry hair.'

'We'd better not push this too far,' said Edward. 'Or we shan't like what emerges.'

They were both now inflamed by the unaccustomed wine. Neither particularly wanted any more but a lifetime's resistance to waste went deep. They drank, doggedly.

'Flat feet and a tendency to be frugal are nothing very terrible. You aren't like her in any other conspicuous way. Nor is Louise.'

'And nor are you,' Edward put in, promptly.

'Look at us, though – sitting here talking about her.'

Edward pondered. 'When she was alive we hardly ever did, do you realise?'

Helen nodded. Tacit acceptance; the occasional glance of collusion; unspoken shared expertise in methods of evasion and camouflage. 'There was no need, was there?'

'Then why do we do it now?'

'Exorcism,' said Helen briskly. 'Or something of that order.'

'Don't you feel guilty? I do.'

'Of course.'

Edward tipped the last of the wine into their glasses. 'When did you first realise other people's mothers were different?'

'When I was about five, I think.'

'You were always more sophisticated. I was twenty-one at least.'

'In any case,' said Helen, 'we mustn't exaggerate. Other people have difficulties with their parents.'

'Do they? Good.'

'We could always have moved out, both of us, but we didn't. Why not?'

'Inertia,' suggested Edward.

'Do you honestly think so?'

Edward avoided her eye.

'In your case, possibly,' she went on. 'Or at least inertia certainly comes into it. In mine, I think the whole situation is more dubious.'

'Helen . . .' Edward began, warningly,

'I can see, with detachment, a certain lack of enterprise, to put it mildly. Perversity, even. Masochism.'

'Oh, don't be silly,' said Edward.

'What woman of any initiative would have spent almost her entire adult life living in discord with a difficult mother?'

'You . . . coped with her. She'd have been lost without you.'

'No she wouldn't,' said Helen. 'Mother was entirely self-sufficient, and you know it.'

They regarded one another. 'I told you we shouldn't push this too far,' said Edward.

'At the time one justified it in various ways. There was always next year, and the one after. One was just biding one's time.'

'Of course,' agreed Edward. 'And anyway . . .'

'One was always about to get the serious, definitive job.'

'Exactly. And in any case . . .'

'Or get married.'

Edward, furiously scouring his plate, rambled on about Dorothy.

'Instead of which suddenly I'm fifty-two and mother isn't there any more. I wish I could subscribe to your theory of mother-as-obstacle. It would be comforting. It looks to me, frankly, like a clear case of chronic timidity, laced with apathy.'

'Oh, well in that case, what about me?' said Edward wildly.

They looked at each other.

The waiter, practised at the disruption of moments of intimacy, plumped the bill down beside Edward's plate.

'In fact,' said Helen, 'I'm not feeling particularly glum about all this. It's a question more of assessment. Taking stock.'

Edward picked up the bill and examined it.

'Mother's part in it is one thing. One's own is quite another.'

'This seems to say three hundred and seventy-five pounds,' said Edward. 'Can that be right?'

Helen took the bill from him and indicated a decimal point.

'Oh, I see.' He examined his wallet. 'I still don't have enough. I hope this doesn't mean you're going to rush off and become County Librarian now. Or . . .'

Helen laughed. 'I shouldn't worry. Neither is likely.'

The waiter hovered. Helen fished in her purse. Between them they came up with a pile of notes and coins. Neither of them possessed a credit card, and it did not occur to them to offer a cheque. The waiter watched this display with patient interest and carried the loaded saucer away ceremoniously, as though it were a church collection plate.

Outside the restaurant they paused. 'I rather enjoyed that in a funny way,' said Helen. 'Have you ever noticed that we seldom talk to each other at meals normally?'

'Of course we don't,' said Edward. 'What is there to say?'

'Quite a lot, it seems. Oh well . . . What shall we do now? It's only half past two. We could go to an exhibition or something.'

Edward looked unenthusiastic.

'Or do some shopping.'

'Shopping!' Now he was aghast.

'It's Louise's birthday next week, you know. And she's coming down this weekend. We ought to buy her a present.'

'We don't know what she wants,' said Edward, fighting desperately.

'As a matter of fact I do. She's got all these photos she took with that new camera – all jumbled up in an envelope – and she was saying she ought to put them into something. We'll get her a photo album.'

'We – you – could get a photo album in Spaxton.'

'We can get a better photo album in London. A more Louise sort of photo album. An up-to-the-minute photo album.'

Edward gave her a surly glance. 'It's the wine. I knew a whole bottle was a mistake. All right, then, if you insist. Where?'

'We're not far from Knightsbridge,' said Helen. 'Big smart shops. That should do.'

She still felt interestingly exhilarated. Maybe the wine. Or maybe the sun on white stucco (really London was much prettier than one remembered) or the cheerful scarlet of buses or the continuously satisfying recollection of the terns and the oblivious complacency of pink tie and striped shirt in their sealed air-conditioned office. Or maybe something else; this curious sensation one had all the time now of the blood running a little faster, the senses being more keenly tuned, of tomorrow or next week being more inviting. Giles Carnaby might be phoning Grey-stones at this very moment, the phone ringing in the empty hall . . . Maybe he was putting the receiver down and picking up his pen to write a quick note instead, handing it to his secretary to pop in the post, saying 'Mind you don't forget that one, it's rather urgent.'

Or maybe not.

'Surely this'll do?' said Edward. 'It looks quite big enough and smart enough.'

Hoisted back to the London street, she saw them both reflected in the plate-glass of the shop window, superimposed in transparency above silk and fur, gilt and leather, the swaggering dummies with blind inscrutable gaze in their preposterous clothes. Their reflections, gliding above these sumptuous displays, showed a shabby pair, distinctly down-at-heel, as sharply contrasted as the proletarian flotsam in some Victorian street scene, dingy specta-tors of the nobs in their satin and feathers. The dummies in the windows wore clothes so unlike Helen's that they might have stepped from some other culture: rainbow colours, fabrics of wondrous texture and design, skirts like puffballs or split like a dancer's. The chairs upon which they sat or leaned were gilded or of shining chrome and glass; bales of material were half unfurled to spill around more silk and satin; jewellery was flung down in handfuls upon tables or simply on the ground. Prices, where stated at all, were scribbled in decorative script upon tiny cards, an afterthought. Helen watched her own face swim above these rich and glowing caverns; did it have a lean and hungry look, deprived, excluded? Well, no, not really. It was her usual face, homely, familiar – diminished merely and made incongruous by the setting; it wandered ghostly, with Edward's alongside, across the Aladdin's caves beyond. Any more of this, thought Helen, and I shall have doubts as to who I am, like Alice. I'll be getting into conversation with one of these fibreglass ladies. 'Explain yourself!' she'll say, and I shall be hard put to it to do so. Her preoccupations would not be mine at all. 'What are you worth?' she'd ask; I'd certainly have trouble with that one. 'What do you cost?' would be a bit easier; around £4.50 an hour would be correct I think. Plus second-hand value of what I stand up in, which by current jumble sale rates would be maybe ten pounds or so. She, on the other hand, top to toe, comes out at well over two thousand; as for structural costs . . . does one buy or hire her, I wonder?

'Come *on*,' said Edward. 'I can't hold this door for ever. You're the one who wanted to come here.'

Within, there was that rich smell of better-class department stores: an expensively achieved amalgam of perfume, out-of-season flowers, new leather and virgin fabrics. Pace seemed to have slowed up; people did not walk but drifted; sound was muted, mopped up by space and carpeting. The Glovers hesitated. Edward looked accusingly at Helen. 'This way,' she said firmly, and plunged off into a perfumery hall of gleaming marble, as lush as some Byzantine church. Edward followed; she heard him skid on the floor, in whose black and shining depths were reflected the chandeliers above their heads. All around were Arab women, heavily robed, sniffing their wrists. A bottle of perfume, Helen saw, could cost £110. Edward now wore the manic look of some animal transferred into the wrong environment, as though he might run amok, or bite. Each counter had an assistant behind it, none of them doing anything. Helen headed for the nearest one and asked about photograph albums. They were directed onwards.

Perfumes gave way to leather goods, and leather goods to food. The air was scented now with chocolate, coffee and freshly baked bread. They passed a counter above which hung trusses of pigeons, pheasants and other less identifiable but more disturbing birds; Helen grabbed Edward's arm to hurry him on but he was already gazing at a row of hares suspended by their feet from a rack. He turned and caught her eye. 'The butcher in Spaxton has hares,' she said defensively.

The assistants behind the counter wore what appeared to Helen to be fancy dress: boaters with scarlet bands and elaborate aprons. One of them – an adolescent with the fair, downy looks of a choir boy – reached up with a pole to bring down a clump of unidentifiable silvery speckled birds. Both Glovers had come to a halt now, mesmerised despite themselves. The boy reached for a chopper and began briskly to decapitate the birds. Enough! thought Helen; she turned to Edward – and he was not there.

She looked round. Everywhere, expensively dressed people were buying food with an air of dedication. She couldn't see Edward. She walked from one end of the hall to the other; no Edward. Irritation gave way to a feeling of panic. She told herself to calm down: at the worst they had lost each other and would have to go home separately. She had Edward's ticket, which was a nuisance, but never mind. But even as she went over all this she continued to hurry from one section of the store to another, searching, her heart thumping. It was ridiculous. Once, when Edward was five, she and Dorothy had mislaid him in Woolworths. Dorothy had glared phlegmatically around and said that would teach the silly little wretch to wander off on his own; it was Helen who had rushed to and fro and eventually found Edward, white with shock, cowering beside one of the tills.

She moved from handbags through gifts to the flower shop and eventually reached a men's outfitting department where, suddenly, she saw Edward. He was sitting on a chair beside a display of furled umbrellas; he had his head in his hands and was being eyed dispassionately by two male assistants in dark suits. As she approached, one of them broke ranks and went to stand over Edward, apparently addressing him. Edward neither looked up nor moved.

Irritation now displaced concern. 'I've been looking everywhere for you,' Helen snapped.

'We have a First Aid Room on the second floor, if the gentleman isn't feeling well.'

Edward took his hands from his face and sat up. He was shaking, Helen now saw. He quivered, very slightly, all over, as though he were perished with cold. He simply sat there, shaking.

'The nurse is always in attendance.'

'I'm not ill,' said Edward. He glanced at Helen as though he had never seen her in his life, and made no attempt to get up. The assistant inclined his head diplomatically and when an American was heard to make enquiries about cashmere sweaters he stepped aside.

Helen said, 'Are you sure you're all right?'

Edward nodded. He stood up. She put a hand on his arm and felt the rhythmic shivering through the stuff of his jacket. 'Let's get Louise's photo album and then go.'

She steered him into a lift. She tracked down, at last, the right department. Photograph albums, it turned out, could also cost £110, or thereabouts. They came in tooled leather, they came gilded and embossed and with special paper made in Florence. They also came, if you insisted and were prepared to accept a measure of mild public humiliation, in plastic and plain paper. Edward stood in silence while Helen negotiated. The shaking appeared to have stopped but he looked dazed. She guided him back to the lift, down to the ground floor and the street and into a taxi.

Just before they reached the station she said, 'Was it the birds?'

'Birds?' He seemed almost normal again; he had been staring out of the window and had commented on a street name he remembered from his London period.

'Those silver birds. At the butcher's.'

'They were guinea-fowl,' said Edward. He spoke quite composedly. The whole thing, Helen saw, whatever it had been, was to be ignored. 'I can't imagine why anyone would want to eat them,' he went on. 'There'd be nothing on them. You'd get twice as much off an ordinary chicken.'

In the train, Helen thought about money. Money, she realised, had changed its nature over the years. There was both less of it about, and more. Today's world was one in which five-pound notes gushed benignly from the walls of banks at the touch of a button, in which people had only to scribble their names and anything they wished for was theirs; a world in which – as she had seen on a television programme – unimaginable sums of money flew about the globe at the whim of shirt-sleeved young men who sat tapping idly at keyboards. A world in fact in which the stuff itself – the coins, the notes – seemed barely relevant and indeed a trifle indecent. Sayings of Dorothy's came to mind: 'It doesn't grow on trees, you know.' 'You've got to learn the value of money.' Impossible nowadays to say such things to children, presumably. As a child she had had a piggy bank; she could recall the physical satisfaction of its jingling weight in her hands. That was wealth. The child of a neighbour in the village had showed her last week his newest share certificate; he had bought British Telecom, he told her gravely, and was thinking of going into Gilts. The family lived in one of the Barratt houses and did not seem to Helen unduly prosperous, but clearly one was losing one's eye for these things.

She looked at Edward. He seemed quite all right again. He had bought himself the latest issue of *Wildlife* and was immersed in an article about otters. The day would be held against her, she knew, if only in the muted way in which Edward was capable of bearing a grudge.

EIGHT

'Thank you,' said Louise. 'It's exactly what I need. However did you guess? Mind, God knows why I keep on recording the children for posterity, the way they are now. When I look back I could weep – dear little things tottering about on beaches. Phil hasn't addressed a civil word to us in weeks. Anyway – thanks.'

'It's from Edward too.'

'I took that as read. Since when did Edward go shopping on his own behalf? Where is he, anyway?'

'In the Britches, I think. He's been trying to do something about the brambles and nettles.'

Louise flopped on to the sofa. 'How did you enjoy your day in London?'

'It had its moments,' said Helen evasively.

'What about the investment people?'

'They made it fairly clear we were too small fry for them. And the place was more like a botanical gardens than an office.'

'Tim knows some other people. I'll tell him to . . .'

'No,' said Helen. 'We have still to recover from those.'

'Think about it,' conceded Louise. 'So what did you do after that – it can't have taken you all day?'

'We had lunch in that restaurant in South Kensington.'

'It doesn't exist any more.'

'Exactly,' said Helen. 'So we discovered. We had lunch on its ashes, as it were. Then we went shopping.'

'Well! Quite a spree! Very good for you both.'

'Don't patronise,' said Helen. 'We're less socially disadvantaged than you imagine. The village provides resources undreamed of in Camden Town. Though I will admit that I find London disconcerting these days. The landscape. Everything

105

seems to be built of mirrors – what on earth has happened to brick? But I grant you that I'm behind the times in some ways. Architecture and offices full of botanical specimens are the least of it. Social etiquette, for instance . . . What's done and what isn't.' She shot her sister a crafty glance. 'Most of it is quite irrelevant to me, of course, but one keeps a sort of technical interest.'

'Huh?' said Louise. 'What are you blathering on about?'

'Oh, I don't know . . . How people behave . . . Men and women, for instance. Such as . . . Do women take the initiative nowadays?' She felt the beginnings of a disastrous blush and busied herself with a dirty mark on the window, getting out her handkerchief and scrubbing, her back to Louise. 'I mean – time was, you wouldn't . . . Nowadays, would they ring up first – that sort of thing?'

'How should I know?' said Louise sourly. 'I'm married, aren't I?'

'Well . . . your friends . . .' Helen persisted. 'For instance, if someone hadn't heard from a man friend for – oh, for a couple of weeks or so – when he'd said vaguely he'd ring – I mean, she might wonder if there was something wrong, if he was ill, or if she'd offended in some way. Would she feel nowadays it was up to her to make contact?'

'Look, what is all this?' demanded Louise.

'I'm just curious. Detached interest. One ought to know how things are. If they've changed or not.'

'You are a funny old thing,' said Louise. 'You're making that window worse, you know. Haven't you got any Windowlene? Actually so far as I can see it's sod's law for women, just as it always has been. You know my friend Judith? Well, she's been having an affair with this bloke for the last year or so and then out of the blue he turned round and . . . Here's Edward. Open the window and he can come in this way.'

Edward was advancing across the lawn. 'What did he turn round and do?' said Helen.

'Oh, some other time . . . Hi! Thanks for the birthday present.'

Edward came in at the french window and stared blankly at

his younger sister. After a moment he said 'Oh . . . Yes.' And then, 'Many happy returns of the day. How old are you?'

'It's next week, not today. And I'll be forty-three for Christ's sake. There's this piece of contemporary mythology that the forties are the best time of your life. A load of cock, so far as I'm concerned. What about you?'

But Edward had lost interest, apparently. He turned to Helen. 'Have we got any wire anywhere? I want to mend the fence.'

The question of age, in fact, filled his head these days, but it was not a matter he wanted to discuss with Louise. Or indeed with anyone. He did not want to be young again – that time had had particular and transcendent horrors – but the thought of being any older filled him with panic. He could not imagine finding tranquillity of soul in old age; if he could only be allowed to mark time for a while all might yet be well, one might suddenly achieve equilibrium, certainty, serenity. There would still be possibilities. Hopes.

When his mother died it was as though his youth began to slip out of sight. Her existence, he now realised, had implications far beyond her abrasive and insistent presence: it had tethered him to a distant shore. Now, the shore was fading and there was no going back.

And every now and then there came these appalling moments when feeling boiled, when, it seemed to him, he became slightly mad. Most of the time one was all right – or at least as all right as one had ever been – and then out of the blue it struck, a hideous uprush of fear, of longing, of shame. It could be prompted by anything, or nothing. It could come in the wastes of the night, or at the most humdrum moments of the day. It had surged forth in that dreadful shop in London, when he had stood transfixed – not, as Helen thought, by bunches of guinea-fowl but by the bare arms of the butcher's lad adroitly trimming a carcass on a block beneath. The boy was done up in a long striped apron and straw boater in arch Victorian pastiche but his arms were all that Edward saw: young, dusted with golden hairs and somehow indisputably male. Beautiful arms; he looked at them and wanted to cry.

He could fend them off, the appalling moments. Fight them. The thing was to keep occupied. He banged about in the scullery, hunting for wire. He would make the Britches impenetrable, tackle the dead trees and plant saplings.

As soon as Louise had left, Helen went to the telephone. She picked up the receiver, dialled Giles Carnaby's number, and then replaced the receiver before the connection was made. She wasn't quite ready yet, after all. In fifteen minutes' time, she told herself sternly. Just a little longer to get oneself into the right frame of mind, run over the right casual, uncommitted phrases. 'It just occurred to me you might like to . . .'; 'If you're free on Wednesday, I thought maybe . . .'

She too resolved on activity. She had been intending for days to make a start on clearing out the cloakroom; now was the moment – she would make a preliminary survey, set aside what should be kept, see if there was anything good enough for Oxfam. Then, suitably relaxed, she would telephone Giles. Properly.

The cloakroom led off the hall. It was large, ill-lit, exceptionally cold, and housed a primitive washbasin; the lavatory was separate, an internal room of its own. The walls were lined with layers of raincoats of a uniform dun, as though their colours had run together; they went back years – some had even belonged to her father and were so stiff and cracked that they could have stood unsupported. There was a pair of mackintosh waders; there were shooting-sticks and an Egyptian fly-whisk and an alpenstock. The pegs above the raincoats were occupied by assorted headgear – berets and peaked caps, a riding bowler, sou'westers, knitted hats, deerstalkers. Everything had associations – Dorothy's, Edward's, given by so-and-so, bought on a particular holiday, left behind by relative or friend; Helen saw an insistent kaleidoscope of references, shimmering tiresomely behind the garments and the implements, as ineradicable as the blackberry stains on a sleeve or the ingrained mud on everything.

And the whole lot smelt – a pervasive stench of damp and mildew. High time something was done about it. Starting in one corner, Helen began to lift garments from pegs and drop them on the floor in a pile – a mack of her father's, something of Edward's not worn within living memory, a very ancient corduroy jacket of Dorothy's, also unused for many a year. It occurred to her that it might be wise to go through the pockets; her father's garment yielded an old penny and a broken pipe. In Dorothy's jacket was a letter.

Unopened and addressed to Helen.

She knew the handwriting at once, of course. Until ten years or so ago a bundle of similar envelopes had lain in a drawer of her desk; one day in a fit of vigour she had torn them up and thrown them away.

She sat down on the battered settle and opened the letter. 'Dearest Helen,' he began; that was interesting – the letters in the destroyed bundle usually began with 'Dear' or 'My dear'. He went on to say that he felt they were both being rather silly and he wanted to make amends. He was missing her, he said. He had phoned a couple of times but she had been out. Anyway, maybe he could say what he felt more easily in a letter. She knew he wasn't good at expressing himself. If she was still cross with him please would she stop. He was sorry about what was mainly a misunderstanding. He wanted very much to talk to her. There was something in particular he wanted to talk about. Please would she meet him for a long dinner on Friday – he would expect to hear from her tomorrow or the next day. He signed himself 'With a great deal of love – Peter.'

The postmark on the envelope was March 10th 1965.

The hand of fate is brutal but impersonal. The hand of one's mother is something different. Witting or unwitting? Carelessness – the thing picked up off the hall mat, thrust into her pocket and forgotten – or deliberate appropriation? If the latter – why had she not gone the whole hog and burned it? Well, one would never know and either way the effect was the same.

Helen began to shake. She saw her own hands with a certain detachment, holding the letter and trembling convulsively. She did not otherwise feel at all detached. Her mind raced. A number of things fell into place – click, click, click – with distant muffled echoes like stones dropped into a well. That time. The tiff. The coolness about . . . about *what* had it been? 'A misunderstand-ing'. Those weeks, not seeing him, wondering, too proud to make the first move. And weeks becoming a month, two months, three . . . a year. Anger giving way to misery and then to regret and eventually to . . . nothing. Until now, when one sat here in the cloakroom, surrounded by old raincoats, shaking as though struck down by fever.

One could, presumably, trace Peter Datchett. It would be relatively simple – she could think at once of how it could be done: the casual enquiry of a mutual friend with whom she still exchanged Christmas cards, the phone call to the college at which he had been a lecturer. And then the reply: 'Dear Peter, I have at last received your letter of March 10th 1965. I hope it is not too late to say yes, I'd like very much to have dinner on Friday and I too feel we've been rather silly and it has all been a misunderstanding . . .'

And there is Peter, on the receiving end, opening it over breakfast with his wife and children . . . no, children if any are flown by now, Peter is fifty-six . . . with his wife (and the wife one is of course assuming, merely, but the assumption seems reasonable enough, things being what they are), who says 'Who's that from?' And he shoves it in his pocket with some dismissive remark and wonders what the hell he is to do. How embarrass-ing, he thinks. God – poor old Helen.

No, one will not set about tracing Peter Datchett.

At this precise moment, thought Helen, I hate my mother. It was a refreshing feeling – invigorating, even. And worth indulg-ing: it stifled various other feelings.

She knew that she would not have lived happily ever after with Peter Datchett. No one lives happily ever after. Very likely there would have been a further coolness or misunderstanding and they would have parted. The point was that one would never know, now. And so would wonder, and go on wondering. One would construct alternative scenarios, and brood about them. One would furnish houses and arrange landscapes; one might go dangerously far and people them with . . . children. One would conjure up occasions; things would be said and done.

All this thanks to Dorothy. Still ordaining.

No, said Helen. She rose from the settle. She put the letter in her pocket. In due course she would dispose of it, but not just yet. Think of what was, she told herself, since only that is relevant. What might have been is neither here nor there. She tried to reconstruct the physical Peter Datchett: tall, thin, black hair that tended to flop forwards, a mole on one cheek. He taught at the College of Further Education a few miles from Spaxton; she had met him through a rambling club. His physical presence was all mixed up with muddy tracks, overgrown woodland paths, rain and barbed wire fences and glasses of beer in steamy pubs. And then of course the relationship had become more personal and exclusive: lunches and dinners, films, visits to stately homes or places of scenic interest. Intimacy, of a kind; they were both reserved people, they didn't rush things. She did not remember passion, but a certain eroticism – that, definitely. They were on the brink of sex; it was a matter of time, she had known – next week, the one after. She had explained to him about her mother; he had met her mother; he had seemed to size up the problem, had said the right things in his oblique way. Dorothy had referred to him as 'that chap with the birthmark on his face.'

Love? It had been in the air, certainly – around the corner, along with sex. What she remembered was a sense of expectancy, of confident expectancy. They had been a unit, had shared jokes, exchanged small gifts, written to each other when unable to meet for a week or two; the assumption was always that this would continue, and expand.

Why didn't he write again? Telephone? Arrive on the doorstep? Because, thought Helen, he was as he was. Reserved; a touch diffident. And why did I do nothing? Ditto.

She went out into the hall. She picked up the receiver and dialled Giles Carnaby's number. The ringing tone came: once, twice, six times . . . Out, she thought. Good. Reprieved. But honour is satisfied. You can put the thing down.

'Hello?' said Giles.

'Oh.' The prepared words evaporated. 'Is that . . .? Could I speak to Giles Carnaby?'

'You are.'

'This is Helen Glover.'

'But how very nice. I didn't recognise your voice.'

'I was wondering . . .'

'And I'd been thinking of you only yesterday. How *are* you?'

'Very well. I wondered if . . .'

'Your mother's affairs progress. Slowly, as I'm afraid is always the case. The Probate Office moves in its own mysterious way.'

'Actually,' said Helen, 'that wasn't what I was ringing about. My brother and I are having a few people in for a drink before lunch on Sunday. I wondered if you might be able to come.' There. No going back now.

'But I'd be delighted. What fun. Last weekend I was away but this one I'm as free as air. I shall look forward to it. By the way I've finished the Earl Grey. Things are getting desperate. And you never *did* come and have a cup.'

'Oh. No. You can buy it at the delicatessen in Long Barton, you know.'

'I'm never in that direction. Do you think you could get me a packet next time you're passing?'

'I'll try. I mean yes, I will.'

'Bless you. And thank you so much for ringing. What time?'

'Time?'

'On Sunday.'

'Oh – twelve, I think.'

'Twelve. Splendid. Till then.'

'We're having some people in for a drink on Sunday. Before lunch.'

Edward, dealing out Puffed Wheat to the birds, swung round sharply. 'Whatever for?'

'I thought we should.'

'But we've never done it before.'

'It's the sort of thing that's done all the time, in other households.'

112

'I can't think why. Who, then?'

'Doctor Taylor and his wife, I thought. A few others from the village. And our solicitor, Giles Carnaby.'

'But you went to hear him sing,' said Edward. 'Surely that was quite enough.'

'They will arrive at twelve and stay probably for an hour and a half or so. I'll get the drink but you'll have to help pour it out. Is there anyone you'd like to ask?'

'Certainly not. And I hope this isn't going to be a precedent.'

She made telephone calls. She hoovered and dusted the sitting room. She found glasses that were unchipped and as nearly matching as possible. She bought sherry and white wine and whisky. She bought bags of little biscuity things. 'You make me laugh,' said her mother. 'I never saw such a carry-on. Who do you think you're fooling?' 'Nobody,' Helen replied. Least of all myself. 'And that chap – Giles Thingy – do you imagine he's going to be taken in? A man like that.'

'Enough,' said Helen. 'You have no right. Nor ever did. From now on I'll be mine own executioner.'

'Whatever have you done to the cloakroom?' complained Edward.

'Cleared it out.'

'I liked it the way it was.'

'We've still got nine raincoats and anoraks between us. And eight different hats and an alpenstock and a flywhisk and four walking-sticks.'

'I used to enjoy the way you never knew what you'd come across next.'

'I don't share your feelings,' said Helen.

She considered making a ceremonial pyre. She would burn Peter Datchett's letter and that dress in one fine condemnatory blaze. There you are, mother – there they go, properly disposed of at last. A few years too late. Or did you always think they had been? Were you careless or calculating? And what did you do it for? Were these sins of omission, or a devilish scheme? I can't know if you succeeded in changing the course of my life, but it's possible. And for a person in a somewhat delicate emotional condition, as I believe myself to be, this is hard to contemplate.

She did not believe that marriage, or pairing, or however you cared to define a sexual relationship, was the key to happiness and fulfilment; you only had to look around you to see that this was not so. Which was worse – to have tried and failed or never to have tried at all?

She thought of her father – that grey and distant figure associated only with anchovy paste and a rustling newspaper. It was not comfortable to consider her parents' intimate life; she could recall no demonstrations of affection or indeed even of much displayed interest in one another. Usually, Dorothy had been engaged in shifting her husband around like an inharmonious piece of furniture. His own image was one of compliant self-effacement. He went out to work by day, conveniently, at a firm of accountants; in the evenings and at weekends he made himself as unobtrusive as possible. God knows what went on at night.

In the end she pushed the letter into the drawer of her desk and left the dress where it was, in the corner of the wardrobe. All in good time.

Edward, practised in self-deception, forgot about the guests until Sunday morning and was therefore surprised to discover Helen, at ten-thirty, wearing unexpected clothes and straightening cushions in the sitting room. She was also flushed and evidently in a state of unrest, which made him feel chivalrous and sympathetic. He decided to be nice about the whole business, though he still could not see the point of it, and offered to put the little biscuity things into bowls. He gave some of them to Tam in the process.

It was not so much that he had anything against people in general, more that he saw no purpose in deliberately setting up occasions on which you stood around trying to think of something to say. Moreover, the whole process was self-perpetuating; the guest became the host in an act of social revenge and thus it

114

went on for ever. The only sensible course was never to start it in the first place. He could not think what had got into Helen, normally as rational as himself about all this, or so he had thought.

Nevertheless, when the doorbell rang he was ready and waiting, with an agreeable expression and a fluent command of what to offer by way of drink. He had been feeling a bit better for the last few days. He had repaired the fence between the Britches and Ron Paget's yard, filled two black plastic sacks with rubbish and had embarked on a vigorous assault upon dead and decaying trees. It all felt very positive and forward-looking.

The visitors arrived. There were not enough of them to make the large Greystones sitting room look as though much was going on; people stood in small clumps, eyeing one another; awkward silences broke out. I told you so, thought Edward, ploughing valiantly around with a bottle in each hand. Tam scrabbled at each pair of legs in turn, remembering the biscuits; the more uninhibited guests kicked, furtively. Apart from the doctor and his wife and Giles Carnaby they were all people from the village who had not had an opportunity for a good look at the inside of Greystones for quite a while and were busy taking note. 'I s'pose you may be thinking of selling the Britches now, Edward?' asked a neighbour. 'Oh no,' said Edward. 'There's no question of that.' He couldn't remember her name; her face was as familiar to him as the frontage of the village shop or outline of the church tower; he had always been hopeless at names. The solicitor detached himself from another group and joined them. 'Giles Carnaby – we haven't met. Your sister is busy hostessing so I'm introducing myself.' 'Oh,' said Edward. 'Yes. Hello. This is Mrs . . .' He gazed wildly at the neighbour who said crossly, 'Jean Powers. Actually Edward's known me for ten years, but there we are. You live in Spaxton, don't you?' Edward, thinking with relief that he could leave them to it now, began to withdraw, clutching the bottles that gave him a certain exemption, free to come and go. The solicitor laid a hand on his arm, making Edward wince: he didn't like to be touched. 'Were you talking about the famous Britches? Helen's told me so much about the place. May I have a conducted tour sometime?' No you certainly can't, thought

Edward, and what's all this 'Helen' stuff? He said, 'There's absolutely nothing to see and it's awfully full of nettles'; at the same moment Jean Powers was saying noisily that not a solitary soul had been into the Britches in years and the village wondered what Edward got up to in there – ha ha! – some people said he must be into black magic, or maybe he was growing cannabis. Edward laughed politely, slid from Carnaby's grip and edged towards the group by the window, who were talking about hedges in tones of some desperation. As he did so Helen passed him; her neck was red, a sure sign of agitation. She hissed, 'Do do something about the Taylors and old Mrs Phipson. They've been stuck together for hours.' 'How?' enquired Edward; he meant it – he had absolutely no idea of the mechanics involved. Helen gave him a look of fury. The group by the window turned to him anxiously: '*Is* that hedge yew, Edward? None of us can decide.' Really, thought Edward, people must be out of their minds, submitting themselves to this sort of occasion quite voluntarily.

Kill or cure, Helen had thought. As soon as she set eyes on Giles Carnaby again she knew that whatever it was it was not a case of cure; her heart thumped, she felt unstable. There he was. Here he was. Smiling at her over people's shoulders while she could not move because someone was telling her at length how much she must be missing her mother. And then she saw him talking to Edward and Jean Powers and then someone had mislaid their glass and she had to find another and then there was the problem of the Taylors and old Mrs Phipson. And then eventually she could cross the room towards him. '*There* you are,' he said. 'I have been most restrained – I could see you had your hands full. But I have met your brother at long last and Mrs Powers has been regaling me with the most fascinating pieces of village gossip.' This set Jean Powers off on a torrent of exclamations and denials so that Helen could not have got a word in had she wished to; she stood and looked at Giles Carnaby and tried to be calm. She tried to see him dispassionately as a grey-haired solicitor rather too well endowed with easy charm; indeed, she saw him thus, but she also saw him otherwise, and could not help herself. When he turned to look intently at Jean Powers she felt a twinge of jealousy; his arm, brushing momentarily against hers, made her tingle all over. This sort of thing was bad enough at eighteen, she thought; at my age it is ludicrous and humiliating.

Jean Powers moved away. Giles said 'Dear me, what a demanding woman. She's not a great friend, I hope? Anyway, now that I've got you to myself for a moment can we make some plans? First of all, am I going to be able to persuade you to . . .' 'Oh Helen!' cried the doctor's wife, appearing at their side, 'We're going to have to rush off, I'm afraid. John's on call today. But first I must just have a word with you about . . .'

She attended to the doctor's wife. She got the doctor and his wife into their coats and saw them out of the front door. She returned to the sitting room and struck Tam, who had knocked the bowl of biscuits from the table and was wolfing them off the carpet. She refilled three glasses. She went into the kitchen to see if there was another packet of biscuits. I am not enjoying myself, she thought – but then I was never supposed to, was I? She sought biscuits in the bread bin, the vegetable rack, on the dresser. No damn biscuits.

Giles appeared. 'Is there anything I can do? You look harassed.' 'I am harassed,' said Helen. 'Edward's wretched dog has eaten the biscuits.' 'People can live without biscuits.' 'I know,' she replied. 'But it doesn't seem so at this moment.' I just may burst into tears, she thought. I just might, appallingly, sit down on the kitchen chair and start to weep . . . Giles put his hand on hers: 'Stop worrying about the biscuits and talk to me. We were interrupted. I was in the middle of trying to find out if you'll come and have dinner with me next week. At home. I'm not much of a cook but I do a passable roast. Friday? Saturday?'

She subsided onto the chair. She was not, she found, going to burst into tears after all. The biscuits became unimportant, and the guests. 'Saturday,' she said. 'I'm not doing anything on Saturday.' The kitchen became a warm and friendly place; she sat in it smiling at Giles Carnaby. I'm happy, she thought in surprise, at this precise moment I am happy.

NINE

Hemp agrimony – *Eupatorium cannabinum* – flourished in the Britches, as it happened; Jean Powers was not so wide of the mark. Edward of course was unaware of its connotations and encouraged it as a handsome and relatively uncommon plant. It grew in a boggy area where there was a spring and a small stream which flowed in a desultory way after the autumn rains but almost dried up in summer. Other water-loving species turned up here from time to time also – *Mimulus* and forget-me-not and Water Speedwell. The *Mimulus* was in fact a garden escape, but he allowed it all the same, while conceding that a purist would not. Once there had been kingcups, but none had been seen now for at least ten years. The whole area was much dryer than it used to be, and Edward suspected that something had interfered with the water table; there had been nesting moorhens at one time – now only the occasional toad was left. But the hemp agrimony continued to grow strongly, rather swamping the more genteel species, indeed. Now and then he was obliged to curb it in order to give a chance to the bluebells and the wood anemones, which were both getting sparse to the point of extinction. He sometimes had the feeling that all the more delicate growths were being quenched and ousted by the rougher stuff, if one did not intervene. He saw himself as a wise and benign deity, presiding over his kingdom and seeing to it that evil did not always prevail; a hollow symbolism of course and anyway he rather liked hemp agrimony and ground ivy. The real war was waged against nettle and bramble – now there you really could persuade yourself that some malign force was at work, set upon reducing the whole place to a rank and thrusting wilderness, in which the weakest went to the wall.

Edward felt that he and the malign force were fairly evenly matched. In a few hours of concentrated assault he could destroy months of determined surreptitious growth; but then he would discover some other overlooked area where things had been going to the dogs unheeded and some valiantly struggling patch of wood anemone or bluebells had been choked to the last gasp. One thought, of course, in such terms: malign, surreptitious, struggle, valiant. He was well aware of the anthropomorphism and indeed found it satisfying; it was as though, in the Britches, thigh-deep in lashing nettle and octopus strands of clutching bramble, he was coming to grips at last with a great many things and, as often as not, getting the upper hand.

He spent the afternoon in the Britches, as soon as the last of the party guests had departed. Half of a perfectly good Sunday had been wasted, but there were still several hours till dark. He was working in a thicket of briar, elder and dead wood from a fallen tree. From time to time he resorted to the saw; the noise he was making deafened him to Ron Paget's approach. When he spoke Edward jumped so violently that the saw fell from his hand.

'You're not getting far with that, are you?' said Ron. 'Tell you what, I'll have one of the men come over with some proper equipment. Have that lot out in no time.'

Edward picked up the saw. 'Thanks, but I can manage perfectly well.' And get out, he fumed, you've no business marching in here like this. Through the gap in the fence, I suppose, the place I didn't wire up.

Ron gave him a look of amusement. 'You do like to do things the hard way, don't you, Mr Glover? I heard you at it so I thought I'd pop in and pass the time of day. How's Miss Glover, then?'

'She's very well,' said Edward.

'I'm glad to hear it. I've a lot of respect for your sister. Quiet but got a mind of her own, know what I mean?'

Edward stared coldly.

'I've lost track of how long it is now we've been neighbours. I was saying to Pauline the other day, there's some people you grow old with, willy-nilly, without noticing it – not that we aren't all wearing pretty well.' Ron laughed.

Edward thought of the previous, discarded Mrs Paget. He made no comment.

'You remember my first wife, of course. Well, these things happen, don't they? You pick yourself up and soldier on, don't you? Of course, you're not a family man yourself . . .' – Ron's eyes flickered momentarily – '. . . but we all have our ups and downs, I daresay life's dealt you out one or two, one way or another.'

Shut up, thought Edward. And go away.

'Anyway – it's nice to have a word from time to time. I miss your mother, I really do – we had our differences but we'd got the measure of each other, as you might say. I often think of her. Gary doing his stuff all right in your vegetable garden?'

'I think so,' said Edward. 'It's my sister's preserve.'

Ron's glance had fallen upon the huge mound of nettle roots and bramble stems that was the product of Edward's afternoon. 'I don't know why you bother doing all this by hand. Half an hour with a drum of selective weed killer and a spray and you'd put paid to that lot for good and all.'

'Plus much else.'

'What? Oh, the wild flowers.' Ron smiled indulgently. 'A year or two and they'd be back. But you wouldn't catch me sweating my guts out like that when there's an easy way to set about it. Take advantage where you can, that's what I say.'

'I'm sure you do,' said Edward.

Ron looked at him narrowly. There was a brief silence. 'Well,' said Ron. 'I'd better be off – Pauline'll be after me. And remember, any time you feel like changing your mind about what you're going to do with this place, let me know. I'll be ready and waiting – put a cheque in your hand any time you want it.'

Edward sighed. 'I'll remember.'

He listened to Ron crashing his way out of the Britches. At last there was silence. A robin began to sing, and presently a chaffinch. The light was fading and it was getting cold; Edward decided to pack it in. But first he would have a few minutes of

120

self-indulgence. He sat down on a log and tried to perform what he thought of as the vanishing act, whereby you became insofar as it was possible a part of the surroundings: breathing, seeing, hearing only – merely an aspect of the place, a dimension, like the robin or the moss-covered log or the leafmould on which his feet rested. You tried not to think or to feel – just to be. Whimsy, as he well knew – an affectation, even – but satisfying nonetheless.

There he sat, and the Britches darkened around him.

For Helen, all that week, Saturday shone like a distant sunlit hilltop. She was in no hurry to reach it – contemplation was almost as satisfactory as arrival. Anticipation is one of the choicest forms of pleasure; it was a long time, she realised, since she had experienced it. Conditioned to observe, she noticed what it did to her; the feeling of vigour, the brisker step, the tendency to be nice to others, to talk to those whom one usually avoided. In the library she negotiated a cease-fire between Joyce Babcock and the new trainee, a girl fatally endowed with enthusiasm both for books and for people, and therefore threatening the entire ethos of Joyce's empire. The girl, Lorna, announced her intention of applying for a transfer: 'I don't know how you've stuck it with her so long, I really don't.' Helen replied enigmatically that it was all just a question of experience.

Wednesday gave way to Thursday, the day on which she did not go to the library. She walked to the village shop to collect the bread and was waylaid four times and treated to opposing viewpoints on the two current matters of local dispute. Helen, neutrally listening, anaesthetised by her state of uplift, thought that they nicely illustrated the condition of the place. One controversy was about visual amenities; the other concerned noise. Both had implications about prosperity and the power of cash. Someone had applied for planning permission to knock down an old cow-byre in his garden and build a bungalow; the environmentalists raged at this further desecration, the *laissez-faire* element saw no reason why people shouldn't do what they wished with their own. The village youths had taken to roaring round and round of an evening on highly powered Japanese motorcycles from which the silencers had been removed; those distressed by this were invoking the law, the youths laughed, their friends and relations pointed out that they'd paid their road-tax, hadn't they, like anyone else? Words like freedom and rights were bandied around on both sides.

'Your mother would have been with us,' said one of the waylayers with a touch of reproach, presumably sensing Helen's lack of commitment. He was right. Dorothy, in her time, had been an active member of an organisation called the Noise Reduction Society, which had campaigned valiantly and indiscriminately against lawnmowers and jet aircraft. It had disintegrated (in despair, one assumed) many years ago, but Dorothy continued to bawl furiously at passing vehicles and to write letters to the commanding officer of the local airbase, who returned each time the same duplicated reply of infinite courtesy and obscurity.

What is at the bottom of all this, thought Helen, is that people – some people – have inappropriate expectations. This is the country. The country is supposed to be peaceful and beautiful. Traditionally people – some people – have retreated to it in search of spiritual solace. Others, of course, have seen it quite differently – as a source of income or a place of work. These points of view are now fatally and perhaps finally opposed. Money and technological advance intensify the problem.

She considered all this as she listened to the heated opinions forced upon her outside the shop (where the throbbing engine of the Findus delivery van obliged everyone to shout), on the corner by the church and at two other points on her route back to Greystones. And at the same time, behind her own thoughts and over the faces of those who spoke to her there hovered the mirage of the distant sunlit hilltop: promise and expectation. 'How are you, Helen?' people said, without waiting for a reply, and silently she answered: I am really quite extraordinarily well, thank you, I have something to look forward to, I believe I am happy.

*

122

Edward was crossing the hall as Helen came down the stairs. He halted and stared at her. She had put on a pale green dress that she seldom wore. She had added a largy floppy white collar bought in Spaxton, and one of her few pieces of jewellery – a Victorian cameo on a gold chain. The effect of the collar and the cameo were remarkable, as Helen herself had dispassionately noted a few minutes before in her mirror: they made her look softer, prettier and younger. She saw this again in Edward's stare.

'I'm going out,' said Helen defensively. 'I'm having dinner with Giles Carnaby. I told you.'

Edward snatched off his glasses and began to scrub them. He peered again at Helen. She could see fly across his face a whole sequence of emotions and responses. 'What shall I eat?' he enquired petulantly.

'Anything you like. There are fish fingers in the fridge. Or some ham. Or tins in the cupboard.'

He put his glasses back on and rallied, with dignity. 'What time will you be back?'

'I've no idea.'

'I won't lock the front door, then. I hope he isn't going to expect you to listen to him singing again.'

'Don't be silly, Edward,' said Helen.

He looked at her bleakly and turned back into the kitchen. As she put her coat on she could hear him rattling about in a conspicuous way with pans and dishes, and talking to Tam. Just as she was about to leave he came out and complained that he couldn't find the tin-opener. 'Try the right-hand drawer,' she said.

'Where does he live?'

'In Spaxton. I told you that, too.'

'It's pouring with rain.'

'I'm intending to drive there,' said Helen. 'Not walk.'

Edward returned to the kitchen, banging the door. Helen, ruffled but in control, hurried into the car.

*

123

By the time she reached Spaxton her control was a little less certain. She stood paralysed for several moments on Giles Carnaby's doorstep. Her mother stood behind her, giving tongue: 'He's got you on the end of a string, that fellow, hasn't he? Like some silly schoolgirl. You're fifty-two, Helen. I don't know what you think's going to come of it. Riding for a fall, I'd say.'

She rang the bell, and there he was, suffused in the warm golden light of the hall, his sleeves rolled up, pushing that silver forelock back from his eyes. There was the smell of meat roasting. They both spoke at once: cries of welcome from him, apologies for lateness from her (she was, by sixteen minutes). He drew her inside, removed her coat, shepherded her into the sitting room. 'So here you are,' he said, beaming. 'What a becoming dress, if I may say so.' He glanced at his watch, became distracted: 'Forgive me just a moment – kitchen duties. Make yourself comfortable. A drink? On the side there. Oh, I *have* been looking forward to this evening . . .'

He went. She sat. Then rose and strayed around the room. She looked again at his wife, securely smiling behind the glass of her photograph. She noted the flowers agreeably disposed in a vase on the mantelpiece, the recent issues of magazines arranged upon the table, the *Radio Times* open upon the desk with a programme encircled in red biro (a talk on Handel operas). An orderly man. I know nothing about him, she thought, nothing at all; he could have robbed banks for all I know.

He came back into the room. 'All is well. I tend to panic unnecessarily. And you haven't given yourself a drink. Sherry? Vermouth? Sherry – right.'

No, country solicitors don't rob banks. But there are other offences, less conspicuous. The point is, I seem to be past caring.

'And what has your week been like?' he said. 'Mine has been unspeakably mundane. By the way, we progress a little with the Probate Office – but I'm not going to talk business tonight. That will do for another time.' He came to sit beside her on the sofa; she felt him look at her, intently.

'I've had a good week', Helen said. She told him about dissension in the library, about the village feuds. He appreciated; he laughed; he pressed for further details. She was made to feel witty and entertaining. She expanded like a plant turned to the sun; she flourished and was gay. The room enclosed them both: exclusive and private.

The door bell rang.

'Oh, my goodness!' he said. 'The Watsons. I'd almost forgotten about them. You know them, I daresay? James Watson who's headmaster at St Bartholomew's and, um, Julia.' He hurried out. She heard the opening of the front door. Greetings. The closing of the door.

The Watsons. Ah. No, I don't as it happens know the Watsons.

He never said, she told herself, that it would be just you and him. Never once. So why did you assume that? You have not been misled. You can't complain. So continue to smile and be gay.

The evening progressed. They moved from the sitting room to the dining room. They consumed avocado pears followed by roast lamb followed by a fruit salad and assorted cheeses. Julia Watson, who evidently knew Giles quite well, insisted on popping in and out of the kitchen to help; laughter and exclamations could be heard from beyond the hatch. James Watson told Helen about unrest in the teaching profession, at some length. They moved back into the sitting room and drank coffee. Julia, a dark woman in her early forties, asked Helen in a kindly interested voice about the extension plans for the library. Giles offered brandies; Julia said, 'Giles, you are a wicked man, you know I can't resist – be it upon your head if I have a hangover tomorrow.' Giles said, 'My dear, we shall suffer together. Helen?' Helen replied that she had better not, since she had to drive.

The Watsons eventually rose, and Helen with them. Giles made no attempt to restrain her; he said, 'You're all *going* . . .?' In the hall, he helped her on with her coat, his hand resting on her shoulder for a moment – or so it seemed. The Watsons got into their car, and Helen into hers. She had to drive to the end of the street to turn round; when she passed Giles's house on the way back the door was closed.

She drove home through further rain. Her mother rode in the back seat – silent, exuding complacency.

As soon as Helen had gone Edward was overwhelmed with self-contempt. Bleakly, he sat at the kitchen table eating spaghetti bolognaise out of a tin. Tam watched, drooling. Half way through Edward gave up, scraped the rest into Tam's food bowl and put the kettle on for a cup of tea; behind him, Tam slurped as though rescued from the brink of starvation.

Edward, leaden with gloom, waited for the kettle to boil; as he did so he watched the steady progress of a wood-louse across the wall behind the sink. There were many wood-lice at Greystones; the wood-louse is a kind of prawn, surprisingly – hence its preference for damp places. In an age of central heating and renovation Greystones presumably featured as a rare unspoiled habitat. Dorothy had persecuted the wood-lice, in Edward's view; she stamped on them, swept them up and even poured boiling water upon whole colonies of them. Edward, observing the patient journey of this one (from whence? and why?), experienced a momentary consoling detachment. He put his reading glasses on and looked more closely at it; there were, he knew, dozens of different kinds of wood-lice, all classified, all named, distinguished by minute anatomical refinements, small but significant differences in the antennae or the genitalia. Goodness only knew what this particular one was, toiling down towards the crack behind the sink, but it seemed profoundly satisfactory that it should have the dignity of documentation. Even more important was the fact that people had devoted their lives to establishing the identity of such creatures; that for someone the original distinction between *Porcellio* and *Armadillidium* had been a matter of life-consuming importance. Edward envied such people.

Those who knew of his predilections often wondered why he had not become a botanist, an entomologist, a biologist. At school, the few masters who had noticed him at all had tried vaguely to direct him towards science. In fact, Edward did rather worse in scientific subjects than in others. He was not systematic;

formulae and calculations confused him. Presented with a diagram of the alimentary canal, he tended to marvel at its artistry rather than study its efficiency. As an amateur ornithologist he knew himself to be far behind those people who could identify from a snatch of song or flicker of a wing. He could never remember the names of rarer plant species.

The kettle boiled, spurting scalding water everywhere, as usual. The wood-louse had vanished, and with it Edward's temporary distraction from his gloom. He felt alone. He felt a recurring flash of resentment towards Helen. Tam brushed against his leg in passing and Edward leaned down to pat him but Tam, replete, was staggering towards his favourite sleeping place by the cooker – he shrugged Edward's hand off and collapsed with a noisy sigh. Edward observed him with a certain bitterness; such simplicity of need could seem enviable.

He switched on the radio. The kitchen was filled instantly with a loud snuffling noise, interspersed with grunts; Edward, perking up, poured out his tea and listened attentively. After a few moments the snuffles and grunts were overlaid by a voice explaining in sympathetically conspiratorial tones that we were listening to the sounds made by mating koalas in the Pilliga Nature Reserve in New South Wales. The koalas faded and their place was taken by a studio discussion about threatened habitats and imperilled creatures. The pig-footed bandicoot, the trumpeter swan, the scimitar oryx, the sperm whale, the cheetah, the bower bird . . . the list went on and on. Such has been the destruction of the Brazilian rain forests that only about two hundred of the golden lion tamarin survive in the wild. Their relative, the cotton-top tamarin, fares little better. Edward, who had seen both of these creatures on the television screen, pictured the tiny animals, with their sad wise old men's faces framed by silky manes, their long, long tails, their agility. A few hundred of them, and five billion human beings. The tamarin will be preserved, in all probability, only if zoos throughout the world cooperate in breeding programmes. The programme concluded with a snatch of birdsong, a low trill, repeated several times before dwindling into silence; this, the presenter announced, was the song of the dusky seaside sparrow, a species of which the last survivor had died a few days before in its aviary at Disney World in Florida. This sound would never be heard again on earth.

Edward, much affected, switched off the radio. The unutterably sad sound of the sparrow lingered in his ears. His own depression was compounded now with this global *malaise*, a process he found paradoxically satisfying; it was acceptable to weep for the dusky seaside sparrow, but not for oneself.

He went to bed, and lay awake. At one point tears rolled from his eyes; they crept down the side of his face, and into his ears; he continued to lie rigid. Tam snored at his feet.

'Did you have a nice evening?'

'Quite,' said Helen.

'What's the matter?'

'Nothing.'

'There's no need to snap,' said Edward piously.

Helen poured herself another cup of tea in silence. The phone rang. She jumped up. 'I'll go.'

Louise, in Camden, was in full torrent immediately. 'Is that you? God! As if I hadn't got enough on my plate with Tim throwing a mid-life crisis and Phil doing the disturbed adolescent bit – now if you please Suzanne comes in at three-thirty in the morning, and me lying there sick with worry, she having never thought to phone, and London with rapists on every street corner or so one's told. And then her only response is to burst into tears.'

'Why?'

'She's in love. I thought she was the one with some sense.'

'Ah,' said Helen.

'What's the matter?'

'Nothing,' stated Helen, 'is the matter.'

'Well, you're not being very sympathetic. I'll go, then. I only wanted a shoulder to weep on. I've been awake all night and I've got a hell of a day ahead, meetings from morning till night.'

Helen returned to the kitchen. The phone rang again. She said to Edward, 'You can go this time.'

'It won't be for me.'

128

'Then let it ring,' said Helen.

Edward rose and went into the hall. He returned. 'It's that man.'

'What man?'

'The solicitor.'

Helen stared at him. The kitchen, which had been a uniform grey, was dappled with sunlight, she saw; outside, a blackbird sang.

'He's waiting,' said Edward. 'I suppose.' He dropped a half-eaten piece of toast into Tam's bowl.

Helen went back to the phone. 'Hello.'

'It's me – Giles. Am I interrupting your breakfast?'

'No.'

'Bless you for helping me out with the Watsons. You were heroic – he is unstoppable, once in full flow. I saw you enduring. But then you rushed off and left me without a chance to say the most important thing of all . . .'

Edward appeared, clad for school, briefcase in hand, scowling. 'I'm going.'

'Excuse me a moment,' Helen said to Giles. 'I'll see you tonight then, Edward.'

He went out, banging the door.

'I'm sorry . . . Edward was just leaving.'

'Please give him my regards. We didn't get enough chance to talk at your party. Anyway . . . the thing is, I have tickets for the opera on Friday – are you free? *Don Giovanni* – it's the touring company, you know, usually very good.'

'Well . . .' she said. 'Yes. Yes, I'd like to.'

And so there shone yet another distant sunlit hilltop. How do people endure this switchback of emotion? Helen wondered. They have no choice, of course. She felt as though flung from health to illness and back by the day, by the hour. She thought of Giles Carnaby both continuously and not at all; he was permanently in the head, but as some unavoidable elemental force – she could not consider him as a person, reflect upon character or deeds. He was there, simply. For better or for worse.

She telephoned Louise, who was grumpy. 'And the school term ends in another week, which means the children either mooching around the house all day under-occupied or vanished and one's wondering where the hell they are.'

'Is Suzanne still . . .?'

'Besotted. Yes, poor little wretch. Thank God one is beyond all that. Getting older has some compensations. I occasionally find myself eyeing some bloke and thinking I wouldn't mind popping into bed – but passion . . . no thanks.'

Edward's term too would end shortly. It was high summer. A year ago Dorothy had been in the first, ominous stages of her illness, furiously denying that anything could be wrong, her normal ill temper exacerbated by discomfort and increasing disability. It had not been a pleasant summer. Helen had attended Dorothy and tried to be as patient as possible; the doctors told her, privately, what to expect. Edward kept out of the way. When confronted by his mother he was propitiating to the point of servility.

'What's wrong with him?' demanded Dorothy. 'Why's he being so obliging? I suppose he imagines I'm going to die or something.' She laughed.

Edward had not taken to Giles Carnaby. His usual attitude towards people casually encountered was one of absent-minded indifference. In this case, though, hostility had festered. He told himself that the man was arrogant, self-satisfied, and smelled of after-shave stuff; Helen was an idiot to let him pester her like this. Also he appeared to have corrupted her: she was alternately prickly and forgetful. She snapped at Edward; there was no bread. Edward, brooding, remembered a summer long ago when Helen had brought back a schoolfriend and he had felt pushed aside, abandoned. He saw himself then, and now, and did not like what he saw.

*

Act One concluded. The curtain came down. Giles said, 'We'll stretch our legs, shall we?' The little theatre was full; they joined the crowd moving towards the bar. A woman alongside Helen said uncertainly, 'Well! What a commotion!': the stated purpose of the enterprise was to bring opera to those who do not often experience it.

He went to buy drinks. Helen was greeted by an acquaintance; 'Hello! We spotted you from above – we're in the circle. Isn't that Giles Carnaby you're with? My sister knows him.' Helen said 'Yes.' There was the slightest pause. 'He's very popular, apparently,' said the woman, moving away.

Giles returned, his hands full. 'There – worth the struggle, let's hope. Well – what do you think of it? Personally, I'm wallowing. It never fails, with me. And this isn't a bad production is it? Elvira is a bit weak, but the Don is doing fine, and the orchestra has plenty of dash. And the best is yet to come.'

'The flames of hell . . .'

'Exactly. Operatic plots are so satisfying. Everyone getting their just deserts. Perhaps that's the secret of its appeal – opera, I mean.'

'Oh no,' said Helen. 'It's the singing, so far as I'm concerned.'

Giles shot her a look tinged with disappointment. 'Well, of course, yes. The music . . .'

'I don't mean music. I mean all that systematic expression of emotion. That's why you come away with a sense of release.'

The look changed, rapidly. 'How true.' After a moment he added, 'I don't know you all that well as yet, of course, but I imagine you're not a person who throws emotions around, yourself?'

'No, I suppose I'm not.'

'Infinitely preferable,' said Giles. 'Operatic behaviour in real life is intolerable, of course. One has experienced it occasionally.'

Helen nodded. An image flew into her head of Dorothy as some Wagnerian virago; it was not entirely inappropriate – there had been a whiff of the Valkyrie about her mother, with her alternating hairstyles of frayed bun or plait wound around the head and tendency to long brown shapeless garments. She smiled.

131

Giles also smiled, enquiringly.

'I was thinking of my mother. She was uninhibited in that respect.'

'I wish I had known her. I get the feeling that I have missed quite an experience.'

'Possibly,' said Helen.

'Well, at least she brought us together.' He beamed at her, and took her arm. 'Come along – they're ringing bells at us. Let's go back in and wallow.'

He stopped the car outside Greystones. Only the hall light was on, Helen saw; Edward must have gone to bed – or at any rate was in his room. She hesitated. Giles got out and came round to open her door.

'Would you like to come in for a . . . cup of coffee or something?'

'Do you think I should?'

The query seemed enigmatic. Not knowing how to deal with it, she began to walk towards the front door. Giles followed her.

They went in. Instantly, Tam flew from the kitchen and embarked on a histrionic welcome display. 'Be quiet!' ordered Helen. 'Get down!' Tam continued his staccato barking. If Edward had gone to bed he certainly would not be asleep. Helen waited to hear a door open. The house remained silent. Tam lost interest and returned to his basket. She led Giles into the kitchen.

'No coffee,' said Giles. 'Nothing, in fact.'

'Then we should go into the sitting room. It's not very comfortable in here.'

'But I love your kitchen.'

Helen thought of his – fragrantly warm, humming with appliances. Behind her, both taps dripped. Tam was snoring. There was a smell of rotting dishcloth. Like Dorothy, Helen and Edward used swabs of mouldering grey stockinette; they festered by the sink and were known as dead rabbits. She saw one now, and shuddered.

'It has a sort of museum appeal. One almost expects a mangle, or a posset stick.'

And me? thought Helen. Am I one of the exhibits? Of nostalgic charm?

'The thing about you, Helen, if I may say so, is that you are so refreshingly detached from all that one finds disagreeable about contemporary life.'

'Unfashionable,' said Helen.

'Is that what it is? Then do please stay that way.'

'I doubt if there's much chance of anything else.'

Giles laughed. He moved closer. 'You're not acquisitive. You appear to have no pretensions whatsoever. Your opinions are your own. You're the most attractive person. And you seem not even to know it.'

She stood there. He put his hands on her shoulders. And then leaned forward. He laid his cheek against hers; she felt his warmth, and smelled him. He turned his head and kissed her cheek. At the same time his hand slid down her arm and reached behind her; it slid swiftly over the curve of her buttocks. The erotic effect was electrifying; it could not have been greater if he had plunged his hand into her crotch.

He stood back, releasing her. 'What a lovely evening, my dear. We must talk very soon. Don't let me out – I know my way. We've probably disturbed Edward as it is.'

She heard him close the front door gently behind him. She continued to stand in the middle of the kitchen, ablaze.

TEN

'Where are all the dead rabbits?' complained Edward. 'There's nothing to wash up with.'

'I threw them away. We're going to use those scourer things in future.'

'Why?'

'They're more hygienic. And they don't smell.'

He looked affronted.

'Don't you ever realise,' said Helen, 'that the way we live is unlike the way other people live?'

'On the whole I should have thought that was cause for satisfaction.'

'Actually,' she continued, 'when I come to think of it – you never go into other people's houses, do you? Anyway, if a sanitary inspector came in here I should think the whole place would be condemned.'

'What else are you going to chuck out?' enquired Edward, with resignation.

Helen sighed. 'Oh, I don't think I have the stamina for a full-scale assault. Aren't you going to be late? It's after half past.'

Edward glanced at her with reproach. 'It's the sports day.'

The Croxford House sports day, the culminating event of the year and last day of term, was his annual torment. All the staff, whether sporting or not, were required to be in attendance.

'So it is,' said Helen. After a moment she added, in an offhand tone, 'By the way, have there been any phone calls this week when I've been out?'

'No.'

*

In other years she had displayed appropriate sympathy about sports day. Edward, resentful, set off in an even more dour frame of mind than usual. He knew all too well what to expect: several hours of bad behaviour from the children – over-excited and freed from the constraints of routine – and importunate conversation from the parents. He would have to dredge up an interest in his least favourite pupils and submit himself to a barrage of child-obsessed monologues from people he barely remembered from the year before. Parenthood brings out the worst, it seemed to him; vicarious ambitions and frustrations raged all over the lawns and games fields of Croxford House on sports day. The sports were in fact more of a backcloth than the central event; the real purpose of the day was for the parents to prowl around the school inspecting the various displays of work set up in the classrooms, and compare the achievement of their offspring with that of others. They all expected each member of the staff to express – discreetly – particular and intense interest in their child.

The whole process was, it seemed to Edward, a fine manifestation of the single-minded ruthlessness of species in pursuit of survival and improvement – if you considered Willmots and Handley-Smiths and Stannards as species.

He arrived late. Things were in full swing. Posses of girls rushed about shrieking. The parents moved in couples, greeting one another with false enthusiasm and competing for the attention of the staff. Mrs Fitton patrolled continuously, displaying a feverish combination of anxiety and benevolence. From time to time she hissed instructions at teachers or senior girls. Edward, hoping to slink past unnoticed, was pounced upon and told to hurry to his classroom, where the Lower Fourth had an exhibition with a literary theme. Edward had conceived and arranged the exhibition himself and was aware that it lacked verve: he was not good at these things. In desperation, the previous week, he had ordered the children to select a favourite passage from books he had been reading with them, write it out in their best handwriting and then add some comments on what they enjoyed about the piece and about the book in general. Those with artistic inclinations were encouraged to illustrate as well. Most of the children said they couldn't remember any bits they liked; eventually, with much prompting and nagging, everyone came up with something. The results were pinned up around the walls of the classroom. Edward, re-inspecting them, saw even more clearly the perfunctory effect, and blamed himself. He sat down gloomily behind his desk to await custom.

He knew that he would never have survived as a teacher in the state sector: he was both not good enough and not bad enough. He could never have been one of those charismatic men and women who inspire and enthuse; equally, he could never have achieved an indifferent acceptance of failure. At Croxford House the luxuries of small classes and lavish facilities, plus moderately compliant children, cushioned his inadequacies. Here, he was not a particularly good teacher, but he was by no means a disaster. He did the best he could. Quite often he enjoyed what he was doing.

Not, though, at this particular time. Small groups drifted through the classroom: mothers and fathers, large numbers of children – Edward's pupils along with older and younger siblings. It was all very noisy. No sooner had Edward attended to one lot than he was seized upon by another. In addition to the literary exhibition the class performance lists were displayed, at Mrs Fitton's insistence. Edward disliked these intensely. Croxford House deployed a competitive system within which girls were ranked according to performance in every conceivable area; since intellectual ability was not all that highly valued, marks were given for trying, for behaving well, for being punctual and helpful and energetic and tidy, indeed for anything at all. These various ratings adorned the walls. The parents studied them intently.

Edward, spotting Sandra Willmot's mother, hastily crossed to the other side of the room. He was at once ambushed by the Stannards. Mr Stannard was a partner in one of the leading county estate agencies; his name graced the pages of the local paper each week, spread like a banner above photographs of houses all priced, it seemed to Edward, at a quarter of a million pounds. He was a big man, crammed into a tweed suit despite the weather, and flanked by his wife, done up in what even

136

Edward recognised as a seriously competitive dress. Their daughter Caroline lurked behind them; she was a small pale child of determined anonymity. Edward rather liked her. She appeared to have no qualities at all to speak of, either positive or negative, and spent her time trying not to be noticed. He had made various bids at drawing her out, to no avail; now he felt in sympathetic collusion – thus had he survived his own schooldays. Today the entire Stannard family was present – three more children, all strapping creatures like the parents. Caroline, evidently, was the runt of the litter.

'You've seen Caroline's display?' Edward enquired. Caroline smiled wanly.

Her choice had surprised him. She had been the only one to choose a piece from *Alice in Wonderland*. Mr Stannard was inspecting it closely.

> At this moment the King, who had been for some time busily writing in his notebook, called out, 'Silence!' and read out from his book, 'Rule Forty-Two. *All persons more than a mile high to leave the court.*'
> Everybody looked at Alice.
> '*I'm* not a mile high,' said Alice.
> 'You are,' said the King.
> 'Nearly two miles high,' added the Queen.

Beneath this Caroline had written: 'I like this bit because it is funny. The reason it is funny is because a person could not be a mile high. I like *Alice in Wonderland* because of the funny creatures and because they talk like people except it is not what you expect. Mostly in real life you know what people are going to say.'

Edward had been startled when first he read this. Now, reading it again, he was positively awed. One could only pray for Caroline, given her circumstances.

Mr Stannard turned from the display and said heavily, 'The second line isn't good grammar.'

Edward explained that in order to encourage freedom of expression he preferred not to jump on every solecism.

Mrs Stannard said, 'Don't you read Roald Dahl with the children?'

Edward replied that he did not.

'He's very good, you know.'

Edward inclined his head, without comment.

The books from which the children had taken extracts were laid out on Edward's desk. Mr Stannard picked up *Alice*, riffled through the pages and put it down again. His expression was that of a bibliophile rejecting a volume of neither commercial nor idiosyncratic appeal.

'It's a classic,' said Edward craftily.

Mr Stannard's confident manner faltered for an instant. His hand hovered over the book as though to give it a second chance.

'The boys adore Roald Dahl,' said Mrs Stannard. Caroline's brothers grinned alongside her, clones of their father. Behind, an older sister manifested sophisticated boredom.

Mr Stannard had turned his attention to the class performance lists. Edward, knowing that Caroline's name appeared towards the bottom of all these, sought a distraction. He tried to interest Mrs Stannard in some art work.

'The best Caroline's done,' pronounced her father, 'is thirteenth for effort.'

'It's a shame,' said Mrs Stannard. 'The boys were in the top three for everything this term, and Emma had the tennis trophy.'

Mr Stannard shook his head. 'Is she being pushed enough, one asks oneself?'

Edward, who could see Caroline cringing behind the blackboard, lost control.

'Frankly,' he snapped, 'if I had my way those lists would go into the dustbin, the lot of them. They serve no purpose whatsoever.'

The Stannards stared at him, evidently rocked by this heresy. Even the boys dropped their look of unshakeable well-being and gaped.

'If a child can't see how it's performing,' demanded Mr Stannard, 'how's it to know if it's doing well or not? Just tell me that?'

'Achievement isn't necessarily measured by competition,' returned Edward.

'Oh, I can't agree with you,' said Mrs Stannard. 'I mean, in this day and age you don't get anywhere by just sitting back, do you? We've always felt Caroline's got it in her if only she's handled right.'

Mr Stannard was now contemplating Edward with the air of a man who wonders if he is getting his money's worth. There was a silence. 'Well,' continued Mrs Stannard briskly, 'we'd better get on. We've not had a chance for a word with Mrs Fitton yet. Nice exhibition, Mr Glover.'

The Stannards departed. Before Edward had time to simmer down he was buttonholed by Mrs Willmot, who had been lurking. Sandra was at her side, looking smug; her name topped several of the lists. If that woman utters one word about God or evolution, thought Edward, I shall do something irrevocable. But Mrs Willmot had more important things on her mind, it seemed: she wished to enlist Edward's support for the Parent-Teacher Association fund-raising concert in the autumn. 'Do you sing, Mr Glover? We're in desperate need of a few more tenors for the choir.' Edward declared himself without musical talents of any kind. Sandra stood by, quietly amused: she wore a sugar pink track suit with matching plastic hairslides in the shape of elephants. Edward could see quite clearly behind her shoulder, like the aura visible to spiritualists, the woman she would be in thirty years time. There is probably nothing to be done about people, he thought, nothing at all, nor ever has been: processed, from the cradle to the grave. Most neither know nor care, which makes it worse. Mrs Willmot was now going on about a film evening in October: 'I thought you could lay on some nature things – I know that's your *forte*.' Sandra, from time to time, performed a little pirouette, as though warming up for *Swan Lake*. Nature, nurture . . . thought Edward, and God knows which does most harm. He had a sudden vision of families in endless reproduction – Willmots and Stannards and the rest replicating themselves down the years, perfecting their most infamous capacities. Sports like Caroline, of course, would be quietly extinguished, a dead-end. And that, of course, was the other side of the coin: what people do to their children. Wittingly or not. He stood there in the crowded classroom, half listening to Mrs Willmot, and thought of the inexorable process going on all round him – the lives whose courses were being decided at this moment, behind the innocent-seeming chatter, the smiles, the faintly carnival atmosphere of families having a day out. He knew that those who are not parents only glimpse the awful forces at work. Equally, he was never sure if he had missed something or escaped it. He thought, inevitably, of his mother. At the same moment he became aware that Mrs Willmot was talking about Helen.

'I know your sister, of course. I see her in the library. Such a nice unassuming person.'

Don't, thought Edward dangerously, patronise my sister.

'And we waved to each other last week at the opera. She was with Giles Carnaby, wasn't she?'

'I believe so.'

'Charming man,' said Mrs Willmot. 'Slightly elusive. I've tried without success to recruit him for the CPRE and the Friends of Spaxton Theatre. Anyway, it was nice to see your sister looking so relaxed.'

'She enjoyed the opera,' said Edward in frigid tones.

'Oh, of course – it was super.' Mrs Willmot smiled knowingly. 'Well, I mustn't monopolise you. Now don't forget about that film, will you? Come along, darling – I want to see your art display.'

Edward, his nerves jangling, turned to his next client.

When, by Thursday, Helen had heard nothing from Giles the words that rang in her head began to turn from music to mockery. 'I don't know you all that well as yet'; 'We must talk very soon.' She ceased to savour them and tried to drive them away. Unsuccessfully. Equally, half a dozen times a day she felt again his hand on her, and she burned. She also raged. She raged because she no longer controlled her thoughts or her body. She felt humiliated. It seemed perverse that love – if this was love – should be a state traditionally celebrated in literature. She did not feel as though she had anything to celebrate.

She went to the library with some relief. At least, there, one was busy and distracted. During her lunch hour she shopped, deliberately avoiding the part of town in which Giles's office was situated. When she returned Joyce Babcock sought her out at once.

'A man came in, asking for you.' Joyce's eyes glittered with prurient interest.

'Oh?'

'Fiftyish. With that sort of greyish-silver hair. Very friendly. We had quite a chat about the Lakes. He was asking for a fell-walking guide. Our only one is out.'

'That would have been my solicitor,' said Helen crisply. 'Giles Carnaby.'

'He's very attractive, don't you think?'

'That's not the sort of thing I notice about a solicitor. Professional efficiency is what one is after.'

'Well, I thought he was a real charmer. Lucky Helen, I thought.' Joyce eyed her closely. 'He seemed very disappointed to have missed you. I suppose there's a lot of to and fro over your mother's affairs?'

'A fair amount,' said Helen. She began to sort through some reservation cards. After a moment she added, 'Was he going to look in later? There is something we're supposed to discuss.'

'He didn't say,' replied Joyce. She continued to observe Helen with attention. 'You could always ring him up at his office, of course.'

'It's nothing that can't wait,' said Helen.

The afternoon progressed, but was moved now on to a different plane, lit by the glow of expectation. Helen watched the door, through which Giles did not come. She checked that the fell-walking guide was indeed out on loan. Each time the phone rang she reached it before Joyce. Eventually it was five-thirty. She drove home to find Edward returned from the sports day.

'How did it go?'

'It was awful,' said Edward morosely. 'Worse than usual.'

'Well, at least you've got it over with for another year.'

'I suppose so.'

'Cheer up. It's the holidays now, at any rate.'

The six weeks of the summer school recess were the high spot

of Edward's year. He would settle down to a contented programme of long walks, daily spells of observation in the Britches,
and some leisurely reflection on work projects for his pupils next
year. He usually also went off somewhere under the auspices of
some ecologically minded group. This year he was not doing so,
claiming that he had left it too late to make arrangements.

'You should get away for a bit,' Helen continued. 'Surely
there's still something you could fix up.'

Edward shrugged. Helen felt a wash of irritation. Come on
now . . . I have my own troubles. Edward made himself a cup
of tea and vanished to the Britches, where he stayed late into the
dusk. Helen listened to a concert on the radio, with the sound
turned low lest she should miss the phone ringing.

It did not ring. Neither then nor for the next four days. All
right, she said to her mother, who trailed Helen once more,
watching her with an impassive stare, all right – you win.
Consider yourself vindicated.

Why, then, did he say those things? Do what he did?

Perhaps he didn't, said her mother. You always had a ridiculous imagination, as a child.

I am not a child now, said Helen.

On the Wednesday of the following week Joyce Babcock said,
'That Lake District book's back, by the way – Wainwright. I
should think you'd want to give your friend a buzz.'

Helen put the book on one side. It lay there, inescapable.
After lunch, she told herself – at three, at four. Eventually, at
four-thirty, she telephoned Giles's office. 'Could I speak to Mr
Carnaby?' Her stomach churned.

'Mr Carnaby's away this week. Can I take a message?'

'Oh. It's not important. It's the library here, just to say the
book he asked for is in. Wainwright on fell-walking.'

'Oh, what a shame,' said the girl. 'I expect he wanted that for
his holiday – he's up there now, in the Lake District. Anyway,
I'll tell him.'

'Thank you,' said Helen. She put the receiver down and placed

142

the book on the pile due for shelving. Where, later, Joyce would see it, with tedious inevitability, and ask questions.

Funny he didn't mention, said her mother. That he was going on holiday. You'd think he'd have said. You'd think he'd have told you he wouldn't be around for the next week or two. More, maybe. 'We must talk very soon'; so much for that.

Wonder who he's with? said Dorothy. He'd be with some woman, no doubt, a man like that.

That's all he came into the library for, of course – to get that book. Not looking for you at all.

What's the matter, Helen? I know that po-faced look.

It turned hot. A sullen grey July gave way to sultry August. Everything shot into growth, fortified by weeks of rain. The Greystones garden was like a jungle, parts of it as impenetrable as the Britches. When Gary Paget reappeared, offering his services again, Helen accepted with alacrity. She had planted some runner beans in the patch of the old vegetable garden he had dug earlier; they were flowering energetically and seemed to have been worth the trouble. She set him to work on a further area of deep neglect. 'I'm afraid it's very weedy. You'll have to dig it over more than once.' Gary, a stoically silent boy, merely nodded. He peeled off his T-shirt, revealing a chunky tanned torso that reeked of Lifebuoy soap.

Helen went into the kitchen and began to cut up onions. She had bought a recipe book and was attempting a rather complex casserole, involving red wine and many ingredients. When in low spirits, seek gainful employment. The Lord helps those who help themselves. The only cookery books at Greystones were yellowing volumes from the twenties and thirties, smelling of damp and telling you how to make spotted dick or pickle eggs in isinglass. No wonder we have always eaten as we have, she thought; if nothing else comes out of my *malaise* I may at least learn how to cook in the spirit of the times.

She was struggling to cut the meat into what the book described as bite-size chunks when Edward appeared at the kitchen door.

'Why has that boy come back?'

'Oh, for goodness sake!' exclaimed Helen, maddened by the recalcitrance of the meat as much as by her brother. 'He's come back because I want him. And he's called Gary. You know that.'

'I simply don't see the point.'

'The point is to get things cleared up a bit. The garden is a disgrace.'

'We could do it ourselves.'

'Yes. But we aren't going to, are we?'

'He's digging up all the groundsel. There'll be no cinnabar moths next year.'

Helen flung down her knife. 'Oh, Edward, don't be ridiculous! The point of a garden is to grow things. We'll have potatoes instead of moths, which makes a lot more sense.'

He was panting, she now saw, as though he had rushed from somewhere. He clutched the door frame. We're having a quarrel, Helen thought. This hasn't happened in years. Whatever is the matter?

Edward wiped a hand across his forehead. He walked into the room and headed for the door, without looking at her. She heard him cross the hall and go up the stairs. A moment later a flop on the mat announced the arrival of the post. Helen stood over her bleeding bite-size chunks of meat in a state of agitation; annoyance with Edward was fused with some nameless, indefinable anxiety. She went into the hall. She could hear Edward overhead, moving about in his room. She hesitated. No, she thought, he's being absurd. She stooped and picked up the post. There was an electricity bill and a postcard from Giles Carnaby.

He said: 'I won't say wish you were here since it rains incessantly and I am not a sadist. However, we contrive to have a very pleasant time. But perhaps you too are kicking up your heels elsewhere by now. If so, I hope all goes well. Do you know this lovely spot?' It was signed, merely, Giles.

She turned the card over. Tarn Howe glowed beneath an unsuitably blue sky.

Helen returned to the kitchen. She had forgotten Edward. She put the card upright on the dresser and gazed at it.

We? said Dorothy. Who's *we*, I wonder? Funny he should

think you might be on holiday. He never enquired, did he? Take it or leave it sort of fellow, if you ask me.

Be quiet, said Helen. She returned to her task. She chopped herbs; she peeled mushrooms. Every few minutes she glanced again at the postcard.

Upstairs, Edward sat on his bed. He sat quite still, with his hands clenched in his lap. Tam, excluded, scrabbled indignantly at the door. Eventually Edward heard, and let him in.

'What is this?' said Edward. He put his knife and fork down and stared at his plate.

'It's called *Boeuf* something or other. Don't you like it?'

'It's very nice.'

'Then aren't you going to finish it?' she asked, a few minutes later.

'I'm not particularly hungry. Sorry.'

Helen cleared the plates. 'Look – I'll tell Gary to leave part of the vegetable garden undug. For the moths or whatever. All right?'

'It doesn't matter,' he said. 'It's not important.' He looked at her – evasive, placating – and picked up the local paper. He began to read a piece about the proposed transformation of a disused mill into a luxury hotel. Helen started to say more, and then changed her mind. Oh, *Edward*, she thought impatiently.

The days inched by. Helen went to the library, did what had to be done, returned from the library. She persisted in her relationship with the new recipe book; the kitchen at Greystones was filled with strange aromas. She was experimenting with a risotto when Ron Paget appeared at the door. He was so tanned that for a moment Helen failed to recognise him. The whites of his eyes gleamed from a chestnut face. He stepped into the kitchen and put something on the table.

'Thought I'd bring round the little brown envelope – for the guttering and that.' He inspected the pan simmering on the stove, and sniffed. 'Very nice. Pauline used to be keen on that sort of thing, but she's gone off it since we gave up Italy as a holiday venue. She's into seafood at the moment. We tried the Seychelles this year. You ever been out there, Miss Glover?'

'No.'

'Amazing skin-diving. Quite something, let me tell you. I should think your brother might fancy that, being as he's so keen on wildlife.'

'I doubt it,' said Helen. 'Scotland's more Edward's line.'

Ron nodded sagely. 'It's pricey, of course, but I said to Pauline – come on, we owe it to ourselves.'

'I thought Gary was looking very sunburnt,' said Helen.

Ron laughed. 'Oh, Gary's been in Wales with the school camping trip. I'm not for taking the kids on holiday. Grown-up amusements, that's the idea. Pauline likes some fun at the discos. Fair enough – it's not exactly the bright lights living down here, is it? I'm not fussed for myself, but Pauline's younger and she's been used to town life, see what I mean?'

'Really?' No, Helen thought – I will not ask where Pauline hails from because that would prolong the conversation and anyway I don't want to know.

'East Croydon, Pauline grew up. I daresay you're wondering how we ever came to meet – Club Méditerranée it was. I'd gone along with some of the lads – my first wife was never that keen on travel – and there she was. So abroad's always a bit nostalgic for us. You going away this year?'

'No, I'm not.'

A strained expression appeared on Ron's face which Helen eventually interpreted as being intended to convey concern, or sympathy, or both. 'I've kept that bill as low as I possibly can, Miss Glover. I think of you as a special customer.'

Helen turned to the stove; the risotto looked to be heaving over-enthusiastically. She wished Ron would go. 'Very kind of you. I'm not doing without a holiday because I'm feeling hard up though, but because I don't particularly want one.'

'Well, I suppose you don't miss what you've never had. You've always been one for a quiet life, haven't you?'

146

This is impertinent, she thought. My mother would have thrown you out by now. If indeed you had ever got in.

'Still – it's never too late to break loose, is it?'

Helen faced him. Enough. 'Look, Mr Paget, I don't think . . .'

'And you've got the means right there at the bottom of your garden.' He waved a hand in the direction of the Britches. 'You should give yourselves a chance, you really should. And I'll tell you something else – in my opinion there's going to be funny things happen to the market in a year or so. You might see prices fall.'

'That's a risk we'll have to take, then. I wish I could convince you, Mr Paget, that we're not interested in selling the wood. Not now and quite probably never. There really is no point in going on about it.'

Ron shrugged. 'You're a mystery to me, Miss Glover, you really are.' His glance strayed around the kitchen. Assessing the extent of our poverty, thought Helen. Wondering how long we can hold out. He moved towards the door. 'I'd say you could do with a touch more garlic in that, by the way – Pauline always used to go quite heavy on the garlic. Cheers, then.'

Later that day, she went into the Britches. Edward had gone to a meeting of the local ornithological society. Looking from the sitting room window at the shaggy mass of the copse, she thought again of Ron, and, on an impulse, opened the french windows and walked across the garden to the gap that marked Edward's comings and goings. She hadn't been in there for months. It seemed a good idea to see what it was she was defending with such tenacity.

Edward's regular trail led to the nest-box area in the centre, where there were old trees and the open space with the big fallen mossy trunk on which he sat. Helen, too, sat for a few minutes. Less attuned than Edward to the internal noises of the Britches – the birdsong, the hum of insects – she was conscious of the insistent presence of the world beyond. She heard distant traffic from the road that skirted the far side of the wood; she heard machinery and men shouting in Ron Paget's yard; she flinched as an aircraft ripped the sky, miles above. When she got up and walked again – struggling through the exuberant growths of high summer – she noted Edward's recent efforts at clearance and control. Left alone, the place would rapidly choke itself to death, it seemed. Edward's interference in fact made adjustments that favoured his own view of the direction nature ought to take; nature itself generated a free for all. And in a free for all there are those who survive and those who perish. Edward's attempts to manipulate seemed both touching and, eventually, fruitless. The Britches will outlast us both, Helen thought, carrying on in its mindless way until scuppered at last by economic circumstances and the likes of Ron Paget.

She started back towards the house. The telephone might ring, with no one there to pick it up. She forged her way through the tangle of growth and decay, thinking of Giles Carnaby.

ELEVEN

'I saw your friend,' announced Joyce Babcock, 'that solicitor.' She watched Helen, covertly. 'Crossing Market Street. Going to his office, I should imagine. He had a briefcase.'

Helen continued to check through a publisher's catalogue. Quite calmly. 'Did you? He must be back from his holiday then.'

I wonder when? said her mother. Hasn't hurried to get in touch, has he? It's Wednesday now. He'd have come back at the weekend, most likely.

'I thought you'd like to know, anyway. Of course it's too late for that book. But I suppose he might want it just to see what he's missed. It's still on the shelf. Shall I put it in Reserve?'

'I shouldn't bother,' said Helen.

She took her lunch an hour late. There were some food items to be bought; she was persisting, doggedly, with the recipe book. She made her purchases carefully, forcing herself to consider the quality of meat, to search out some stem ginger. Then she set off back to the library. There were two routes she could take. One kept to the main streets; the second, marginally shorter way, passed through the side road in which Giles's office was situated. She took this one.

They met, in fact, in the main shopping street, several minutes from his office. She saw him from fifty yards away, coming towards her; then he spotted her and when they came together he was smiling and had a hand outstretched with which he took her elbow. 'So there you are! What a nice surprise! You're not off gadding somewhere, then . . . Did you get my card?'

'Yes. Thank you.'

'And you rang about that book. My secretary said. Bless you. Frankly, with the weather the way it was fell-walking lost its

149

charms. We had to find other diversions. I was about to get in touch with you – there are faint signs of life on the part of the Probate Office. Which way are you going?'

She walked beside him past Boots, past Baxters, past Rumbelows. Giles talked about Rydal Mount and Ruskin's house. She listened to him intently – and not at all; I am not cured, she thought, indeed things are worse if anything.

He halted. 'Well, I must leave you here. So – I'll be writing you a boring letter about business matters, but can't we meet? Saturday I am tied up, but Sunday . . . How are you fixed on Sunday?'

Helen said that she was not fixed on Sunday. Not at all.

'Then let us do something nice together.' He pressed her elbow. 'I'll give you a ring. Goodbye, Helen.'

That was a bit of luck for you, wasn't it? said Dorothy. Running into him like that. Good luck or good management. But now you'll never know whether he'd have made a move or not, will you?

Edward started to make unusual entries in his diary. All his life he had kept a diary; it was a detached record of matters like the arrivals of the first migrants, the occurrence of various plant species in the Britches, and the prevailing weather. The years went by in a bundle of exercise books, seasons succeeding one another as flycatchers came and went, orchids were noted and then vanished, temperatures varied from the normal. He himself featured not at all. It would have been a sad disappointment to anyone ferreting in the top drawer of his desk. He had at one time suspected his mother of doing precisely this.

Now, no one would pry. Edward, alone in his room in the long wastes of those summer days, looked back into the exercise books and noted his own absence. The first chiff-chaff had shown up exceptionally early in 1970, he saw; the last kingcup had been seen in 1967. Neither of these facts seemed, now, of much interest. He had been thirty-two in 1970; there had been certain events that were crucial to his life. Suddenly he wanted to recover his responses to these, not the arrival of the chiff-chaff. He would have liked to be able to confront and examine his own previous self. The diary was mockingly silent.

'August 15th,' he wrote. 'Cleared bramble from area by the big beech. Very few speckled wood butterflies this year. Counted four young magpies. Cool; thunderstorm p.m.' He put the pen down. And so on and so forth, he thought. As though I did not exist; as though it were an automaton who cleared brambles and counted magpies. He began to write once more. 'Next year I shall be fifty years old. I shall die when I am between seventy-five and eighty, in all likelihood; Helen will outlive me – women live longer, it seems. Neither of us will leave progeny. Less successful, in that way, than anything around.' He looked out of the window, at the fecund garden. 'If the purpose of life can be said to be replication, then we have both failed dismally.' He sat motionless, staring out at the Britches, for five minutes. He then wrote: 'It is only so, of course, in a biological sense.'

'Had you forgotten?' said Giles. 'You hadn't – oh good. And the weather forecast is promising – now, what do you fancy? A long walk? Some gentle carriage exercise and a pub lunch?'

'I could make a picnic,' Helen said.

'What a lovely idea! Excellent! Should I collect you at about eleven, then? In that case . . . Wouldn't your brother like to join us?'

She hesitated. 'I doubt it. But I'll ask.'

'I'm making a picnic. Giles Carnaby is coming. Do you want to come?'

'No,' said Edward without hesitation.

Giles drove decisively, with a hint of aggression; the car was powerful, and more fully furnished than any Helen had experienced. He put on a tape of Vivaldi and then switched it off

151

because he said they had too much to talk about. It was he, in fact, who talked. He was a considerable talker, Helen realised. What he said was informative if a touch inconsequential; you didn't remember too much of it but the effect was cumulative. It was a kind of verbal display; listening, she was disconcertingly reminded of a bird idly preening, limbering up with bursts of song, stretching a wing . . . It came to her, in fact, with dry detachment, that Giles was a somewhat self-centred person. Most of what he said pertained to himself. Occasionally he asked a question or sought an opinion; you had the impression that the answer had glanced off his surface. He appeared to listen with flattering attention; you also felt that possibly he had not heard.

Perceiving all this, she knew also that it made no difference. None whatsoever.

They had decided to make for a small river valley in which there was an isolated church reached by a footpath across fields. Helen had gone to some lengths over the picnic; the recipe book included a relevant section, she discovered. Flaked tuna with mayonnaise was new to her but she had managed and was quite proud of the results. Giles, when they had parked the car, dived into the back and produced a bottle of wine. They set off across a water meadow rich with buttercups and decorated with Friesian cows, like a television advertisement for some environmentally dubious product: petrol or fast cars. A heron rose from the river and flapped away into a clump of tall trees in the distance.

They inspected the church. Giles was not, evidently, much interested in churches. Helen, for a moment, came into her own; she pointed out salient features, found some medieval paving and a battered Norman font. Giles listened – or not – and then put a hand on her arm to steer her towards the door. 'Come on, I'm starving – time to find an idyllic spot in which to eat.'

The river seemed the obvious place. They chose a point at which the bank reached steeply down to a pool, a slight bend in the course having eaten away a miniature beach on the far side. It was thick with alder and willow; the water, green and shaded, flashed from time to time with coins of reflected sunlight.

'Perfect!' said Giles.

Helen unpacked the food. He poured the wine (he had

remembered glasses, too). They ate and drank, sitting tucked into long grass that screened them from the river; they could hear the flow of it, and the occasional plop of a fish. I suppose, Helen thought, this is one of those moments in life that will live in the head. Whatever comes of it. Giles declared the sandwiches excellent. He ate everything she had brought, and then lay back, glass in hand. 'What heaven!'

Helen said, 'We've got company.'

On the far side of the river a dog appeared – a collie, leaping in excitement. Followed at once by a young man, dark-haired, sunburnt, wearing jeans and a T-shirt.

The man, if indeed he realised they were there, paid no attention to them. He threw a stick into the river and the dog went after it in a flying leap, landing with a huge splash and paddling furiously, its black head sleek like a seal. It came out, shaking so that water spun off in silver spray. The man threw more sticks and it jumped again, ecstatic, diving and swimming, in and out. And then he sat down and stripped off his shirt.

'Now he's going in too,' said Giles. 'I wish he'd go away. Our peace is wrecked.'

The man pulled off his jeans and stood up. He was naked. It seemed to Helen that he must surely be aware of them; if so, they were of no interest whatsoever. She heard Giles say – embarrassed? – 'A proper child of nature, evidently . . .' The young man stood for a moment on an overhanging ledge of the bank, looking down at the water; the dog swam round and round below; the man's body was flecked all over with light and the shadow patterns of leaves, so that he seemed some human extension of the place. He was spare, muscular, young. Then he threw up his arms and dived into the river.

He swam vigorously, ducking his head in the water and flinging back his wet hair. The dog circled him, barking. At last they both climbed out onto the little beach. The man dressed, put on his shoes, stood up, and then bounded up the bank into the field, followed by the dog. They were gone as suddenly as they had come. The water of the pool was still muddy and heaving where they had swum.

'I don't think I'd fancy it,' said Giles. 'Too much weed.'

It had been, while it lasted, electrifying; now, it was as though neither man nor dog had ever been. The shape and texture of the man's body were still before Helen's eyes, but as an image, a picture once seen. Giles reached for the wine and emptied the rest of it into their glasses.

She was intensely conscious of him. When his leg brushed against her it seemed to burn her. I'm not sure how much of this I can endure, she thought. She glanced at Giles; she had no idea if he felt anything, or nothing. He was sipping wine and talking about dogs. He had seen a sheepdog trial in Cumbria: amazing creatures. It seemed to Helen that they might sit there thus for ever. All my life, she thought, I have let things pass me by.

They were sitting side by side. She turned to face him. He stopped talking and, presumably, saw. Afterwards, she thought perhaps she had touched him, but could not remember. Giles leaned forward; he took her face between his hands and kissed her on the mouth. She felt his tongue. Then he drew back and looked intently at her. 'Helen, my dear . . .' he said. He sighed, 'We mustn't . . .' He stood up. She heard herself say, 'Why not?' but if the words reached him he made no sign. He began to pack things into the picnic basket. He said, 'Now what I have in mind is a stroll to the end of the valley just to see what goes on there, then back to the car and home for tea, how about that?'

'I'm coming down for a night,' said Louise. 'Thursday. O.K.? I've got to get out of London. The office can bloody do without me for a couple of days. Everyone else is swanning around the South of France anyway. The children are a pain, frankly, and Tim has sinus and won't give you the time of day. So what's new with you?'

There was a spell of hot weather; mosquito larvae hatched in the stagnant pond on the far side of the Britches. Some children broke in and trampled down the surviving patch of ramsoms. A cat killed one of the young magpies. A decaying treestump sprouted a collar of saffron fungus of a kind Edward had never seen before. He observed all these happenings but wrote: 'Dogs: four including the one that got run over when only six months. Tam is fifth. I have always wondered if mother left the front door open deliberately; he was a spaniel mixture, very nice. Pickle was first – tan and white terrier, died of cancer at eight. Best, too, in many ways. Then Jess – collie from Canine Defence, had to be put down eventually. Then the run-over puppy. Then Minnie – terrier type again, very loving, strayed a lot, died suddenly, probably ate something. Cats: the tabby next door, when I was a child – but of course that wasn't mine. Then the ginger kitten I hid in the garden shed and mother found it and there was a monumental scene and Helen called her a beast; funny, I can hear it now, mother going on about the kitten and Helen suddenly exploding and mother's face. It was Louise who said things like that, not Helen. The kitten lived to be nine, so came out of the whole business best, I suppose. Then Prince – black and white tom. Then no more cats because of problems with birds.' He paused. He pushed his chair back and wandered around the room. Everything in it was old and shabby; little had been chosen by Edward himself. There were some World Wildlife Fund posters and a carving of a red-throated diver he had once bought in Orkney. There was a small case of books. The candlewick bedspread on his bed dated from his schooldays; an area at the end was worn completely bare by the five dogs. The rug on the floor had once been in his father's study. A Victorian jug on the mantelpiece had been given him by Louise one Christmas. The dressing-gown on the back of the door had been bought by Helen to replace one twenty-five years old.

Edward returned to the desk. He wrote: 'I cannot sleep at night. There is nothing to be done. The boy came again last week.'

He could not remember now the precise moment at which he had realised, once, time out of mind ago, that he found male bodies inviting and female ones not. He could remember a period of engagement with art – with Greek statuary and the young gods of Renaissance paintings, those bodies officially sanctified on the page or given sexual neutrality as museum displays. Here, you were licensed to admire without discrimination: the body as

155

aesthetic object, pure and simple. Edward had come to realise that he found some bodies more appealing than others, and that the contemplation of them aroused feelings that had nothing to do with artistic appreciation. He made the connection between these bodies and those he saw all around him – clothed, partially clothed, or unclothed in the roaring maelstrom of the school changing rooms. He had had to conceal his revulsion at the creased and thumbed photographs handed round from desk to desk at school – those grey girls with their balloon breasts and gaping hairy forks. And presently revulsion gave way to indifference: he ceased to see the flaunted female bodies of advertisements and magazines because they had nothing to do with him, they were irrelevant. It was other images, now, that disturbed, from which he turned in anxiety and in guilt.

And, over the years, he had learned to avert his face, to sidestep, to damp down the fires. On the rare occasions when sharp eyes had penetrated his facade, when complicity had been invited, he had fled in panic. When, once, he had thought himself on the brink of an alliance for which he yearned, he was suddenly and shatteringly rejected. Thereafter, he turned inwards.

Five days after the picnic Helen received a postcard from Giles Carnaby. The picture was of a well-known local church. Giles said: 'I can see I must brush up on my Perp and Dec if I am to keep up with you. Thank you for a gorgeous outing. Will be in touch very soon.' No signature.

You don't know where you are with him, do you? said Dorothy. From one week to the next. Blowing hot and cold like that. Time to put it to him, fair and square, I'd say. Mind, you may not like what you hear.

She loomed large these days, as in the weeks after the funeral. Her airy presence filled the house. Above all, her comments rang in Helen's ears.

'Is Edward all right?' said Louise. 'There's something distinctly odd about him lately, you know. I mean, even odder than usual.

156

He never was much like other people. And you're looking a bit off-colour, to be honest. Seedy, as mother used to say. Not that I can talk – I've got almost as many spots as Phil. Maybe adolescence is contagious. God – what's going on here?'

They were walking through the village. Louise wished to visit Dorothy's grave, where the memorial stone was now in place. A confusion of lorries and cement mixers defaced the area just past the green. Helen explained that someone was converting the disused Baptist chapel into a house. They entered the churchyard. She said: 'Is Phil still being . . . difficult?'

'Of course he's being difficult. And Suzanne. Do you know, I am nostalgic for nappies and broken nights. I look in prams, with a soppy smile on my face. At the time, I thought one had hit rock bottom. There's a bloody great silent conspiracy that goes on, and it's the conspiracy of those who've had children against those who haven't yet. What you don't know, till you're in it, is that it's a life sentence. The other thing of course is that you haven't got any choice anyway, because the yen to have children is about as basic as the yen to have sex. It's all devilishly neat. Contraception is merely cosmetic. You breed, willy-nilly, and lo and behold! you find life isn't ever going to be the same again. Even mother – even *mother* – I now realise, must have gone through some of this. Even mother must have had the odd twinge, incredible as it seems. And the whole process is made as simultaneously agonising and amazing as it could be – you *labour* to give birth, that's the right word all right, and it's about as ghastly as possible and then at the end there's this absolutely wonderful feeling, that the conspiracy has never hinted at, when you hold it and see it and you suddenly realise there's a whole new emotion you didn't know anything about. Nobody's ever mentioned that. And from then on you're done – they've got you by the short hairs. You're going to spend the next few months hanging over them with your heart thumping in case they've stopped breathing and the next few years after that stopping them committing suicide because a perfectly ordinary house has turned into a minefield of electricity and stairs and windows and boiling kettles. Every day the newspapers are telling you what happens to other people's children. They're being run over and

157

raped and burnt; there's leukemia and meningitis and muscular dystrophy; it's all out there waiting to spring, if you're fool enough to relax. But at the moments you wish you were shot of the whole thing you know perfectly well that it's precisely because you couldn't endure to be without it, now you know about it, that you've got to go through all this. You've lost your innocence. And then they get bigger and they start thinking and watching and you realise you're fouling them up yourself too and there's not much you can do about that either. And you know that at the same time as you could clout them you'd actually die for them also if it came to the point. It's a fiendishly clever system for making sure the human race continues and most people over twenty never have a tranquil moment. God – what a spiel! I don't blame you for looking edgy.'

'Sorry,' said Helen. 'I didn't realise you were talking to me, in fact.'

They had arrived at the grave. 'Do you think it's all right?' Helen enquired, after a moment.

'The stone? Fine. Nice lettering. Simple and straightforward.'

'It's considered a bit austere by some.'

'Of course. Look around. It sticks out. Offends against the prevailing taste. Well, that would have given mother quiet satisfaction.'

They stood in contemplation. 'You know something?' said Louise. 'She's changing. In the head, that is. I'm beginning to see her differently. She's losing her edge, somehow. Fading. What about you?'

'Fading? I wouldn't say that, no. I'm seeing her differently. I wouldn't say that I'm seeing her faded. Interesting. And even more interesting is the way in which I see myself differently. What I am and what I'm not, and why. All of which slots in with what you've just been saying. Did mother foul me up? As you put it. Or does one hammer the nails into one's own coffin? As mother used to have it. Sorry about the language. Inept. It slipped out.'

'What do you mean – fouled up? You're not . . .'

'Of course I am. As are we all. To a greater or lesser extent.'

'Oh, gawd . . .' said Louise, turning from the grave. She

dumped herself down on the low stone wall that skirted the churchyard.

Helen joined her. 'Mother, I now discover, once scuppered my romantic prospects. Do you remember Peter Datchett? No – I daresay not – and in any case who's to say what would have come of it? I might at this moment be living in anguish with Peter Datchett. Perhaps I should thank mother. But one would prefer to have made one's own mistakes. And there's the question of the yellow muslin dress – not on the face of it a central matter but . . . but again there is this sense of one's fate having been manipulated by another. By mother, to be precise.'

Louise was staring intently. 'I do remember Peter Datchett. I always wondered why he disappeared without trace. What did she do? And what yellow dress? I simply can't see you . . .'

'No, I'm sure you can't. And you would have been about seven at the time. What bothers me is not so much the loss of either Peter Datchett or the yellow dress, but the awful glimpse of my own acquiescence.'

'I don't understand,' said Louise after a moment.

'Why should you? Neither do I, in a sense. I see, simply, that at some point I became pathologically compliant. The habit of avoiding confrontation with mother became a habit of not confronting anything. Of accepting without question. You used to go on at me about getting out. You were of course entirely right.'

'Oh, goodness . . . One *said* that sort of thing. I didn't always mean . . .'

'It's all right,' said Helen. 'I'm not bemoaning the past. I'm merely casting a beady eye on it. Hoping, perhaps, to learn something.'

Louise, dissecting a cushion of moss, laid green fronds upon her knee – and switched tactics. 'What *did* mother do?'

'Oh – failed to hand over a letter. A sin of omission rather than of commission, quite possibly. One will never know. I'm more interested now in what I didn't do. Put up a fight. Rage against the universe.'

'You aren't that kind of person,' said Louise.

'Ah, there you have it. And why not?'

'Nor is Edward . . .' continued Louise, shredding the green fronds, sweeping them to the ground.

'Precisely. Whereas you are. Odd, isn't it? I can see you now – it's my earliest memory of you, incidentally – I can see you now *biting* mother. Aged about one.'

Louise laughed. 'What did she do?'

'She put you in a cot and shut the door on you. You yelled for an hour without stopping.'

'No wonder. It's surprising I'm as normal as I am. That we all are.'

'Hmn . . .' Helen rose. 'We'd better get back. I haven't done anything about supper. Edward will be getting restive.'

'Where is he, anyway? He was around for five minutes when I arrived and then he vanished.'

'In the Britches, I expect.'

'Edward's relationship with that place would keep half a dozen psychiatrists busy. Oh, that sounds snide. It's not meant. *You* know. When I was little I thought the light shone out of Edward's eyes. Now I get frightened for him. The world's a brutal place and he wanders around worrying about toads and orchids. He wouldn't have enough sense of self-preservation to come in out of the rain. In the dark ages people like Edward got crucified or burned as witches. He lives in a jungle today and he doesn't know it.'

'Hardly,' said Helen. 'Here.' They were turning out into the village street again now, leaving behind them the stone ranks of the dead, with their propitiatory offerings of flowers and foliage. A clutch of young mothers gossiped outside the shop, with children eddying around them. Radio One leaked from the open windows of a house.

'Of course. Social violence is universal, and I don't mean mugging and burglary. A place like this has fangs like anywhere else, given the circumstances.'

'Edward's rather popular in the village.'

'That's not what I'm getting at,' said Louise. She appeared to lose interest in the subject and began to talk about Suzanne. Suzanne wished to leave school at sixteen and become a hairdresser. Louise fulminated. Helen heard Dorothy, twenty-three years ago, screaming at Louise. Louise, glancing at her sister, caught the silent comment and said, 'There is absolutely no parallel. Mother was obstructing, purely and simply. *I'm* trying to stop Suzanne making an idiotic mistake.' Then she started to laugh and added, 'Do *you* always know what *I'm* thinking? God – it's as bad as marriage!'

By the time they got back to the house it was past eight. There was a rich and spicy smell; Helen had left the dinner in the oven. 'Coriander . . .' said Louise, sniffing. 'You really are into contemporary cuisine, aren't you? Mother would have a fit. Here – I'll lay the table.'

Edward came down from his room. Helen served the meal. They began to eat. After a few mouthfuls Edward put his knife and fork down and said, 'Oh – the lawyer rang. Half an hour or so ago.'

'Funny time to ring up,' said Louise. 'Out of office hours.'

Edward started to eat again. 'She goes to the opera with him.'

Louise turned sharply to Helen, who felt herself turn a treacherous red. 'What's all this?'

'And picnics,' said Edward.

'The probate thing will be sorted out in a month or so,' said Helen in strangled tones. 'Apparently.'

'*Picnics?*' demanded Louise. 'Picnics where?'

'He uses after-shave stuff,' said Edward. 'I don't really like him.'

'So what?' snapped Helen.

Louise, wide-eyed, looked from one to the other. 'What on earth is going on?'

'Nothing,' said Helen, 'is going on.' She got up. 'Would anyone like some more of this?'

Louise turned to Edward. 'What did he want?'

'He didn't say,' said Edward smugly. 'He just chuntered on a bit and then rang off.'

Helen dumped a spoonful of stew on to each plate except her own and sat down again.

'This is delicious,' said Louise, in a social tone. 'You must give me the recipe.'

*

161

After three days Helen dialled Giles Carnaby's number. There was no answer. The next evening, too, he was out. She rang his office, and then panicked at the secretary's voice, and put the receiver down without speaking. This, she thought, is how adolescents behave; to this is one reduced.

'I hate August,' said Joyce Babcock. 'Nothing but overdue books and kids fooling around. And the town jammed with coaches. Nothing *happens* in August. Everyone's away – even the people you never think you'd miss, like the neighbours. I've not spoken to a soul in the last fortnight, except for you – sorry, no offence meant. No, I tell a lie – I saw Kate Blackford outside Marks. You know – from Oxford Central. She's living up here now. So we had a nice chat. Oh – and this'll interest you – while we were talking who should go past but your solicitor friend. Again. I'm always seeing him, aren't I? Anyway, he didn't see me but Kate recognised him too – her sister works in his office, apparently. And the thing is he wasn't alone, he had someone with him – that woman who runs the Choral Society, I can't remember her name, with black hair, youngish. And Kate says her sister says he's quite a one for the ladies. Apparently he led his wife an awful dance. You know his wife's dead? Apparently she was ever so nice. Anyway, I thought you'd be interested.'

I know, said Helen to Dorothy. Of course I know. I've always known, probably. It makes no difference. Unfortunately. No difference whatsoever.

And how do I know she's not just a friend? Like I'm just a friend.

Why did he send another postcard? Telephone? He didn't have to. And of what value is the testimony of Kate Blackford's sister?

*

Why does he not telephone again?

'So . . .' said Louise. 'Back in the nest. Where things have not changed. Tim has seen a new specialist and is going in to have his tubes drained. Phil disappeared for twenty-four hours and had me ringing up the local police station. Who demonstrated what you might call a profound lack of interest. So I took it out on Phil when he did show up which was natural enough I suppose but probably unhelpful. Now he's off again. God knows where. It was lovely seeing you. Listen – what *is* going on? This bloke . . . You haven't gone and fallen, have you? I remember him now. The Older Man type who came to the funeral. I know you were getting pissed off with Edward needling you like that, but you can tell *me*, surely. I worry about you.'

'Continuing humid,' Edward wrote. 'Cuckoo-pint in the corner near the road has increased – eight specimens this year. Wood spurge also doing better. Green woodpecker fledglings have flown. Neither spurge, cuckoo-pint nor woodpeckers will feel satisfaction at this, of course, nor indeed anything at all; they exist, simply, and that is that. Exist, replicate – if circumstances permit, and expire. The entire wood does that and nothing else, year after year – the dominant emotion is fear. When it sings and blossoms in the spring it is not happy; it merely does what its genes tell it to do. Such subtleties as happiness and misery are contributed by me, along with satisfaction at increase of cuckoo-pint and survival of woodpeckers. The point of all this being that . . .' He put down his pen and stared out at the Britches, which shifted gently and continuously in the light wind. Edward was not a great reader but he knew quite well that he was broaching the oldest and most central concern of literature; he felt appropriately diffident. '. . . I don't know if it is a comfort or a mockery. The beauty of it. The permanence. Everything that is in my head, everything that I feel; the fact that the natural world thinks nothing and neither laughs nor cries.' He pondered again. 'Though that is true only up to a point – last year after the dog fox was killed on the road the vixen called for three nights, the saddest sound I ever heard.' He paused again. On his bookshelves were the tattered copies of *Tarka the Otter* and the works of Cherry Kearton that he had read and re-read as a schoolboy, weeping the while. 'But is the vixen sad or do I attribute sadness to her? All that can be said for certain is that I respond to all of it – vixen, trees, plants, birds, the lot – but it does not respond to me.' Tam, who had been sleeping on the bed, woke suddenly, scratched himself, jumped down and marched to the door, where he stood, whining imperiously. 'All right,' said Edward. 'In a minute.' He wrote: 'And also that it sustains me, in ways that I can't explain. Especially now. Things still bad. Not sleeping etc. Was churlish to Helen.' Tam, at the door, continued to whine.

TWELVE

I suppose, Helen thought, that the interesting thing about my condition is the loss of self-control. Eventually one will see this as interesting rather than demoralising. It will be possible to look back and observe that those in love become utterly self-destructive. Oneself in love. At the moment I can no longer act with common sense and deliberation, because there is only one course open, and that is determined by obsession. I am obsessed by Giles; all I can think of is whether I shall see him again, and when. What the outcome of seeing him might be is beside the point; I have become incapable of calculation. Normally behaviour – or at least my behaviour – is governed by certain processes; weighing one course of action against another, thinking about consequences. In this predicament, one does nothing of the kind. One responds to some basic drive, like an animal. In youth, I found this exhilarating, I remember.

She tried, as therapy, to recall previous experiences. She was probably, she realised, shorter on this than most people. Apart from that early sexual encounter, which did not count as love, there had been Peter Datchett and two others. With Peter Datchett, it had been a question of ripening interest rather than obsession. The others, in so far as she could recover her feelings of the time, seemed to have involved love – inflammation of the senses, certainly. At eighteen – the period of the *mousseline de soie* dress – she had found herself hanging around a certain area of Twickenham, where they were then living, in the hopes of encountering the doctor's son, with whom she had had a strangled conversation at some social gathering. He had subsequently taken her to the cinema, where she had been startled to feel his hand creep into hers. Four weeks later she had seen him in the cinema queue with another girl, and had perceived that her day was over; in between, she had known disorientation and obsession, diagnosed her trouble, and felt exhilarated. Later, in her twenties, she had become quietly and patiently infatuated with a married colleague. The man had never behaved towards her in other than a friendly and decorous way; nevertheless, she burned. When after a year he moved away to another job, she felt acute distress and thought continuously of him for many months. It was that experience, in recollection, which most closely reflected her present state.

Late one afternoon Giles came into the library. Helen had taken over the 'Returned Books' counter temporarily from one of the juniors and looked up to find him standing in front of her, smiling.

He held up empty hands. 'I'm not a customer. Nothing to declare. But I did have something in mind – a biography of Mahler.'

'We have Donald Mitchell. I'm not sure if it's on the shelf. You'll find it in . . .'

'I'd hoped for personal service,' said Giles.

Helen glanced round. 'When Janice comes back from her tea I can hand over here.'

'Good. I'll fend for myself till then.'

Five minutes later she joined him in the Biography alcove. 'I'm sorry I was out when you phoned – Edward did remember to tell me this time.'

'Did I phone? Yes, so I did – this week has been hectic, though not in any interesting way. Nothing to report on your mother's affairs, I'm afraid. Now – what do you advise? Mahler is out. Shall I embark on two volumes of Henry James?'

They discussed books for a few minutes. Giles made his selection. He glanced at his watch. 'I must be off. Choir night, so I get myself an early supper. Thank you for your invaluable help – what luck to find you. I was afraid I might have struck one of the days you aren't here.'

There was to be no arrangement made, then. Choir night. Helen thought of the dark woman; in the mind's eye she saw her – laughing and talking with Giles. She felt a gust of despair. For a moment she was quite faint; the library rocked around her – the browsing readers with shopping baskets set down beside them, the books in their bright rows, the humming strip lights. She took a deep breath, gathered herself, the room settled; Giles was tucking his pile of books under his arm, picking up his briefcase. She said, 'Then what were you telephoning about?' 'About?' He looked at her in surprise. And something else: something chilly, something that warned. Stop, she told herself, stop.

And continued. 'If there's nothing to report . . .'

'Oh,' said Giles. 'Yes . . . Let me see now, what *did* I have in mind? Mahler, perhaps. And to say thank you for that lovely picnic. I was telling Edward about the heron we saw.' He was about to go; he turned to her. Well – goodbye, my dear, he was about to say, so glad I found you. And would be gone, leaving her to stare into blank days ahead. No, she thought, no.

'I should like to see you,' she said.

'Helen . . . Of course.' He laid a hand on her arm, placating. 'Very soon. It's difficult to talk here, isn't it? And I have the blessed choir. We must organise something – very soon.'

'And you've given me the impression you wanted to see me, too.' Appalled, she heard herself forge on.

'But my dear . . .' A woman edged past them into the alcove, murmuring apologies. Giles continued, his voice losing its solicitous intimacy. 'We must talk again. Soon. Definitely. And thank you again for your help.' He smiled: a public, neutral smile. The woman looked at them for a moment over the book she had pulled from the shelf.

He went. 'I can never find R to Z,' said the woman plaintively. 'Something funny happens after P.' Helen supplied assistance. She could hardly hear the woman's queries; her stomach twisted; his bland little words ticked in her head – soon, very soon. Well, said her mother, I should think you may have gone and done it now.

She was having dreams of unabashed sexuality. It was not Giles, though, who featured in these dreams. She consorted, these nights, with strangers – men who were temporarily vivid when she awoke but who faded as the day progressed until, after a few hours, they vanished entirely. Since the picnic, the young man by the river had joined her twice; she herself, interestingly, had not been the Helen of today but her own younger self and indeed not even that – some other girl who was both alien and deeply familiar, a *doppelgänger*, a mirror-Helen. She had bathed naked from a deserted beach with this man, and lain with him afterwards among sand-dunes. In the morning, while the dream remained with her, she felt searingly deprived, as though she had been abandoned, as though she had lost someone known and loved. And the loss was in part the loss of some aspect of herself, as irretrievable as past happiness.

She remembered that somewhere Dorothy had kept old photograph albums and, on a whim, began to search for them. They were not where she had expected to find them, in the big tallboy in the sitting room, in which lurked an unvisited confusion of old magazines, moth-eaten balls of knitting-wool, paper patterns, Edward's school reports, Louise's sketch pads, buttons, string. She ran them to ground eventually in the bottom of Dorothy's wardrobe, an area she had not yet steeled herself to clear. Pulling them from under some old blankets, she sat down on the bed and began to leaf through the pages: photographs fell out, battered, uncherished, not stuck-in – this was no lovingly tended relic. Here was a curly-haired Louise, smirking in a sunsuit on a grey, shingly beach; here was Edward in knee-length shorts, hair clipped to his scalp and ears sticking out. And here was Helen, a forgotten Helen with anxious chubby adolescent face, wearing a crumpled cotton dress and tilted sideways – her mother had been a careless photographer. All these prints, indeed, were under- or over-exposed, with their subjects askew; heads were chopped off, feet and hands loomed giant in the foregrounds. Nevertheless, photographs had been taken; there had been a deliberate attempt to record, to retain. Helen, shuffling through them, remembered Louise in the churchyard: even mother must have had the odd twinge . . .

Here was her father, too. Always on the edge of things. He stood diffidently to the side of a group, or featured as a background – the pair of legs clutched by baby Louise, a blurred figure in a field beyond Helen and Edward who sat on a rug eating sandwiches. That particular snap prompted the memory, the afternoon returning as she stared at it – the sandwiches had been of marmite, Edward had found a hawk-moth caterpillar. But what was their father doing, lurking indistinctly over there under a tree? That Helen could not remember. And nowhere did he appear alone: never, it seemed, had Dorothy turned the view-finder of the old box Brownie deliberately upon her husband.

Equally, she was absent herself; naturally enough – she had been the photographer. At the back of the album was a clutch of glossy professional pictures, and in these Dorothy could be found, glaring out from Louise's wedding group, standing rigid beside Edward on his graduation day. For both occasions she had worn the same hat – an uncompromising chenille turban; Helen had disposed of it a month ago with the rest of her things and, as she looked at the photographs, felt again the curious dry but slimy touch of it. And there also, in an earlier picture, was the brown bear fur coat: Dorothy, flanked by Helen and Edward as children, stood on a pavement against a background of London taxis and buses – they must have been caught by a street photographer on one of those pantomime or ballet outings. Dorothy looked determined rather than festive; she would have been in her forties at the time but already stood as though planted, like an elderly woman. She had never seemed young, Helen realised; not even in the haziest reaches of recollection.

But it was not for Dorothy that she searched, nor even for her father. She hunted herself, putting aside all those pictures in which she appeared – not as child but as a grown woman. There were not so many. The sequence ended abruptly in the late fifties; the camera had packed up. Helen could even remember the occasion; the shutter jamming, her mother's fit of temper, the thing flung into the dustbin. And never, of course, replaced; such a purchase would have been an unjustifiable extravagance. The last photograph of herself showed her at about twenty-five, here in the garden at Greystones, sorting apples into baskets. Clearly Dorothy's principal intention had been to record the apple harvest – a prodigious one; Helen's presence was incidental, like one of those figures introduced for purposes of scale or composition. But she had turned her face to the camera and it had caught a look that she could find nowhere else and indeed that seemed to belong to another girl; she barely recognised herself. She saw a person who was young, yes, but – more than that – who wore an expression of arresting vivacity and expectancy. And who looked thus at her mother – what had she seen? Of what had she been thinking? Helen turned the picture over and saw that Dorothy had pencilled on the back '18lbs Laxtons; 27lbs Coxes.' One of those trees had blown over in a storm a few years later; the other survived as a diseased and sterile relic.

She sat on her mother's bed and studied her own distant and alien face. The eyes, indeed, met hers – alive, expectant, vulnerable. She felt as though confronted by a child: it'll be all right, she wanted to say, I'll see that it's all right.

A letter came from Giles: a typed, official letter concerning her mother's affairs. But folded within it was a handwritten note – 'So good to see you at the library, albeit briefly. Though I thought you seemed not quite yourself, and trust all is well now – do let me know if there is anything I can do. Yours affec. Giles.'

What am I supposed to make of this? she wondered. And with the thought came a spurt of irritation. I am supposed to make anything, or nothing, of it; obscurity and ambiguity are built in, whether deliberately or because that is his habit. Just as he has behaved since we met in a manner that avoids interpretation.

She telephoned that evening, before she could change her mind. She picked up the receiver without planning what she would say.

'This is Helen.'

There was no hesitation, no coolness to his voice. 'How nice – and how *are* you? You've had my letter? As I explained – we should be able to get those shares transferred next month, and then you can go ahead and sell them, or re-invest or whatever you wish. It might be as well to . . .'

'I understand,' she said. 'And thank you for your note.'

'Ah . . .'

'There is, in a sense, something you can do. Perhaps we could meet.'

Giles said at once, 'Of course. Let's see . . . Tomorrow? What about tomorrow – Saturday? I am bespoke in the evening, but the daytime is free, once I've done my domestic chores. Why don't we have a pub lunch and a breath of fresh air somewhere pleasant?'

He had suggested the landscaped grounds of an eighteenth-century house, noted for their expression of the picturesque: 'I'm not a great one for stately homes, but you can have a good walk there.' They had lunched in a crowded riverside pub, where Giles had talked smoothly and continuously on a general level. He continued to talk thus now, as they walked down the grand vista, away from the formal gardens and into the woodland rides, where classical figures loomed from the undergrowth and the serpentine rill wound away towards a distant temple. They stopped at the balustraded terrace overlooking the small lake, and leaned over; below, enormous golden fish lay around in the green water.

'Carp?' wondered Giles. 'Or orfe, are they? There's something called an orfe, isn't there?'

Helen said, 'I think I should find myself another solicitor.' She had not considered the words; they arrived, simply, and once said, seemed right.

He turned to her. She saw him, for the first time ever, startled. There was a sudden nakedness to his face. Then the nakedness was covered: he had seen what lay ahead. He said, with deliberate care, 'But of course, my dear, if you feel we are not coming up to scratch. You have a perfect right.'

'It's nothing to do with professional things. It's because I am in love with you.'

There was a silence. 'Oh dear, oh dear,' said Giles. He sounded entirely artificial. He looked down at the fish. 'My dear Helen . . .'

'Which is my fault,' said Helen. 'But it makes life difficult.

171

And I have to say that although what I feel is my fault, and my responsibility, you have, up to a point, encouraged me. Or at least you have left me not knowing what to think.'

Giles sighed. 'Then I am to blame. Please let me say, Helen, that I have the very greatest affection and respect for you. Please realise that. I value your friendship enormously, and I'd hoped to continue to do so.'

She watched the fish. Carp, or orfe. They lay at angles to each other, drifting very slowly so that the gold-splintered pattern of the lake changed continuously. She heard what he said and she thought, so that is how it is, and how it is going to be. She felt nothing very much, except the sense of moving inexorably from one moment to the next, and accepting what each brought. She followed the slow gyration of one very large, cream-coloured fish and said, 'But you aren't in love with me, which would make it, I'm afraid, an awkward friendship. Of course, my feelings may change – I'm well aware of that – in which case all this will seem rather silly. I'll probably wish I'd never mentioned the matter, but it seems necessary to me at the moment, so there it is. What isn't very important to you has become important to me – disturbingly important. There is an imbalance, and I feel that I can't allow it to go on. For my own sake, I suppose.'

It was surprising how easily the words came, now that she had allowed them. She did not look at Giles at all as she spoke and the sentences piled one upon another, without restraint, like a flow of thought; there was even a low level of enjoyment in the sense of release.

'Another woman would cope with this differently, I daresay. You have appeared at a time when things are rather . . . odd. For me, I mean. Maybe that's partly why I've reacted like this. I'm conscious of not abiding by rules, in saying all this. You'd much prefer that I didn't.' She caught, out of the corner of her eye, his gesture of disagreement. He started to speak but she interrupted. 'Don't think, though, that I am dishing out blame. The problem is – has been – that what was one thing to you was quite another to me. Probably I misinterpreted, from time to time. Thought you meant things you didn't mean.'

She paused, and Giles leapt in at once. 'I am at fault. The

trouble is . . . my trouble is . . . Oh dear. I'm susceptible, I suppose. Even now I'm finding your honesty charming. Does this really have to end our friendship? Surely not. As you rightly say, your feelings may change. Oh – will change, certainly.' Was there an edge of doubt or complacency to his tone?

'I don't really think,' said Helen, 'that either of us would feel very comfortable after this.'

Giles sighed. 'You're so much nicer than I am, Helen. You make me seem insincere. But I'm not, you know. I'm just . . . well, I meet someone like you with whom I feel instant affinity, to whom I'm instantly attracted and . . . I get carried away, I suppose. It isn't insincerity. It's . . . susceptibility. A weakness, I suppose, but there we are.' He turned on her a rueful expression – rueful but placating, like a boy caught out in a misdemeanour.

She was to be wrong-footed, she saw: made to feel ponderous, portentous. 'I never saw you as insincere. Merely perplexing, at times. At least perplexing to me, but that is probably to do with my own shortcomings. In relationships, that is. That's what I mean by things being different for you than for me.'

She was watching the fish again. And now she caught him in another gesture, but a surreptitious one this time – the quick shooting of a cuff to glance at his watch.

At some other level of consciousness she registered amazement, a flick of anger, and the distant recognition of her own recovery: eventually, she would remember that movement. A pair of collared doves were moaning in the trees overhead; the day was absolutely still – sunless and oppressive.

Giles laid his hand on her arm. 'You know, I have this feeling that too much introspection will get us nowhere. Shall we move? I'm getting rather tired of these fish.'

They walked on into the thickening woodland. Giles still had his hand under her elbow; she stopped to adjust the strap of her sandal as a pretext to shake it off. I can get through all this, she thought, so long as he doesn't touch me. I think I can.

They were following the concrete channel of the serpentine rill, which emptied itself into a pool of stygian blackness. Giles paused to peer into it. 'No fish. Really, this place can be extraordinarily melancholy on occasion. Perhaps I shouldn't have brought you here.'

'I would have said what I have if we'd gone to a fun-fair,' said Helen.

He laughed. 'There! That's what's so engaging about you – but of course you're the one person who can't see that. I hope I am not to be cast absolutely into the outer darkness, Helen – I should find that very wretched.'

I see, she thought, he is to be the one who is rejected; that is how it is to be.

They came out into the open. A little temple presided over a sloping hillside with a prospect of open fields and river lined with reeds and willows. A pair of swans cruised, with cygnets, and swallows were zipping to and fro above the water.

Giles said, 'Something's on fire.'

'Stubble burning.' Helen realised now that the sky was over-cast not by cloud but by hanging palls of smoke. The edges of the landscape fumed. At the far end of the valley, beyond the river and the water-meadows, was a rim of red; they could hear crackling.

'It's a disgrace,' said Giles. 'It's been allowed to get quite out of hand. There should be new legislation.'

They walked on, past a classical arcade, past an Apollo and a sequence of nymphs. Waterlilies swung at the edge of the river; willows rained down. The air was now quite acrid; Helen saw that the sleeve of her shirt was covered with dark specks of ash. Giles was talking of childhood holidays in Devon; hayfields filled with wild flowers, corn-sheaves, butterflies. A vanished country-side. And horse-drawn waggons and smocked farmworkers, I daresay, thought Helen: everything is embroidered by recollec-tion. Even today, no doubt. Eventually.

They reached the car. He drove her back to Greystones, still talking fluently of things that mattered not at all. As he opened the door of the car for her to get out he smiled, a smile that appeared eloquent both of regret and appeal. Then he laid his hand on her shoulder for an instant, got back into the driving-seat, and was gone.

She walked up the path towards the front door. You could

smell burning here, too. The sky above the Britches was sepia-coloured, as though a storm were imminent. She registered all this, opened the front door and knew also, immediately, that there was something alien about the house. She called 'Edward?', and then remembered that he had gone out with the ornithological group. She walked into the kitchen and Phil was sitting at the table.

He got up. His green crest, she saw, was now tinged with brown at the roots. So it did grow out. He looked extremely unhealthy; the anxious eyes of a child peered at her from a white mask. He said 'The front door was locked, so I got through the window at the back. Edward wasn' here either.'

Helen removed her coat and filled the kettle. She felt an unusual surging lust for a cup of tea. 'We weren't expecting you, Phil.'

'I thought I'd come and stay here for a bit. You and Edward don' min', do you? I mean, I thought since it's my house, sort of, it would be all right. But if you don' wan' me I'll go somewhere else. I mean, I don' care one way or the other. Fact is, I'm a bit pissed off at home.' He watched her, tensely; his eyes were those of a five-year-old.

She took two cups and saucers from the dresser and put them on the table; she got the milk from the fridge. 'That's all right. You can stay if you want to. I'll find some sheets presently and you can make up a bed in the spare room. But I do think you should tell your parents. Ask your parents,' she amended.

'That's fine,' said Phil. 'I rung mum. She said it sounds like a good idea, till I get myself together.'

'She did, did she?' said Helen in a different tone. The kettle spurted. She made the tea, poured two cups.

'Thanks,' said Phil.

Helen took a gulp of tea, and felt herself begin to rally. She looked at Phil; he was encased from top to toe in black leather, as always. 'Don't you want to take your jacket off – you must be awfully hot?'

Phil, vaguely, shrugged off the jacket which fell to the floor with a metallic clatter. Beneath it he wore a T-shirt of quite astonishing filthiness.

175

'The thing is, I'm not getting on with Mum and Dad. I mean, we're all pissed off with each other.'

'That can happen.'

'I 'spect,' he continued magnanimously, ''s'partly my fault too.'

'I daresay,' said Helen. After a moment she added, with sudden hope 'What about school? Surely the term starts soon.'

'I can't remember,' said Phil evasively. 'Anyway, that's not important. The thing is to get myself together. I got problems.'

Helen refilled both cups. Phil slurped his with one gulp. He seemed restored; his crest stood perkily again. 'I got to sort myself out, see.'

'Well,' said Helen. 'We've all got problems, but you're welcome to stay here for a bit.'

Phil looked at her over his cup with kindly reproach. He ignored the first part of her statement. 'Thanks, Helen.'

'Actually,' said Louise, 'it's the perfect solution. I don't know why I didn't think of it myself. I mean, you and Edward aren't involved emotionally like we are, and he's not going to get up your nose in the same way and I'll know where he is and that he's all right. It's the obvious arrangement. At least he rang. Though of course you would have done anyway. Not that he was what you'd call forthcoming. A series of grunts, which is mainly what I get these days. There are points when I wonder if he actually hates me, or if he's not yet got beyond the level of contempt and indifference. I look at him – when I can bear to and frankly if you can persuade him to use a clean T-shirt you'll be doing all of us a favour – I look at him and I remember dear little chubby hands clutching one, and the way their faces used to smell of soap and milk. What *happened* to all that? Anyway, at least he rang. Maybe it indicates *some* normal human responses. And I'll know where he is and roughly what he's up to. Though . . . is there a drug scene in the village yet? All *right*, I daresay you don't – but there's no need to snap, I have been pretty well at the end of my tether. You don't know what it's like – wondering what the hell he's up to now and where he's gone and when he'll be back. And the grunts and the glares and the

176

slammed doors and that bloody T-shirt. Do try and get him to eat some decent food. And keep me informed. Unless of course he deigns to ring again himself. You might point out that one has feelings. Anyway . . . So how are things with you?'

'How long for?' said Edward.

It was Helen who made up the spare room bed, in the end. Phil, it appeared, had spent his life under a duvet; the technical problem posed by sheets and blankets defeated him. He dumped himself in the battered armchair and watched her, chatting cosily the while. He seemed to have taken on a new lease of life. 'I like it here. S'a nice house. S'not smart. I don' like smart houses. Actually, that's what I like about you and Edward. You're not smart either. Not like Mum and Dad's friends. They know some shocking people, really shocking.'

'Mmn. Could you pass me that pillow.'

'All right if I put up some posters? S'a bit boring the way it is, this room.'

'I suppose so. I can't think quite what you're going to find to do here, you know, Phil.'

'You don' need to worry about me,' said Phil reassuringly. 'I'll probably be spending quite a lot of time writing poetry.'

'Oh. I see. What sort of poetry do you write?'

'Protest poetry, mos'ly,' said Phil in a business-like tone. 'Edward won' min' if I borrow his typewriter, will he?'

She had given tea to Phil. Had drunk tea herself, telephoned Louise, taken Edward aside and explained, made up the spare room bed. And all through this she did not think of Giles. She did not take those hours out and contemplate them; she simply let them lie somewhere in the head, to surface no doubt at some point of low resistance. The small hours of the morning, conventionally. From time to time that evening she was visited by the sight of the lake with its gold fretwork of fish; she wondered how many years it would be before she could go to that place with equanimity. And, thinking this, she knew that the thought itself was the first, faint, early signal of recovery. It was as though, at the height of a fever, you experienced a fleeting moment of well-being. Eventually, she thought, it will all be over. I shan't care. But before then there is a long way to go. Now, tonight, there is nothing to look forward to, no reason to get up in the morning or move from one day into the next. I have been someone else these last few months; now I have to learn to be myself again.

THIRTEEN

'No thanks,' said Phil. 'I've had something.' It was the following evening; he was declining, with all civility, the cottage pie that was on offer for supper.

'Basically, I jus' eat fish and chips,' he explained. 'There's a van comes to the village at tea-time. I sussed it out yesterday.'

Edward, impressed, said, 'I never knew that. It might be useful.'

'Outside the pub. I'll bring you some tomorrow, if you like.'

Edward glanced guiltily at Helen. 'Well, we'll see . . .'

Helen, pushing her way through the day, had forgotten all about Phil for long periods. He had vanished into the village for a while, then had come back and wandered around the garden and even penetrated the Britches, she noted.

Later, he could be heard clacking away on Edward's old Remington, which he treated with the reverence usually accorded to rare works of art: 'S'a lovely job, this. Dad's only got a stupid Amstrad.'

Edward, after his initial alarm, appeared to be unaffected by Phil's arrival. When he came across him, he looked surprised but not especially put out. Helen, through the encompassing distraction of her own feelings, was aware that he too seemed locked into some private anxiety. She found him gazing out of windows. When the milkman appeared at the back door he swung round in agitation. Helen found him irritating; she felt as raw as an invalid, stepping cautiously from hour to hour in a daze of self-protectiveness. Edward and Phil were impedimenta she would have preferred to be without at this particular time; she would have liked to crawl away somewhere, like an animal, and sit

179

things out. As it was there were meals to be provided, interruptions to be faced. When the phone rang her spine crawled. She said to Edward, 'Could you answer that?' Edward, as though deaf, continued on his way across the hall and up the stairs. Helen picked up the receiver and heard Joyce Babcock's voice with a curdling mixture of relief and disappointment.

Did you really think he was going to ring? said her mother. After that? You've burned your boats now, haven't you? Didn't you realise? You're your own worst enemy, you are, Helen. What's that you're muttering about? Self-respect? Well, if you want to use language like that you're welcome, but a fat lot of good it'll do you.

Another day passed. And another. Helen went to Spaxton, drove unflinchingly past Giles Carnaby's office, attended the library and carried out her duties. Back at Greystones, the kitchen drain flooded and Tam discovered one of Helen's trapped mice and began to eat it before he was noticed. Helen, dealing in succession with both these crises, was surprised to find Phil at her elbow, offering assistance. He rummaged enthusiastically in the drain and then embarked on a brief and vigorous tussle with Tam, from which he emerged triumphant with two-thirds of the mouse. Tam, snarling hideously, slunk out into the garden. Phil disposed of the mouse in the dustbin. 'That's an awful dog. I mean, I don' like dogs anyway but that one's really disgusting.'

'Edward's very fond of him.'

Phil nodded. There was a silence. Helen continued mechanically to prepare the supper (or lunch, was it? or breakfast?) She rather wished Phil would go away but could think of no means of dismissing him and anyway it didn't matter to her all that much. She had been visited by one of those moments of desolation that struck, out of nowhere, at irregular intervals, crippling both thought and action; she peeled a potato, put it in the kettle, stared at it for several seconds and then took it out again.

Phil said, 'Edward's a nice bloke.'

'Yes, I know.'

'He don' go on about things. That's what's wrong with mos'

eople. They're so pretentious. I mean, almos' everybody I know
pretentious. Edward jus' doesn' bother.'

' see what you mean,' said Helen. The desolation was ebbing
le, like a fever, but she didn't feel up to a considered review
o. vard's character.

n' mean *you're* pretentious,' Phil continued solicitously. 'I
mea. ..mos' everybody else *excep'* you. You're pretty much like
Edward.'

'I'm glad to hear it.' It was time, she decided, to wrench the
conversation in a different direction. 'Are you . . . do you feel
you're anywhere nearer . . . getting yourself together? Since
you've been here.'

Phil gave her a look in which injury and dignity combined.
'Takes time, dunnit? I mean, if it's psychological.'

'I suppose so,' said Helen meekly.

Edward was having difficulties with chronology. He slept so
badly that he moved around in a continuous grey fog of weariness. He never knew where he was within the day. Sometimes
he found that he had lost his way within the year also. He would
surface from his churning thoughts and look blankly at the world:
what date was it? What month? He had to turn his eyes to the
window and learn whereabouts he was from the state of the
vegetation beyond: high, straggling growth, leaves tinged with
yellow – early September. He realised that he was probably
unwell in some way, but it did not seem to be a state of ill health
about which anything could be done; you could not go to the
doctor and say that you didn't know what season it was. He
seldom left the house, except to visit the Britches. The previous
week he had been out with the ornithological society; the bird-
watching had been therapeutic but he had found the company
disturbing. It was preferable, on the whole, to be alone. Helen
did not count, really. Phil's arrival had been briefly disconcerting, but he was easily ignored. After a few days Edward ceased
to notice him. He was not noticing much except his own grinding
needs.

*

181

'I thought I'd get a bus to Spaxton,' said Phil. 'Get myself some new tapes. All right with you?'

They were having breakfast. The back door was open on to a golden morning; the garden glowed; the hedge was white-veiled with spiders' webs; a robin sang piercingly from the apple tree.

'S'a nice day,' Phil continued breezily. He embarked on his third piece of toast. Helen glanced at him in surprise; one would not have expected sensitivity to the physical world to come high on Phil's list of responses.

'What's that bird singing, Edward?'

'It's a robin,' said Edward after a moment.

Phil smiled benignly. 'S' nice. Well, I'll push off, then. See you later.'

He rose, and at the same moment they all heard footsteps on the garden path. Edward was drinking tea; he put the cup down with a slight crash. Gary Paget appeared at the door. He simply stood there, as was his custom, awaiting instructions. Helen, with an effort, concentrated her attention on the matter in hand and told him which bit of the vegetable garden he should dig. Gary and Phil looked straight through each other, like dogs whose territories have embarrassingly overlapped. Helen was aware, as she talked, of the violent contrast between them. Gary, two years younger than Phil, appeared to come from another decade – another century, even. Seen together like this, both seemed to be wearing fancy dress. Gary, in his baggy brown cord trousers and open-necked cotton shirt, with his thatch of corn-coloured hair and well-scrubbed face, looked like some Youth Hostelling hiker on a railway poster of the thirties. Phil, in skin-tight black leather glinting with metal chains and zips, his hair shaved to the scalp at either side and rising to a green crest at the top, his eye-sockets perfunctorily daubed with rainbow colours, recalled an operatic demon. They appeared not to see each other at all. Phil said 'Cheers, then,' and departed. Gary stumped away to the vegetable garden.

Helen had decided to redecorate the bathroom; activity was the thing. She brought up a bucket and some sugar soap and set about washing down the walls. Obstructed by the bathroom cabinet, she took it down. Within was a welter of half-empty pill bottles with obscure labels, all of them Dorothy's, and sundry ancient packets of aspirin or indigestion tablets; neither she nor Edward resorted much to medication. The whole thing should be turned out, but could wait. She scrubbed the wall energetically, creating great pale swathes down which trickled rusty water. She thought of nothing at all, lost in this satisfactory redemptive action. When she paused for a moment she could hear through the open window that robin, and the intermittent thwack of Gary's spade.

When she had cleaned a whole wall she ran out of sugar soap and went to search for more. As she rummaged in the scullery cupboard she heard Edward come downstairs with an odd hesitant step. She said 'Edward?' but he did not, apparently, hear. He crossed the hall into the sitting-room; Helen heard him opening the french windows.

Unsuccessful in her search, she went into the kitchen. She looked into the garden; there was no sign of Edward; he, too, must be standing at the window. Gary's spade could be heard now only spasmodically; several times it ceased altogether as he took a lengthy breather. The enthusiasm with which Gary worked depended on how closely he thought himself to be observed.

Edward appeared suddenly on the lawn. He stood there for a moment. Helen expected him to head for the Britches. Instead, he began to walk slowly towards the gap in the hedge that led to the kitchen garden. Helen watched him; she felt a little creep of mistrust. Why?

Edward vanished through the gap. The spade sounds were resumed and then ceased. There was silence. A long silence, it seemed, overlaid by blackbird song, shrill and metallic. And then Gary came through the gap, empty-handed, walking fast, putting on his anorak as he went. Helen froze. It was ten to eleven; Gary should not be leaving until twelve. She heard the click as he closed the garden gate and then the whirr of his bicycle. And then Edward walked slowly through the gap and across the lawn towards the house.

She met him in the hall. She said, 'Why has Gary gone?'

He stared at her. 'I don't know.'

Her heart was thumping, she noticed. Bang bang. Bang wallop. 'You'll have to tell me, Edward. What happened?'

And his face contorted. He turned away. He muttered something. She couldn't hear.

She pulled him into the kitchen, pushed him into a chair. He sat there at the table with his head in his hands. She sat down opposite. And saw that he was crying. Trying not to cry. She thought: I cannot endure this. I have borne a good deal in my time, but this is beyond all of it. O God, what sort of swine are you?

'Please tell me. It's better if you do.'

'I touched him,' said Edward.

There was a long silence.

'Just that?'

He nodded.

Helen got up. She put the kettle on, waited for it to boil, made tea, poured it for them both. Then she sat down again. All this while Edward remained silent. Tam wandered into the room, pushed his food bowl around noisily and then leaned against Edward's leg in sycophantic appeal. Edward put a hand on his head.

'What will happen?' said Edward at last.

'I don't know. I should think Gary may tell his horrible dad.'

She saw Edward flinch.

'Don't answer the phone,' said Helen. 'Don't go down to the village for a day or two. I'll deal with Ron Paget, if it's necessary.'

Edward raised his head. 'No. I did this, not you.'

'Yes. But you must let me, all the same. I'm better at Ron Paget than you are. And it may not come to that. Nothing may happen at all. More importantly . . .' She stopped.

Edward looked directly at her. 'More importantly what?' His voice was bleak.

More importantly, what is to be done about you? Now and forever. How are you to be got through whatever it is that is going on within?

'I've always known, you know.'

'Yes,' said Edward. 'I realised you did.'

They sat in silence, not looking at one another. Helen thought of Gary Paget, and winced. Edward, as though she had spoken aloud, suddenly put his head in his hands and groaned. 'Oh God, that boy . . .'

Helen reached for the teapot. She refilled both their cups. 'There's nothing you can do about him. And I doubt if he's been done any irreparable harm, if what you say happened is what did happen.'

'It is,' said Edward dully. 'That was all.'

'Then Gary will recover, I daresay.'

But you may not, she thought. And I cannot help. She would have liked to walk round the table and put her arms about him, and knew that this would not do. Edward shrank from physical contact. Even Louise had learned, long ago, to keep her hands off him.

The hall clock thrummed, and then struck eleven. The last note came out as a strangled clunk, owing to some fault in the mechanism; it had been like that for ten years now. Helen, awaiting the sound with maddened fatalism, thought suddenly that it symbolised everything that was wrong at Greystones. She determined, wildly and too late, to get something done about the wretched thing. From outside came the sound of a passing car and children shouting. And out there, she thought, are thousands – hundreds of thousands – of people like Edward who live in perfect tranquillity with their natures, at least in so far as any of us do. Who are neither guilty nor lonely, or no more than the rest of us. It is not fair. It is deeply and profoundly unfair. Why Edward? Why harmless Edward, when people like Ron Paget walk the earth unscathed? Ron Paget, and muggers and rapists and child batterers and swindlers and drug pedlars and corrupt politicians. Villains are going their way unhindered the world over, and the axe has to fall on Edward.

The phone rang. Both Glovers froze. Edward looked at Helen; his face was a pasty grey colour. He rose. 'No,' she said. She went out into the hall and lifted the receiver.

'What on earth are you doing?' said Louise. 'I was just going to give up. Is he all right?'

'All right? Who?'

'Phil, for heaven's sake. I don't want to talk to him, I'm not

185

geared up for that yet. I just want to know he's O.K. Helen? Are you still there?'

'Yes, I'm here. Phil seems fine. He's gone to Spaxton.'

'Spaxton?' cried Louise suspiciously. 'Whatever for?'

'He wanted to buy something. Tapes.'

'Oh. Well, let me know when he's back, will you. Are you sure there's nothing wrong? You sound funny.'

Edward came out of the kitchen. Helen put her hand over the mouthpiece and said, 'It's Louise.' Edward looked at her without expression. Then he walked over to the front door and opened it. Helen said 'Where are you going?' Edward hesitated: 'I don't know.'

Louise was quacking inaudibly. 'I've got to go,' Helen said to her. She put the receiver down. 'Don't go out, Edward. Not just for the moment.' As soon as she had spoken she regretted it; of course Edward had to go out – now or tomorrow or sometime. She waited for her mother to say 'He's made his bed and he's got to lie on it,' or words to that effect. But Dorothy was curiously absent today.

'I don't mean don't go out,' she amended. 'I mean if you see Ron Paget just don't get involved.'

Edward stood for a moment, irresolute. He said nothing and seemed barely aware of her. Then he turned and headed up the stairs. She heard the door of his room close. Tam also went up, and sat outside, whining. The door did not open.

'I bought something for you,' said Phil. 'It's a present.' He stood by the kitchen sink, grinning complacently. On the draining-board stood a chrysanthemum in a pot, partially shrouded in a tube of white paper. 'S'a flower,' Phil explained. He delved in the pocket of his jacket and produced a small box of Cadbury's Dairy Milk chocolates: 'That's for Edward.'

Helen felt, for a few seconds, dangerously close to tears. She swallowed, blinked, and said 'Thanks very much, Phil. That's very nice of you. Edward will like those.'

Phil continued to smirk. He gave the chrysanthemum a proprietorial prod: 'You got to give it water sometimes, she said.'

'Yes. I won't forget. By the way, I think you should give Louise a ring. She called this morning, wondering how you were.'

'Will do,' said Phil dismissively. He sat down. 'Where's Edward? Isn' it time for supper?'

'I'm afraid it's just soup and cheese tonight. I haven't got round to cooking anything. Perhaps you'd like to go up and tell Edward. He's in his room.'

'Will do.'

After a minute Phil came clumping down the stairs again. 'He says he don' wan' anything to eat. He's got a bit of a headache. I gave him the chocolates. I should think he'd eat those.' Wearing a benign expression, Phil picked up a spoon and began to slurp tinned tomato soup with relish. 'S' good, this. You had a nice day, Helen?'

She murmured something noncommittal. Phil continued to radiate well-being. 'I been lookin' round Spaxton. S'a funny little place, innit? I mean, it's got really stupid shops and there's nowhere you could hang out with your friends, but you can't help quite liking it. But I should think people would get pissed off if they got to live there.'

Helen said, with an effort, 'Actually it's rather sought after. People retire to it, or commute to London from it.'

'I mean people like me,' said Phil kindly. 'All right if I have some more soup, Helen? Anyway, I seen Spaxton now so I don' need to go there again. There's mos'ly rubbish there but I got myself some tapes. So tomorrow I won' be busy an' I thought I'd help you here. Do things for you.' He beamed graciously.

'Oh,' said Helen, startled into response. 'I don't know really that . . . I mean, I can't think of anything that needs doing.'

Phil looked hurt. 'Mum's always on at me about doing things for her. Never stops. It's a real pain. That's one of the reasons I got pissed off and come here. But you an' Edward don' go on at people. You're not bothered. Anyway, it's partly my house, innit, so I ought to do things, right? I could paint this room,' he continued with enthusiasm. 'I like painting. An' it's a bit of a mess, innit?'

'Well,' Helen replied hastily, 'I'm not sure . . . We'd have to think about that. I'd need to talk to Edward. Maybe . . . Perhaps you could cut the lawn. I was thinking the other day that it badly needs doing. The old mower's in the garden shed.'

'O.K.' said Phil. 'Will do. All right if I watch the telly now?'

Helen nodded. She began to wash the dishes. From the sitting room came the sound of the television, tuned to some unfamiliar programme; periodically it would burst into staccato cracklings and she would hear Phil clout the side of the set, wise now to local practice. Edward remained in his room.

That night, both Helen and Edward lay sleepless through long hours. Helen, noting that anxiety had either alleviated or blunted her other distress, decided that accumulated trouble must be a perverse form of mercy. The thought of Giles Carnaby was still painful, but it had receded to a dull undefined ache somewhere behind and beyond the sharp drill of worry. Her mind flitted between Gary Paget (compunction), his father (uneasy speculation) and Edward (raw chafing pity). The entire soup of emotion served to give her a grinding headache and a sick stomach. Once or twice she got up, took aspirin, drank water or visited the bathroom. The night passed, measured out by the hall clock. Eventually, towards dawn, she fell into a stormy sleep, passing from unquiet but rational thought into the frenzied illogical landscape of dreams. Her mother featured, restored to youth and vigour, and Giles, who walked arm in arm along a river bank with a strange woman, and passed her without acknowledgement, and Edward, who had turned into a dog, and howled.

Edward lay flat on his back and stared at the ceiling. He made no attempt to sleep, knowing it to be probably fruitless. He too thought of Gary Paget, with horror and something far beyond compunction. He thought of Gary's father not at all; formal retribution, at this point, was the least of it. He forced himself to go over what had happened, or what he thought had happened. The whole episode seemed now quite unreal; he doubted the testimony of his own memory, which made it all the more nightmarish. He could remember sitting up here, in his room, tense and restless; hearing the sound of the boy's spade from beyond the yew hedge. He remembered getting up, going downstairs, standing for a while at the sitting-room window. There was some idea in his head, he knew, of going out there to talk to Gary, simply talk, he had barely ever exchanged more than two words with him. He had this compulsion to look at him, to stand there in sunshine and watch him digging. He remembered opening the french windows, walking across the lawn. Then, somehow, he was beside Gary. Had he spoken? Gary had turned towards him – there had been an expression of surprise on his face. And that whiff of Lifebuoy soap, and the swell of his brown arms below his rolled-up shirt sleeves. But then what had happened? Edward had wanted to touch him, that he knew. He had wanted, overwhelmingly, to lay his hand on that blooming flesh, to feel its warmth, to make contact. The boy, indeed, had at that moment ceased to be himself at all – to be Gary Paget – but had become universal, anonymous and accessible. Edward had been filled with tumultuous thoughts and feelings, topped by an overwhelming need. And affection, there had been that also – a compulsive, joyous affection. He had seen Gary as someone else, as everyone: as a specific person known and lost, as a person unknown and of wondrous promise. He had reached out and his hand arrived not on Gary's arm but at his crotch.

If anything had been said, Edward could not now remember. He had a vague impression that he might have spoken. The next distinct memory was of Gary's disappearing back, his anorak hooked over his shoulder. And then, of standing there alone beside Gary's spade, which lay where he had dropped it. Going back at last into the house. Being with Helen in the kitchen. By which time that suspended moment of madness and of hope had passed, and he was hitched once more to the remorseless world in which everything is related to everything else, in which actions beget consequences, in which we are all answerable for what we have done, but some of us are called upon to answer more fully than others.

*

When Helen woke the clock was striking nine and rain battered the windows. From the back door came muffled staccato barks; Edward must have let Tam out and failed to let him in again, cavalier treatment so unusual that Helen was instantly wide awake and apprehensive. She washed and dressed hastily, admitted the soaking and indignant dog, and went up to knock on Edward's door. 'Don't you want any breakfast?' Edward replied that he would be down presently; partially reassured, Helen returned to the kitchen where Phil appeared, yawning. 'Stupid rain. I can't cut the grass.'

'Phil,' said Helen sternly, 'did you telephone Louise yesterday?'

Phil, looking evasive, began to slice bread. 'Do you an' Edward wan' toast, Helen?'

'Then you must today. She's worried about you. And you've really got to think things out, you know – how much longer you're going to stay here.'

'If you don' wan' me I'll go,' said Phil in an aggrieved tone.

'It's not that we don't want you. But your school term either has started or is about to start, your mother is concerned, and frankly you wouldn't be at all happy living here indefinitely.'

Phil, sidestepping neatly, said in conversational tones, 'I s'pose Edward'll be going back to work soon. I should think he's a really good teacher. Not like ours. There's some horrible blokes at our school.'

Helen was silent; she had forgotten until that moment about Croxford House. Yes, Edward would be going back next week, presumably. A further complication. Or perhaps a blessing.

Phil, through a mouthful of toast, said indistinctly and in an offhand tone, 'What did mum want, then?' Helen looked across the table at him and his eyes met hers. To her amazement, her mother looked at her for an instant out of Phil's face: a curve of the nostril, something about the set of the mouth. Then it was gone: Phil was not really like his grandmother at all – he resembled his father, had his hair, his build. But even so . . . Well, thought Helen, well, well; genes, hurtling through body after body, willy-nilly, set on a course of their own.

'She just wanted to know how you are. Naturally. She's your

190

mother. Mothers – most mothers – are like that. And she's missing you.' This piece of poetic license was not only justified but expedient, Helen decided.

Phil stared at her. The five-year-old peeked again out of his eyes. 'You think so?'

'I do,' said Helen firmly.

Phil took another slice of toast and appeared to reflect. After a few moments he remarked that he would give Louise a buzz this evening.

The rain continued to fall. Phil vanished to his room, from which came the muffled rhythmic thump that passed for music. Edward also remained upstairs. Helen sat for a while in the kitchen and watched the rain. It drove across the garden in white curtains. If it had rained yesterday Gary Paget would not have come; what happened would not have happened. Thus does the world dispose. Except, Helen thought, that it would probably have happened at some other point, or differently and maybe worse – it was part of a programme whose flexibility is maverick and unpredictable. She thought again of genes, simmering away in the body like invisible volcanoes, harbouring intelligence and irascibility and shape of nose and the tendency to particular diseases.

It will pass. It may pass without further ado. Leaving damage but not destruction. She wandered into the sitting room where rain still lashed the windows. The dark mass of the Britches heaved and shuddered. From time to time rooks were shaken from it and rowed desperately across the slate-grey stormy sky. Helen returned to the kitchen, made a fresh pot of tea and some more toast and put them on a tray which she carried up to Edward's room.

'I've brought you some breakfast.'

He opened the door. He was dressed but unshaven. 'I'm not ill.'

'I know you're not ill.'

'I'm just not hungry.'

Helen marched into the room and put the tray down on the table. 'I daresay you're not. Neither was I. But it helps to keep up the blood sugar level. I read it in a magazine.'

'It's just that I dislike myself so much,' said Edward in a blank tone.

'Then you shouldn't. Nobody else does. You're about the least dislikeable person I know.'

Edward shrugged. He seemed about to say something else, and then sat down.

'Thanks, anyway. I'll have some tea.'

Helen stood for a moment at the door. 'Look . . . things have to go on. It's the only way. This isn't the end of the world. It seems appalling to you – to us – because of the way we live. Have lived. If you'd lived differently . . . What I mean to say is that most people who – feel like you – live perfectly ordinary happy lives.' She stopped, floundering. Better shut up than utter such banalities.

'I'm glad to hear it,' said Edward. 'Nice for them.'

'I mean that you don't have to feel all this guilt, Edward. All that happened is that you touched . . .'

'Please go away,' said Edward, in tones of the utmost courtesy.

She returned to the kitchen and washed up, violently. As she did so she saw that the leaden clouds had split and were tipping away; crevasses of pale blue appeared, infused here and there with the suggestion of sunlight. The rain stopped; the garden began to glitter; a blackbird patrolled the grass, head cocked. She could hear Ron Paget's yard, which had been silent, start into life: the chainsaw, a lorry revving up. Tam whined to go out; he chased away the blackbird and completed a bossily investigative circuit of the garden. Helen felt a flicker of the spirit, a momentary reviving uplift. We just have to get through all this, she thought. Time has to pass, for both of us. The world must turn.

Phil appeared. 'It's not raining now. Where d'you say that mower was?'

'In the shed. But I should wait till after lunch – you can't do it when the grass is still sopping wet.'

They had eaten together, the three of them – Helen and Edward perfunctorily, Phil with zest. Then Phil had bustled off to the garden shed, had returned demanding an oil can, disappeared again. Edward had said, with an effort, 'Sorry. It's just that I . . .' 'Forget it,' Helen said. 'It doesn't matter. You know, Phil grows on one in the most unexpected way. But I am beginning to wonder how much longer he intends to stay here.' Edward nodded uncomprehendingly, back in his private prison; he went upstairs again.

Three minutes later Helen heard a step on the garden path. She stiffened. Not Phil – Phil could be seen on the lawn, wrestling with the old hand mower.

There was a knock at the door. She stood for a few seconds, gathering herself, then opened it. Ron Paget. Of course. He was wearing a suit, she saw at once, not the usual jeans and anorak; this seemed, as no doubt it was intended to be, indefinably threatening.

'I'd like to come in for a few minutes, Miss Glover. I think you'll know what I'm here about.'

She held the door open for him, closed it.

'You're on your own. I'm glad of that. I wouldn't like to answer for myself if I were face to face with your brother just at the moment. You do know what I'm talking about, Miss Glover?'

'I know that something happened with Gary yesterday,' said Helen. 'And I know too that whatever it was my brother is deeply distressed and sorry.'

Ron drew in his breath sharply. Then he shook his head. 'Oh dearie, dearie me. That won't do. That won't do at all. This is a bad business. Being sorry isn't going to do, is it, Miss Glover?'

So this is how it is to be, she thought: extract the last ounce of blood. 'Mr Paget, my brother would make no excuses, and neither would I, all I can say is . . .'

Ron pulled out a chair and sat down. 'You know what your brother did, Miss Glover. He groped him. Not to put too fine a point on it. Know what I mean? Made a grab at his goolies.' He watched her. 'No point in being mealy-mouthed, is there? We're both grown-up people.'

'Yes,' said Helen. 'I gathered that was what had happened.'

'The lad's fourteen. Your brother's illegal, apart from anything else. I could go to the police.'

'You could indeed. And if that's what you want to do then I have no doubt that you will.'

Ron spread his hands. 'Now look – have I said that's what I want to do? We've been neighbours for a long time, haven't we? I'm as upset about this as you are. But I've got my boy to think of.'

'Nothing like this will happen again, that's out of the question,' she said. Unwisely.

He pounced. 'It's not what might happen, is it? It's what's already happened. But I'm going to look at things reasonably, Miss Glover. I want to behave in a neighbourly way. Right? Do you a good turn – you and your brother. And you may well feel you want to show you're a bit grateful.'

There was a short silence. 'I'm not sure that I understand,' Helen said.

'You might want to do a bit of business over that waste ground of yours.'

'Let me get this straight,' she said slowly. 'Are you saying that if we sell you the Britches you won't go to the police about Edward?'

Ron's expression was that of a man being offered suspect goods. 'You're tying things up, Miss Glover. Nothing's ever that cut and dried. I'm saying that we can help each other out. I don't want to see your brother dragged through the courts any more than you do.'

Helen stared at him for a few moments in incredulity. Of course. One should have thought of it oneself. It even inspired a perverse kind of awe. Eventually, she could speak. 'What my brother did was wrong. Whatever it was he did. Gary is not much more than a child and it is wrong to make sexual overtures to children. But what you are doing is wrong also. Quite differently wrong. You are attempting blackmail. How do you justify that?'

'Oh come on, Miss Glover,' said Ron. 'That's strong language, that is. What I'm suggesting is an arrangement between ourselves, for mutual convenience.'

'That is not how I see it,' she replied coldly.

'I mean, if I was to do the right thing, I'd be reporting your brother to the police straight off. But I've got some sympathy for the both of you. I'm prepared to . . . well, to turn a blind eye. I'll take your word for it there'll be no more. I have to think of the boy, right? I'll do you a favour and you do me one.'

'Paternal concern seems to be being overridden now by other considerations,' she retorted. 'I find myself getting quite interested in this. I wonder who is to decide the price for which we sell you the wood. I imagine it will be you?'

Ron eyed her. Unpleasantly. Gone now was the look of pained indignation. He rose. 'I'm sorry you're taking this line, Miss Glover. You're making a big mistake. I don't see how I've any choice left but to . . .'

'You'll have to act according to your principles, won't you?' snapped Helen. 'As indeed we all do. And now please go.'

Ron walked to the door. He turned, looked full at her and shook his head. The expression of regret and moral outrage had been recovered. 'It's up to you, Miss Glover. And your brother. I'd talk it over with him if I was you.' He went. She heard him go down the path. From the lawn came the sound of the mower; Phil's cockatoo crest could be seen, bobbing up and down above the shrubbery as he heaved the machine through the long grass. And now Edward was coming down the stairs. She turned to face him.

'That was Ron Paget, wasn't it? I've just seen him out of the window. Why didn't you tell me he was here, Helen?'

'There was no point.'

'What happened was my fault, not yours. Why should you have to see him? You should have called me.'

'There was no point,' she repeated.

'What did he say?'

'Oh . . .' She turned away. 'He was being offensive. What you'd expect. I said you were distressed and . . . sorry.' She could not look at him.

'What else did he say?'

'Nothing much else.'

'What else, Helen?'

'All right,' she said. 'I suppose you've got to know. He threatened to go to the police. And he tried to blackmail us. If we sell him the Britches he'll . . . do nothing. I said he'll have to . . . do whatever he intends to do.'

Edward stood there. 'Yes. I do have to know.'

Phil appeared at the window. 'S'a stupid thing, this. It don' work properly. You can't do a good job with it. Why don' we get a real one, with an engine?'

FOURTEEN

So now we simply sit and wait, Helen thought. The whole process will now begin, in its own time. There is nothing to be done, no decision to be made, no course of action to adopt – which is a curious sort of relief. It will happen; the worst part will be not knowing in exactly what way, or how quickly. Or what, precisely, the outcome will be. Will Edward lose his job? That is a possibility that has to be faced. If he does, it will not be easy to get another teaching position, and if he does not teach what else is he to do? Fifty-year-olds are not readily employable. There will be sympathy – and those inclined to sympathy may well include that scatty headmistress and her board of governors. They may decide to close ranks. But there will also be condemnation, now and for ever. There will be the averted eyes, the muttering. Down in these parts, there is neither the anonymity nor the tolerance of metropolitan life. Edward is visible, and will be watched with interest, and judged.

'He rang,' said Louise. 'As no doubt you've gathered. I could hardly believe my ears. "That you, Mum? How's things, then?" First civil word I've had in months. What on earth have you been doing to him? We *talked*. We actually talked for about five minutes. It could be called a chat. We chatted. This is communication, I kept saying to myself. Real, person to person stuff. Nothing much was said, mind. All strictly neutral. I didn't dare raise the question of coming home. Or school. One step at a time, I thought. I felt quite weepy afterwards, I don't mind telling you. And furious, as well. The way they can do what they damn well like with you. Because all the cards are stacked their way. Parents haven't a hope. Well, they'll find out. Their turn will come. Though frankly the notion of Phil as . . . But it's all in the scheme of things. Even Phil, I daresay. Breed, and be damned. Well, no, not damned but deprived of free will. Watch yourself join the animals. Except that of course for them there's an end to it. Get the offspring fledged or self-supporting and then they're shot of them. Ready to start all over again. The extra bonus for the human race is that it's for ever. That's the price of intelligence. Intelligence *plus* instinct is a wicked refinement. You're nailed. Hooked. Strung up and crucified. Not a thing you can do about it. Reason suggests one thing, and the body rages for another. Reason, frankly, told me not to get involved in the first place. And then the day I realised I was pregnant I was on cloud nine. And now listen to me. No, on second thoughts, don't. I'm hours late for the office already. Anyway, he *rang*. We'll talk again soon, Helen. Everything O.K. with you? I must fly.'

We wait. It is just possible, of course, that nothing will happen. That Ron Paget will decide that the whole thing is too much trouble, or that the glare of publicity might be distressing for Gary, or that he might be stricken with charitable feelings. It is possible, but unlikely, I'm afraid.

She continued with her work on the bathroom. It did not occupy the mind, but it passed the time. She finished washing the walls, moved the medicine cabinet, its contents, and all other small items out on to a table on the landing, and prepared the room for painting. There was a tin of emulsion in the cloakroom which would do – left over from some distant and abandoned project. She fended off Phil's enthusiastic offers of help. Edward emerged from his room, glanced vacantly at her and walked past. She said, 'We'll have to use the cloakroom for general purposes till I'm finished.' He nodded. She saw that he was quite unreachable, and flinched. She had known him like this before: that time long ago, and in the weeks after he left that school in the north. She heard him go downstairs, wander from room to room, and come up again. She said, 'Were you looking for something?' He shook his head, and went back into his room. She had no idea what he might be doing in there; the silence was absolute.

Half way through the afternoon she realised that she needed white spirit with which to clean paint brushes. The village shop would probably have some. She disliked the prospect of going out, and fought it. I cannot skulk in the house for ever, she told herself. Do it now and get it over with. She put on a sweater, picked up her purse and walked out of the front door into the sunshine. A van passed, driven by one of Ron Paget's men, who lifted a hand in greeting. Helen waved back. She made her way to the shop, bought white spirit, exchanged comments on the weather with two people, smiled at three more. Ten minutes later she was back in the house. Now Edward has to do it too, she thought. Going upstairs again she saw that the door of his room was open; he was not there. She went down again.

Phil appeared. 'I been looking for you. We got a spanner anywhere? I found this old bike in the shed. I thought I might use it, but the seat's all funny.'

'Where's Edward?'

'I think he went into the wood.'

'Oh,' said Helen, relieved. 'There might be a spanner in the kitchen drawer. Or in that box in the scullery.' She went back up to the bathroom.

Phil put his head round the door. 'I can't find it, Helen.'

'Edward may have moved it. I seem to remember he was using it the other day. I should go and ask him.'

'O.K. Will do.'

She selected the largest brush, loaded it with paint, climbed on a chair and set to work on the area above the window. Re-charging the brush, she saw Phil cross the lawn and plunge into the Britches. She swept the brush up and down, creating a glossy silken surface; there was a bland and mindless satisfaction about the activity. I should do more of this sort of thing, she thought.

Outside, a blackbird repeated a snatch of song, then improved it with a final flourish. A wood-pigeon climbed from the Britches and tumbled, clapping its wings – once, twice. Helen got down from the stool to stir the paint. She watched the pigeon. Why do they do that? Edward would know.

There was movement, suddenly, on the track into the wood. Phil came bursting out of the shrubbery. Not just Phil – Edward also. But Phil was supporting Edward, dragging him – Edward's arm was hooked about Phil's neck, his feet weaving around in some sort of stumbling dance.

She dropped the brush, ran down the stairs. She met them half way across the lawn.

'Can you get round his other side . . .' Phil panted. 'I keep dropping him.'

They heaved Edward through the french windows and into the sitting room and lowered him into a chair. His head lolled. Helen said, 'Has he hurt himself? What . . .?'

'He's eaten something.' Phil reached into the pocket of his jacket; Helen recognised pill-bottles from the pile she had dumped on the table outside the bathroom. 'We got to make him sick.'

They hauled Edward to his feet again and got him across the hall and into the cloakroom. 'You got to put your fingers down his throat,' said Phil in anguish. 'I dunno how. You do it.'

They propped Edward over the basin. She reached into his mouth. 'I'm sorry,' she told him. 'I've got to do this.'

He retched. A trickle of vomit appeared. She reached again. Edward heaved and was copiously sick. 'That's better,' said Phil. He kept patting Edward's shoulders. 'Poor ol' Edward.'

She went on, brutally. He kept slipping from their grasp, so that they had to prop him up again. At last she said, 'I think that's all.' They dragged him back into the sitting room and lowered him into a chair again. He seemed dopey to the point of oblivion. Phil straightened and looked at her. He said, 'Edward's tried to kill himself, hasn' he?'

'Yes, I suppose so. I think he'll be all right, though. In a minute I'm going to ring the doctor and find out what we should do next.' She felt dizzy. She sat down.

'Thank goodness I went to look for him then.'

'Yes, thank goodness.'

Edward groaned. Helen went out into the hall and dialled the number of the surgery. Phil followed her. She talked to the doctor, put the receiver down. 'An ambulance will come. He'll have to go into hospital overnight. Where are those bottles? They'll need to see them.' She put the pill-bottles in her bag. 'I'll go with him . . . No, I'll follow in the car so I can get back. You stay here, Phil.'

'But what's the *matter* with him?' he said. His eyes were enormous, horror-struck. He was almost as white as Edward. 'I mean, it's awful when someone's so miserable they want to kill themselves. I didn' know. Did you know, Helen?'

She gathered herself. 'Yes. That is – I knew he was unhappy. I didn't think he was going to do this.'

'But what's *wrong* with him?'

She took a breath. 'Edward is homosexual. He – made advances to Gary Paget. Gary's father came round here yesterday. He is probably going to the police.' She started back to the sitting room.

'But that's awful!' cried Phil. He trotted behind her. 'I mean, Edward can't help it if . . .'

'I know. Let's not talk about it now. The doctor says Edward must be made to walk up and down. He mustn't go to sleep.'

Phil nodded. They got Edward up again and slung him between them. They trundled him up and down. Look, Helen said to her mother: your son, your grandson. Now what have you got to say? But Dorothy was nowhere, today; nowhere at all.

When, two hours later, she let herself into the house again Phil was waiting in the hall. 'How's Edward?'

'He's all right. They pumped his stomach out, to be on the safe side. He can come home tomorrow.' Tam was greeting her with exaggerated enthusiasm, drowning what she said in a volley of barks. 'Shut *up*, Tam.' She had to repeat herself before Phil could hear. 'I must have some tea.' She headed for the kitchen.

Phil stumbled behind. 'D'you know what that dog was doing, when I found Edward in the wood? It was just sat there chewing something it had dug up. An' Edward might of been dying.'

'Well, he isn't, thank heaven.' She felt drained, wrung out. She didn't want to revisit the previous hours, not yet. She wanted tea; rest. She put the kettle on.

'I mean, what I can't understand is why he's so pissed off about being gay. I been thinking. I mean, so what? S'matter of fact if you ask me as many people's gay today as aren't. Actually when I was younger I thought I was probably gay. In the end it's turned out I'm not, but there you are. You see what I mean? It's no big deal, being gay.'

'Edward didn't try to commit suicide because he's gay. He did it because he's unhappy.'

'But he's unhappy because he's gay,' said Phil sagely. 'Right?'

'Up to a point,' said Helen, after a moment. 'It's also because he's the sort of person he is. And you have to remember that Edward grew up at a time when . . . when homosexuality was illegal. Quite apart from being socially unacceptable – at least in the circles we moved in.'

'That's ridiculous. You can't help it if you're gay.'

'Reasonable people have always thought that.'

'Exactly. Poor ol' Edward. S'a shame. An' Gary's a right berk. Why didn' he jus' tell Edward to sod off? He didn' have to go running to his dad. He should've jus' told him to push off, he wasn' interested. I mean, that sort of thing happens all the time, doesn' it? It isn' anything to get in a sweat about.'

The kettle was boiling. Helen got up and made the tea while Phil babbled on about the prevailing sexual climate. This isn't happening, she thought; surely I'll wake up soon. It's some nightmare. Soon I'll come to and I'll be upstairs in bed, not down here in the kitchen, and none of it will have happened. Edward will be out in the Britches, attacking nettles or whatever it is he does there. Phil will be at home in North London, doing whatever it is *he* does.

'You feeling all right, Helen?'

She opened her eyes. 'Yes. I'm a bit exhausted, that's all. Perhaps you could give us both some tea.'

'Sure. Will do.'

'You've been a great help, Phil. Thank you.'

He presented her with a cup of tea, most of which was slopped into the saucer. He was beaming graciously. 'No sweat, Helen.' He sat down. 'You know what? Edward ought to go to a therapist. You got therapists down here?'

Helen took a long drink of tea. 'What would a therapist do?' she enquired. 'Show him how to be happy?'

'What a therapist does,' explained Phil, 'is help you come to terms with yourself, see.'

'Ah,' said Helen. They sat in silence. Tam pushed his food bowl around the floor, ostentatiously demonstrating its emptiness. Phil shoved him with a booted foot. Tam withdrew to the door and sat there with his ears back, twitching. Helen thought of Edward, ten miles away: doing what? Feeling how?

Sunlight flowed through the slats of a blind and made a rectangular golden stain on the wall beside his bed. The rim of this stain dissolved into a blur of rainbow colour. He tried to remember the principle of the refraction of light, failed, and saw that some small winged insect was making its way slowly across the rainbow. It turned from red to blue and yellow as it moved; he could see lacy wings and the quivering of antennae. Then it arrived on the unlit part of the wall and became an undefined grey blob.

There was a curtain round the bed. He could hear the clack of shoes on linoleum floors, voices, the rumble of a trolley. The sounds were loud and individual; they rang in his head. In the same way light was very bright, shape and texture were distinct and interesting; he stared at the shadow cast by a fold of the sheet, at the glinting silver surface of a tray on the bedside table. There was a glass of water. The water itself contained light – circles and streaks of light – and the enlarged distorted brilliantly blue image of a pen lying beside the glass.

It had been like that all along: the exaggerated, insistent sense of the physical world. And he had known, also, that he was clinging to it, clutching with his finger tips: that he had been wrong, wrong. He heard a blackbird, and the clapping of pigeon wings, and then Helen's voice, and Phil's. He felt himself moving, being moved. He felt himself vomit. He tried to say

203

something, and could not. He wanted to sleep, and fought to continue hearing and feeling. He saw light and movement.

He had begun to slide into that fog so quickly. He had crammed the pills into his mouth – two of the bottles were almost empty so he had shaken everything out, frantically, chewing and swallowing as fast as he could. And then he had sat there, watching Tam digging under a bush. And the fog had closed in. But through it had come the blackbird, that pigeon.

The curtain parted. A nurse stood there. She smiled. She spoke. Edward turned his head. He said, at last, 'What time is it?'

'I could come now,' cried Louise. 'I want to come. I can get in the car and be there by midnight. I want to talk. How can this have *happened* . . .? *Edward* . . . And I'm going to strangle that man Paget. I'm going round there to strangle him with my bare hands. You what? Going to *bed* . . . I don't know how you can go to bed, frankly. I doubt if I shall. I mean, how can none of us have realised that he might . . .? How can we have been so bloody ignorant? Yes, of course one always had the odd twinge . . . the way he would shut himself up inside himself, you know what I mean? You couldn't ever *talk* to him about it. And after the *débâcle* with that school one realised how vulnerable he was. But this I never imagined. You know what I want? I want to get him up here to see a marvellous man I know about who does a new sort of . . . Well, there's no need to be quite so dismissive. You always condemn things you don't know anything about. Oh, I'm *sorry*. God, what's the matter with me? It shows what a state I'm in. *Can't* I come now? All right, then – tomorrow. And go to bed and sleep, you need it.'

Edward is coming home today, she thought. Who might not have been. I might be waking into an entirely different day. It is not a good day, it is dangerous and difficult but it might have been something quite other. It feels in some curious way like a beginning, not an end. All is not right with the world, not by any means, but nevertheless I have this interesting sense of a future. A sense that things can be done: by me, by Edward.

And her mother, she noted, remained absent. Dorothy had nothing to say about all this; she was elsewhere, on another plane of time and experience, going about her business. With a jolt, Helen realised that she could not conjure up her face. She could no longer see her, or hear her.

He sat beside her. She found herself driving with exaggerated care. She said, 'Louise is coming this afternoon.'

'Why?'

'Oh, Edward . . . Why do you think?'

'I'd rather there wasn't any fuss,' he said after a minute.

'There isn't. There won't be. She wants to see you, that's all. See us.'

He made no further comment. She saw him looking intently out of the window, as though they were passing through new and intriguing landscapes. And Edward, for his part, saw not the familiar reaches of the road from Spaxton to their home but strange and arresting conjunctions of tree and skyline, of field and hedge. He saw the pale rim of the horizon, grey clouds tipped with lilac, the golden flare of stubble, rich brown plough sweeping up to the dark cushion of a wood. He feasted. His mind was blank; he seemed to be the passive vehicle for a pair of devouring eyes.

The phone was ringing as they came into the house. She saw the look in Edward's eyes. 'I'll answer it. If it's anyone for you they can leave a message.' Edward went into the sitting room.

She picked up the receiver. 'Hello?'

'Helen?' said Giles Carnaby. There was a pause; I knew this, she thought, I knew it before I answered.

'You sound a little . . . distracted. I hope I haven't picked a bad moment.'

'No,' she said. No more than any other.

'Ah. Then I'll be brave and plunge. I wondered if we could

meet. I ask with great diffidence. But it would make me very happy if you'd say yes.'

Helen noted the pattern of light on the hall floor: shifting spheres and bars – like fish, like golden fish in a pond. 'I'd rather not,' she heard herself say.

'Oh.' There was a silence; the fish rippled and flickered. 'I was afraid you would say that. It wasn't, of course, a business meeting I had in mind. Things progress, on that side. We'll be in touch, in due course. What I had in mind was entirely selfish. That last occasion was . . . well, not very satisfactory, was it? I was hoping you might have had a change of heart.'

I see, she thought: I am intransigent, insensitive. 'I don't think it would be a good idea.'

He sighed. A delicate, regretful sound; quite natural, to the untutored ear. She would hear it, she accepted, for quite a while. 'Then I'll say goodbye, Helen.'

'Goodbye.' She put down the receiver.

Edward appeared, and at the same moment Phil came clumping down the stairs. Edward said, 'Tam doesn't seem to be anywhere about.'

Helen looked at Phil. 'Have you seen Tam?'

He shook his head. 'I think it went in the garden. You all right now, Edward?'

Edward blinked. He looked away. 'Yes thanks. I suppose so.'

'That's good,' said Phil. 'Oh – I forgot. Mum rang – they're all coming, Dad and Suzanne too. S'a bit much, innit? They'll be here for lunch, she said.'

The fridge was all but empty. There seemed to be nothing in the larder but decaying potatoes. Helen went to the shop, bought cold meats and the wherewithal for a salad; Louise, on this occasion, would be uncritical. She set off home, rounded the bend in the road, and there twenty yards from the Greystones gate was Ron Paget. Waiting, it would seem. She walked towards him, resolute.

'I gather you've had a bit of an upset. Your brother better now, Miss Glover?'

She eyed him. Who? The doctor? Impossible. Phil? Equally so. One would never know. Villages have eyes and ears. They have their own methods.

'He's all right.'

'I been talking things over with Pauline. We've decided we'll not take this business to the police. It's not going to do our boy any good, and that's the main thing. So I thought I'd let you know.'

'You must do what you want,' she said.

'So the best we can do is put it behind us. You and us both. We're neighbours and have been for a long time and I'm not a man that likes trouble. So that's the way it is.'

'It's entirely up to you. We are not making any sort of bargain.'

He looked pained. 'Miss Glover, who's talking about bargains? I told you, we don't want to see our boy put through any more.'

'Very well,' said Helen. 'And now I must go. I'm expecting my sister.'

'There's something else I've got to tell you. I'm afraid there's been a tragedy with that little dog of yours. One of my men found him just now, outside the yard. Dead. They reckon he'd eaten something. Likely someone's been putting rat poison down. Shame . . . Never rains but it pours, does it? Would you want the men to bring him over or shall I ask them to deal with it quietly, not to worry your brother?' His expression was inscrutable. No, not inscrutable; there was a tremor of concern. Carefully calculated concern.

She took a deep breath. 'I'd appreciate it if the men could see to it.'

He nodded. 'No problem. Right, then. Let bygones be bygones, right? And so far as your bit of land goes – well, you know how things stand where I'm concerned.'

She stared at him, incredulous, and then walked past him to her own gate. She let herself into the house, put the shopping basket down on the kitchen table and went upstairs. The door of Edward's room was closed. She knocked. 'Edward? I have to talk to you.'

*

They had come, and they had gone: Louise, Tim, Suzanne. And with them went Phil. He had appeared in the kitchen as Helen was clearing the table; the others had gone into the sitting room. 'I thought I'd get a lift to London with Mum and Dad. There's some things I got to see to.'

'Oh, I see. Right you are, then, Phil.'

'S'a pity about Tam. I mean, he was an awful dog but Edward liked him, so it's a pity.'

'Yes. We could have done without that just now.'

'Anyway, thanks for having me. And take care . . .'

She had been reminded, wryly, of the hours after the funeral. There they all were, gathered together again in an atmosphere of ritual ceremony in which were combined elements of unspoken relief and of mourning. Nobody referred to what had happened. Louise flung her arms around Edward on arrival; Edward stoically endured this without overt signs of rejection. Tim shook him by the hand. Suzanne gleamed at him from behind a newly reconstructed coiffure which almost obliterated her face. Phil was startlingly genial; he welcomed his parents with the air of some benign Edwardian uncle receiving poor relations. He pressed refreshments upon them and suggested a tour of the garden. Louise, cornering Helen in the kitchen, hissed: 'He claims he cut the grass. Is that true? I don't *believe* it. What the hell have you done to him? And he says he's coming home.'

They had sat around in the sitting room, that least inhabited of the Greystones rooms, always tinged with damp, always chill. They had talked with animation of anything except that of which all were thinking. Edward, from time to time, had joined in. It had been agreed that Helen and Edward should come up to London for Christmas. Helen had heard herself saying that she planned to get a new washing machine and see about some electric storage heaters for the winter. Periodically someone would refer to Dorothy, but her presence now was dimmer, she was no longer the insistent unavoidable black hole that she had been on the earlier occasion. And then eventually there had been shiftings and glances at watches.

*

And so they were alone. Conspicuously alone – it was Tam who was now a hole, a silence, a small absence. His food bowl, standing by the sink, was a mute reproach. Helen, putting it into the scullery, met Edward; they exchanged looks that were filled with some odd kind of guilt. Edward said, 'Do you think Ron Paget poisoned him?'

'We'll never know, will we? I suppose he may have done.'

Edward sat down at the kitchen table. He was still pale, and had the translucent look of someone emerging from illness, but there was also an alertness about him; he had lost the frozen passivity of recent weeks. He kept staring out of the window. 'Poor Tam. I feel as though it were my fault.'

'I know. One does. It may be no one's. Better to assume that. Anyway, Tam is the least of it. You can get another dog.' As soon as she had said it she saw the flaw, and winced.

'Yes,' said Edward. 'I daresay I shall,' he added, quite neutrally.

'By the way . . . I ought to tell you – I've found us some new solicitors. People called Wyndham and Fowler.' Their eyes met. She looked away.

'I see.' Edward paused, then went on with sudden violence. 'I never liked him. I couldn't see what . . .'

'I know you didn't. Let's not talk about him, if you don't mind.'

'He was the sort of person who is all over everyone. Anyone.'

'Possibly. I was aware of it myself. But makes no difference, you know, under the circumstances.'

Edward looked straight at her. He was trembling slightly. 'If I ever saw him again, I'd punch him on the nose.'

She laughed. 'I shouldn't. We've had enough trouble as it is.'

The room was stuffy. She got up and opened the back door. Outside, everything shone in the late afternoon sunshine. She stood for a moment, seeing that the chestnuts in the Britches were showing autumn colour, that the yew hedge was swagged with spiders' webs. She searched for something else; she scanned the garden for her mother, invited that familiar, forbidding brown figure to come stumping across the grass. But Dorothy was not there, nor had been, Helen realised, for any of the last days. She had ceased to comment, had removed herself, it seemed, to some other plane – from which, Helen saw, she might continue to dispose, but differently.

She said, 'Why do pigeons fly upwards and then come hurtling downward clapping their wings?'

'It's a mating display.'

'But this isn't the nesting season.'

'They do it all the year round. Don't ask me why.'

Edward, too, looked out. For him, the world blazed; he saw and heard, in one bright intricate living clamour, leaf and branch, flower and fruit, sunshine and wind and creatures that crept or flew. He saw and heard the pigeons, the silver blink of the big poplar, the quivering shadows on the grass. He was numb, neither sad nor glad; he did not know what he felt – only that all this was here, and so was he.

Helen closed the door and sat down again. The hall clock struck. As its last discordant note died away Helen thought, I shall sell that thing. Edward can spend the money on new trees to plant in the Britches. Edward barely heard it; he saw, now, the room – the bat calendar, the Coronation biscuit tin, that sink. Everything was the same, and yet was not.

The Glovers sat opposite one another, silent, and pursued, independently, the same theme. They saw that there is nothing to be done, but that something can be retrieved. Both sniffed the air; each, gingerly, made resolutions.